PLAYING THE WILD CARD

'The person I'm interested in is Gary Byrne, who moved to play in Italy during last summer on a contract that only lasts a year, as I'm sure you're aware. The other wealthy clubs like Arsenal, Manchester United, Everton, Celtic, Rangers and Liverpool have been keeping their eyes on him, and in addition it wouldn't surprise me if Brian Clough hasn't been following his progress very closely. He's a shrewd character. But I'm also extremely keen to sign him when he becomes available, and the club is prepared to spend money discovering whether he will be a good asset.

'What I want,' he continued after a moment, 'is for you to travel to Italy and find out in close detail what sort of form Byrne is in at the present, what type of life-style he leads, whether he has any particular troubles or vices.' His forehead furrowed.

About the author

PLAYING THE WILD CARD is Philip Evans'
third novel. He lives in London with his wife
and two children and his cat Gigi, who is
named after Gigi Riva.

Philip Evans

PLAYING THE WILD CARD

fl + P

con affetto

Philip

CORONET BOOKS
Hodder and Stoughton

First published in Great Britain in 1988 by Hodder and Stoughton Ltd

Coronet edition 1989

British Library C.I.P.

Evans, Philip *1943 Apr 4.*
    Playing the wild card.
    I. Title
    823'.914[F]

ISBN 0 340 50063 8

Printed and bound in Great Britain for Hodder and Stoughton Paperbacks, a division of Hodder and Stoughton Ltd., Mill Road, Dunton Green, Sevenoaks, Kent TN13 2YA.
(Editorial Office: 47 Bedford Square, London WC1B 3DP) by Cox & Wyman Ltd., Reading.

For my family, and especially for my wife Linda

Acknowledgments

I started to conceive this novel in March 1980 when Roma purchased Paulo Roberto Falcao after Italian clubs had been allowed to end the ban on the hiring of foreign stars. From 1980 until 1982 each club in the Serie A was permitted to hire only one foreign player, but then the number allowed rose to two and in this book clubs are allowed to hire three foreign players. Although I've used the names of several existing players and football clubs, this is purely a work of fiction.

While Nick Sayers has been a very helpful editor I would like to thank June Road, Patricia Hughes, Maureen Thomas and Carol Hawser for giving their opinions on aspects of psychology, and Brian Glanville, Brian Moore, John Moynihan and the England manager Bobby Robson for discussing football with me.

OCTOBER 1987

She who would long retain her power must use her lover ill.

Ovid, *Amores*

obsess, v.t. (of evil spirit, delusion, or fixed idea) haunt, harass, preoccupy, fill mind of (– ed by, with). So obsession (– shn) n.

The Concise Oxford Dictionary

Part One

Of the four people in the Maserati DS5, the only one able to recall the accident was the person who helped cause it.

Everybody agreed that it had been a miracle that the woman travelling in the front of the car had not been killed when it plunged into some roadworks on the Via Lodovico Moro just to the south-west of Milan. When the ambulance men arrived she was still breathing; in a state of extreme shock and carrying a broken leg, but still breathing.

The other occupants had not been so fortunate. The man sitting behind her had been thrown out of the car and spread against the side of the roadworks, the head of the driver had been smashed against the steering-wheel, and the female passenger in the back, who had been sitting directly behind him, had hit her head against the window – causing an injury which disfigured her and put a cruel finish to her new career as an actress.

She'd been taken out to a celebratory dinner by her agent, Salvatore Brini, along with Domenico Mozzolino, the lawyer who handled cases for him, and Mozzolino's Welsh wife Sian, with whom she had struck up a most intense friendship, who had been a vital inspiration in her attempts to speak Italian, and who became her regular companion on visits to the shops and markets of Milan. They had been bonded together by the fact that they were both guarded newcomers to the sophisticated society of the city. The two of them possessed a similar sense of humour and at certain times appeared to be as closely linked as sisters.

When her friends had suggested the evening entertainment on a night when the play was not due to be performed and she had accepted enthusiastically, they'd come to collect her from her large apartment in the eastern part of the city on the Corso Magenta and had driven to the suburb of Corsico along the Via Lorenteggio.

Lying only eight kilometres outside the centre of Milan, La Pianta provided the opportunity to eat al fresco since it was still pleasingly warm even in late September. A background melody provided by frogs and crickets suggested that each was auditioning for parts at La Scala. Being a skilled avvocato by profession, the driver drank only frugally. The two women, however, felt permitted to propose toasts to everybody they could think of so that by the time they left both were laughing happily and neither was in full control of her senses.

During the autumn and winter months the area to the south of the city is frequently blanketed with a thick fog. That particular year it had chosen to make an early appearance so they had driven little further than two hundred metres along the road before the fog suddenly surrounded them.

While the roadworks on the Via Lodovico Moro had involved the removal of a substantial part of its right-hand side, a set of temporary traffic lights, regularly in use, had long before turned from red to green, allowing the driver to travel on with little reduction in speed.

That was the precise moment, however, when the woman sitting in front leant across towards her husband and gave him a kiss that contained raw and sensual lust.

1

Monday, 12th February

The telephone sounded as I was preparing to finish for the night. I'd just completed the paperwork regarding my visit to Bilbao, and had rushed around by messenger my report and impressions to Keith Nightingale, the managing director of KRN Associates, the insurance investigators.

"Mr Armstrong?" asked a smooth, medium-timbred voice.

"Yes."

"Tom Kennart speaking."

Instinctively I sat more upright in my chair, since the only Tom Kennart I'd heard about was the manager of a leading London football club, of which Keith Nightingale was the chairman. Although I went to a rugby-playing school, football has been one of my leading interests during the past fifteen years, and whenever a case takes me abroad I always make a point of going to see a local match – be it in Buenos Aires, Berlin or Bilbao.

"Can I buy you lunch on Friday? I can't make Wednesday since we have an away match in the evening, and Thursday is ruled out completely." It was a Yorkshire accent that had been little affected by living in the South and spoken by a man who sounded as though he rarely took "no" for an answer.

"I understand. Just a moment and I'll take a look in my diary." In fact every lunch-time during the coming week was clear of appointments. "Yes. I think I can manage that."

"Good," Kennart said and named a restaurant in Greek Street. "I'll book a table there at about one o'clock."

"Looking forward to our meeting, Mr Kennart. See you then." I paused. "Could you give me some idea of what you want to talk about?"

"It concerns a footballer who was transferred last summer to a club in Italy. I had a discussion with Mr Nightingale this morning after the board meeting and he suggested that I contact you." He stopped talking at that moment as though fearful that he might reveal information that was strictly private and confidential. "However, I would prefer to delay any discussion until we meet."

"I quite understand, Mr Kennart," I broke in swiftly before he became more self-conscious. "See you on Friday."

I looked forward to meeting Kennart, not least because he was known as one of the most intelligent men in football.

Friday, 16th February

Five minutes before one o'clock on that Friday found me sitting in the Gay Hussar in Greek Street, sipping at a glass of white wine. On the principle that it is always wisest to dress up when trying to impress someone, particularly when they might be about to employ you, I was wearing the soberest of my four suits, a three-piece in charcoal grey, along with a light blue shirt, dark blue tie and well-polished black shoes. Nice and conservative, guaranteed to offend no one.

The restaurant had the smell of success. In my job as an investigator in the insurance business I have to travel a good amount, but nevertheless I recognised a number of the faces present, which belonged to a senior minister in the government, several respected journalists and a few who had made their names in television.

Kennart came in just after five past one, a dark-haired, large-boned man with an open, honest face. I made an inelegant attempt to stand up in the cherry-red bench seat that was holding me in order to shake hands. He was flushed, as though he'd been in a hurry.

"Sorry I'm late," he apologised and sat down opposite me.

"You're not," I said, shaking my head. "You said about one o'clock when we spoke on the phone." Still, it was a useful edge to have in the conversation.

He ordered a gin and slim-line tonic from the Hungarian waiter.

"Do you know this place well?" I asked, before we started to look through the menu.

Kennart shook his head.

"I could easily have dropped by your office."

Kennart nodded. "True. But I thought you might prefer to go out. In any case this place was recently recommended to me by a supporter who lives nearby and likes his food. At the start

14

of the season he persuaded the owner to become a season-ticket holder – so let's see what it's like." He suddenly glanced down at his watch in the manner of someone accustomed to living a twenty-five hour day and an eight-day week.

He selected the wild cherry soup, I the fish mousse, and then we joined forces for a main and chose some *vese-velo tojassal* – scrambled egg with kidney and brains – all accompanied by a rare bottle of 1976 Chardonnay.

"Now that's over, Mr Kennart," I said after the waiter had left, "can you tell me exactly why you want to see me?"

"Forgive me for not having said much on the phone two days ago but it's often wisest not to trust secrets to others until you are sure that your conversation is not being listened to." Kennart made the statement sound like a question, and as though he had been reading too many thrillers. "The person I'm interested in is Gary Byrne, who moved to play in Italy during last summer on a contract that only lasts a year, as I'm sure you're aware. The other wealthy clubs like Arsenal, Manchester United, Everton, Celtic, Rangers and Liverpool have been keeping their eyes on him, and in addition it wouldn't surprise me if Brian Clough hasn't been following his progress very closely. He's a shrewd character. But I'm also extremely keen to sign him when he becomes available, and the club is prepared to spend money discovering whether he will be a good asset.

"What I want," he continued after a moment, "is for you to travel to Italy and find out in close detail what sort of form Byrne is in at the present, what type of life-style he leads, whether he has any particular troubles or vices." His forehead furrowed.

There followed a lengthy pause after he had uttered the final word. The last thing that managers of football teams wish for is players who have a troubled background. They desperately need to channel all their skills and energies into helping to create a victorious side and not have to spend a lot of nervous energy worrying about the psychological temper of their players.

"Vices?" I asked after a moment.

Kennart gave a grimace. "You know what I mean." Kennart was acknowledged throughout the football world as being a manager who preached high moral standards, and lived up to them.

15

"Nothing specific about Gary Byrne?"

He shook his head. "I've not heard any rumours about him from friends involved with the media. In Italy club football has rigid tests to discover whether players are drugged. It won't be that. And after the punishments which were given out following the betting scandal of 1980 it is highly unlikely that Byrne would have become involved with any crooked gambling, searching for easy wins on the Totocalcio, the Italian football lottery that resembles the Pools. As far as I know, he's straight."

"Why the sudden interest, Mr Kennart?" I asked.

Kennart gave a smile. "In one way it's not at all sudden, in another it is. Yesterday I was interviewed by Mick Knight for a piece which he is due to write for *World Soccer*. Just over two weeks ago he flew over to Milan to see the match between Internazionale and Fiorentina. Both teams have a number of players expecting selection for the national team due to play against Switzerland at the end of the month and Mick intended to gain material for a piece that would be a preview of that particular game. With the finals of the World Cup due to be held in Italy this summer, each match played by the host nation is carefully scrutinised. Especially through the length and breadth of Italy." He smiled and paused. "Naturally, when the match was over Mick took the opportunity to have a few words outside the dressing rooms with Gary Byrne."

"How had he performed?" I enquired.

"Not very well, I understand," Kennart replied in a low voice. "That was when Knight wondered aloud which English club would be interested in purchasing him at the end of the season when he is due to return to this country, and went on to wonder whether that might be us." He gave a shrug. "Maybe the fact that his form has slumped might lead Fiorentina to sell him comparatively cheaply. One never can tell in affairs concerning transfers. His value might be better now than it was during the autumn, when he was said to be playing so brilliantly. What we'd like you to do is to travel to Florence and see what might be causing him to play so wretchedly at present. The lad might simply have lost form, and his disappointing failures recently may be totally unconnected with his activities off the field, but we obviously need to know more, to know whether . . ."

"Whether he can fit easily into your team," I finished for him.

He nodded. "Precisely. I've been a great admirer of his since seeing him play against us three years ago, and I've been in touch with one or two people who knew him just before he went abroad. I wonder, though, how well he has been able to adapt to these new pressures, and what effect this has had on his character. Over thirty years ago John Charles fitted in very well at Juventus and in recent seasons Brady especially, Francis, Hateley, Souness and Wilkins have all gone smoothly into Italian football and become popular. On the other side, in the sixties, Baker, Greaves and Law found the style of life there very hard to take, Ian Rush came home after only one season and I just wonder how the boy Byrne has been able to adapt."

He paused and wiped his brow with a handkerchief, although it wasn't particularly warm in the restaurant. "The entire regime, the habits, the manners of the club game as played in Italy are totally different from those known to us. Italian clubs tend to cosset the players much more than we do, to deprive them much more of their sense of freedom. Before important matches they are inclined to ask the players to enter a *ritiro* – a special regime at training camp – for several days. The ways of life are completely different." Kennart was taking a long time to get to the point. "That is why I'd like you to go there for several days and gather information that will tell me whether Byrne will be a good investment, or whether he would be a risky proposition for the club to become interested in."

"Why him especially?" I asked. I recalled reading reports praising his brilliance, but surely there were other players in this country who would be far less risky to sign?

Kennart poured some more wine into our glasses, and looked in front of him – almost as though to suggest he'd not heard me. I was on the point of repeating myself when he gave a smile, which was followed by a brief nod. "I've been told that you know a good amount about football – but before I answer I'll make a few points concerning the transfer market."

"Please do."

"A manager of a team can't avoid relying on advice. He might be the man in the firing-line if and when Failure, with a capital 'F', takes place, but he needs support at all times when purchasing players. Some performers are watched on perhaps a dozen occasions before a club feels confident enough to discuss his merits and make an offer."

"By scouts?"

"By scouts certainly. In recent seasons there's also been a new breed of club chairmen who travel a lot, often abroad, insist on watching football, and pass on their thoughts to their boards of directors. In the main, however, this task of sifting is carried out by scouts, often players who have had experience inside the game. There is always a certain element of fortune involved."

I let him continue.

"For example, when the legendary Bill Shankly purchased Kevin Keegan from Scunthorpe for almost nowt he'd not even seen the lad play, but instead trusted the judgment of his scouts. And look what return Liverpool later made for their investment of only £30,000!" He broke off and gave a chuckle. "So yes, scouts are used by most clubs. But me," he speared his chest with his right forefinger, "me, I like to watch a player several times playing in different conditions before I'm ready to make an offer.

"On those occasions I've watched him, Byrne struck me as being utterly special, one of those players who so often seems to have all the time in the world. Someone who has authentic quality." Kennart looked away for a moment, before continuing with his panegyric. "In fact we were on the point of signing him when he chose to go abroad, but our chairman happened to be away on business and so we were too late. That's why this Monday Mr Nightingale urged me to make contact with you. Byrne has a talent which few over here have fully appreciated but which I am convinced that we can bring out of him. For someone so comparatively young Byrne has the temperament of someone who has performed in the league for about ten seasons. I've always admired the way he played before he went abroad, and watched with interest since."

"I don't remember him having been picked for England," I remarked.

"No, you won't." Kennart gave a short laugh, and shook his head, "It turns out that although his father is English, his mother is Welsh. Apparently he was brought up during his teens by her sister in Yorkshire, and it was the Welsh selectors she approached after she had discovered how promising he was."

"Under-21 level, I presume."

Kennart nodded. "He was chosen four times while he was at

Sheffield Wednesday, and twice after he had been transferred to Stoke City."

"But can't he still be selected by England at full international level?"

Kennart shook his head. "Afraid not. Of course those games took place before he moved to play in Italy, where he has been gaining invaluable knowledge about the grounds and atmosphere that could be crucial when the World Cup finals are played this summer. Imagine how England must be kicking themselves now! Gary might have been perfect as someone to include in the party at the last minute as a surprise selection.

"As far as the club is concerned, in Monday's board meeting I had a long talk to Mr Nightingale about the possibility of signing him. And . . ." He shrugged an ending to the sentence.

"And you don't want to be second in the race again," I said.

He gave a brief nod. "You bet. Although there's another reason. Did you see us in the big match last Saturday?"

"Yes," I gave a nod. "Strong in defence and attack but weak in midfield."

"Precisely. We've been like that ever since David Connolly strained a groin in September. He took the devil of a time to recover completely. In fact I'm not sure that he did, although on occasions he can still be inspirational. That injury might explain why he started to slow up before our games at Christmas. Anyway, he got in touch with me on Sunday and said that after much heart-searching he thinks it best if he were to retire at the close of the season. I'm determined to find a place for him on our training staff. He has given us eleven seasons of superb service since he joined us from Celtic."

"And there are no young players whom you could see taking over?"

Kennart gave a scowl. "At this moment I can't see any of our apprentices stepping up to the first team. On our books is Tommy Phelan, a twenty-year-old Irishman with a Spanish mother whom I envisaged coming into the side just before David had to retire, and able to succeed him. David had taught him a lot – most important the ability to keep calm at all times – but," at this point Kennart hit his knuckles against the top of the table, "his game has stopped developing. In fact it's going backwards. He's started to lose thousands of pounds gambling, and worrying about that has affected his game disastrously. The latest I heard was that the lad was thinking

19

of leaving football and joining a friend as a scrap-metal merchant. Scrap-metal merchant. Ye gods!" Kennart gave a wintry smile.

"Which explains why you want Gary Byrne," I remarked. "David Connolly giving his advice, and Gary Byrne using his ability to thread brilliant passes through to the forwards?"

Kennart gave a nod of satisfaction. "Sounds a winning combination, doesn't it?"

"It could work out fine."

"You mean you're interested?" Kennart's voice rose.

I smiled. "I'll see what I can do."

He frowned and became a bit flushed as he looked me firmly in the eye. "Mr Nightingale suggested that I contact you direct because in addition to knowing a lot about football you've frequently worked for him in Italy. He gave me the impression that if you agreed he would like you to concentrate totally on this particular job. He left me to agree a fee with you by myself, however. This is the first time I've used the services of someone so on the fringes of the game. I simply don't know how these things work."

"What exactly do you mean?" I asked.

"The fee, of course," Kennart answered gruffly. "How much precisely will we have to pay you?"

"Easy, Mr Kennart." I gave a smile. "You make me the offer that I can't refuse, and I'll simply double it."

A look of alarm crossed over his features until he realised that I was joking. "I thought of offering a flat fee of five thousand pounds," he said, when he had recovered himself.

"Half payable now and half when the job is finished?" I suggested. His offer struck me as being most generous, but I knew how wealthy these prosperous and well-organised football clubs must be. I knew that the wealthier football clubs are forced to buy players towards the end of each tax year to prevent the money going straight into the Exchequer. Added to which I'd be saving the club the fee that it might have to pay to a translator. "Six thousand."

He nodded quickly. "That's acceptable," he said and started to look relieved.

"Plus expenses, of course," I said and held out my hand. "By the time I've asked around I should have an idea of exactly what Byrne has been doing with every second of his stay in Italy. Then, if I feel that the case is worth looking into deeper

I could return and continue with my investigations here. However, my first priority is to get to know the player."

"Exactly."

"When do you want me to start the job?"

Kennart gave me a heavy look. "As soon as possible. As soon as possible. I've done everything I can to discover what other clubs have been interested in signing him, but it has often been unrewarding. You desperately need to keep the information to yourself since certain agents love nothing better than to have two or more clubs bidding against each other, hoping to increase the amount of money involved. They're like sharks."

He paused. "Could you do the job using some sort of cover?" Kennart continued, after lowering his voice. "I'm sure that I can trust you not to let on what you are up to, but you do appreciate it is imperative for our interest to remain confined to only two or three people. Imperative. Secrecy in all these operations is so vital."

"A journalist might be expected to know a good amount about football, so that option could be risky." I thought for a moment and then said, "I could pretend that I'm doing research on a profile of Byrne for television." I made the idea into a question.

"I like it, I like it. That doesn't sound at all impossible." A tone of excitement entered Kennart's voice, and a relaxed smile came over his face. "Perhaps you could use that cover when you talk to the lad's agent."

"Who is?"

"A shrewd character called Eugenio Dal Bosco. Don't be fooled by his gushing manner. He makes most of his money from running a small airline, and knows very well that it is charm and reliability that bring the best results. But talking to friends makes me think that he is a man who can be relied on."

"I'll try and see him before I leave for Italy," I suggested.

"Good idea. I'll send you all the details I have concerning Gary Byrne by special messenger this afternoon along with an advance payment on your fees of three thousand pounds."

We shook hands formally across the table-top as though to reinforce our pact, and as a farewell gesture Kennart took out a large envelope from his slim black briefcase and passed it to me.

"It's always been discussed whether football started in Italy or in England. What no one can deny is that the English was the first Football Association to be founded. But inside there," he indicated the envelope, "is a copy of a book that tells the history of organised football in Florence from the last years of the last century until today."

"All the teams, all the players, all the goals and so on?"

Kennart nodded. "It's exhaustive. I've also included some clippings about Fiorentina this season, which you'll find informative. Then there's some information about Gary's agent, Eugenio Dal Bosco, in addition to my address and phone number at home in case you need to contact me at strange hours."

2

Friday, 16th February
When I'd returned to my office, after having climbed three loops of spiralling stairway, I started some preliminary research on the forthcoming case by looking at several useful journals. I also called two well-informed contacts.

Tom Kennart had been a late developer. A Yorkshireman, he had started his career with Leeds and had been transferred to Chelsea, before playing out the twilight of his career with Sheffield United. In spite of having gained no experience at international level, he'd always been respected as a thinker about the game and had taken instantly to the coaching of younger players. It was no time at all before he was snapped up as coach to the junior sides of a team in the top division and after a few years was offered the post of manager/coach to the first team. Now in his mid-forties, he was firmly settled – in as far as any manager is entitled to feel at all safe in a job in which the mortality rate is exceedingly high – and could look forward to the ensuing few years with comparative confidence. Many of the players he had coached for several seasons were still playing for him, and were bound to give him their respect in addition to their loyalty.

I telephoned Eugenio Dal Bosco, the agent involved, to discover any interesting details concerning Byrne's life as a footballer. All I received, however, was a recorded message. I left my name and number in the anxious hope that he would be able to return my call before I had to leave.

Soon after, a motorcycle messenger brought an envelope containing my cheque in addition to a smaller parcel which contained information about Gary Byrne. It struck me as amusing that it hadn't been put in the envelope; Kennart's fixation about security again. I gathered that the people who had been most closely involved with Gary during the period before his transfer to Fiorentina had been not his parents, but instead his aunt and uncle. From a journalist friend who travelled regularly to Italy I learned that Byrne's aunt on his mother's side, Sian, had been married at one time to Domenico Mozzolino, a very successful lawyer who worked in Milan. However, just over three years after their wedding he had been killed in an automobile accident. Although she had been accepted very quickly and easily into Milanese society and had found herself speedily acclimatising to her new country, she had been drawn back towards Britain by links with her family and friends of former times, and had returned only several weeks after her husband's funeral.

Although she chose not to sell the apartment he owned in Milan, she moved to London where she found work as a translator of Italian. Some two years later she met Richard Wright, an elderly barrister who lived in Silkstone, a quiet village just to the west of Barnsley, and practised on the North-Eastern circuit, and, shortly after, they decided to marry. This explained why in due time she went to live in Yorkshire, and gave me a clue as to why Byrne might have played as a youngster for Sheffield Wednesday. However, further information concerning the Wrights and their connection with Gary would obviously be of great help. A call to another investigator ensured that all the relevant material would be available when I returned from my trip to Italy.

Gareth David Byrne appeared an interesting case. Born in Liverpool to an English father and a Welsh mother, he'd first played for the Yorkshire club, Sheffield Wednesday, before being transferred to Stoke City. He was still young, approaching only his twenty-second birthday on 23rd April, and Florence must have been one of the more civilised places to live if a player chose to play abroad.

Before he had been transferred, however, many pundits had expressed their doubts concerning his ability to acclimatise well to the game in Italy. Players in the Italian league are paid vast salaries but on the debit side one always had to be determined to remain cool in the face of provocation, sometimes extreme, and it wasn't certain whether Byrne had the ability to control himself adequately and not be frequently expelled from the pitch.

Drawing conclusions from scant evidence is a dangerous business, but I wondered if his previous transfer was the result of differing styles of play. That would go some part of the way to explaining his move from Sheffield Wednesday where, above all, the supporters like their players to "get stuck in", and often could become more than a little sharp with players who liked to spend time stroking the ball about the field. However, whether this had been the precise reason why Gary Byrne had been keen to leave Stoke City and try his luck inside the more skilful world of Italian football could only be answered by going to interview the people concerned on my return from Italy.

I learned from glancing at the exhaustive history which Kennart had given me that Florence had been the home of an organised football team since the 1890s. First had come a "Florence Football Club", akin to those in Genoa and Milan, which had been the product of English enthusiasts, and gradually there had come into existence rival teams organised by local players. Over the first quarter of this century this passion had been devolved into two or three teams until followed a date crucial to the supporters of Fiorentina: 26th August, 1926 when the club AC Fiorentina came into existence following the amalgamation of two local sides.

The club had been an ever-present member of the Serie A since the 1931–32 season apart from one year when it had dropped into the Serie B. It had been recently taken over by an industrialist whose wealth came in the main from his being a founder and part-owner of a massive clothing combine in Tuscany called Bottoni which was given to producing, with almost paralysing haste, a production-line of shirts, blouses and underwear for the use of ordinary folk. His name was Stirata. Dottore Marcello Stirata.

In the envelope which Kennart had sent were also many clippings from Italian papers which related the present strengths and weaknesses of the team, as well as some papers about former British and Irish players who had taken their talents to the Continent. Several stars had been attracted to Italy during the fifties and early sixties, this rush having been succeeded by a hiatus in the traffic, during which time Italy had barred foreign players from taking part in its game. Since 1980, however, when the doors had been re-opened, many celebrated players had been newly attracted, in no small part thanks to the enormous salaries and bonuses which they had been promised. Italy had again become the Mecca of football.

The British media had not known how to react to this exodus of talent. At first there had been some half-hearted cries of

"Treachery", but this emotional response soon had been balanced by the realisation that, in Italy, such fortunates would be asked to perform on approximately only half the number of occasions which they had back in England and, as a result, might be of considerably more service to national teams thanks to their not being plagued by nigglingly small injuries and the gradual wear and tear that inevitably succeeds overmuch physical effort. It remains a harsh legacy of footballing life that most teams in Britain, particularly in the later stages of a season, are compelled to play two or three players who are less than one hundred per cent fit.

It was only after eleven thirty that evening that Eugenio Dal Bosco telephoned back.

"I have just this moment returned to my apartment. How can I be of help?" He sounded out of breath.

I explained that I was about to leave for Florence the following day in order to gather background material for a profile on Gary Byrne.

"That's marvellous," he remarked, perhaps a little suspiciously. He sounded as though he wished he knew me better. Or not at all. I couldn't blame him.

"My plane leaves tomorrow morning at nine," I explained, "but could I quickly pick your brains about Gary? I gather that you're the agent . . ."

"Let's say I was the man who saw the deal through. My time is mostly spent administering 'Dal Bosco Tours'."

"Fine."

There followed a long pause. "About Gary Byrne – there's nothing wrong, is there?"

"Why do you ask?"

"*Non importa, non importa*," he said very quickly. "I was merely curious, since I've not heard from him for some time." He spoke most confidently but still with the meticulous rhythm of someone who has had to learn English as a second language.

"Nothing as far as I know." I'd tell him more when we met. "I was informed that you accompanied him last June when he visited Florence."

"Who did you learn that from?" Dal Bosco's voice became more measured and seemed to have acquired a sharp edge to it, as though the matter had been secret.

"A journalist friend who works for the Reuter Agency," I

replied, and invented a name and a story, although it had been Kennart who'd told me. "Roger Dale."

"I haven't come across him," Dal Bosco said after a moment.

"He travels a fair amount inside Europe. Spain, France, West Germany, Greece, Yugoslavia, wherever. Name the place and Dale has probably been there. I travelled with him recently when he was investigating a story in Italy, and he recalled that the previous occasion he'd been asked to go there was last June when he caught a plane to Rome. He remembers checking in just after you and Gary Byrne. I don't suppose you will remember him."

"Afraid not."

"Can you tell me the purpose of your visit last June?" I enquired.

"Fiorentina had expressed an interest in signing Byrne. Like most clubs proposing to purchase a player, they wanted to carry out some medical checks before the contracts were signed. It's standard procedure." I could visualise him smiling. "But when we arrived at the offices of Fiorentina at least five hundred supporters were gathered outside carrying banners which said 'VIVA BYRNE', 'FORZA BYRNE' and so on. It made Gary feel very nervous."

"Of course."

"You travel tomorrow?" he enquired after a long pause.

"I should arrive in Florence just after lunch-time."

"Good. Good. And when did you last see a match in my country?" he asked.

"In October, eighteen months ago. Roma versus Inter."

"Ah, two of the best." He paused. "When you land tomorrow you will find the whole of Italy even more gripped by World Cup fever."

That could prove an understatement. Ever since Italy had been announced as the host of the 1990 World Cup it had started to build up excitement as the first European country to act as venue for the tournament on two separate occasions. "Let's hope we see football well away from politics," I said, showing off a bit. "Unlike in 1934."

Dal Bosco took such a long time to reply I thought he might have hung up. "Mussolini." His voice sounded taut. "*Che buffone*. Using the 1934 Cup to make political capital. Disgraceful. And there were many who thought Italy very, very lucky to gain victory. So the propaganda value backfired."

An Italian admitting that! "Almost every team that wins is unpopular," I pointed out.

"I know, I know. But even so."

There had to be a reason for his vehemence. "You seem very bitter, Signor Dal Bosco."

Dal Bosco's voice became heavily barbed. "My father was killed in Russia in 1942. I was only a boy at the time but I've always held that clown Mussolini responsible. I've always found him repulsive."

I began to regret that conversational ploy. If I didn't get things back on to the immediate subject I was going to be in for a much longer talk than I had bargained for. "I'm off tomorrow to do this profile. Shall I remember you to Gary Byrne, if and when I see him?" I gave a laugh.

"That would be nice," Dal Bosco said, his voice starting to sound more trusting.

"And I'll remind him that the telephone was invented over a century ago."

Dal Bosco gave a chuckle. "Please do." He seemed to become more relaxed by the moment. "It has been most mysterious, this absence of communication. Why, when he was in the process of settling in he was in the habit of getting in touch every week to give me a progress-report on how well he was acclimatising. This recent silence is most mystifying."

"I'm sure it's nothing personal."

"I hope not," he murmured, "I hope not."

3

Saturday, 17th February

I flew into Galileo Galilei Airport at Pisa just after 2.30 p.m. and was soon driving towards Florence in the car I'd hired, a new Alfa 90 with a 2.5 litre engine. The brisk drive to Florence along the autostrada, however, provided a constant reminder of the task ahead, the car's colour being almost like that favoured by Fiorentina. I trusted that its violet strip presaged a successful future.

I'd booked into the Excelsior Hotel which had been recommended by Harry Mann, a colleague who'd been involved in a case some years before in Florence. Before taking a shower I rang the secretary of Fiorentina s.p.a. to request a place in the press box for the game the following day, quoting the press credentials I had "arranged" for another job some years before and which had come in useful on more than one occasion since. That would be reserved, came the brisk reply, and I was told that I would have ample opportunity to talk to Byrne *after* the match. The tone of the voice implied that it would not be possible to make any contact before the game. "*Dopo la partita*," he had stressed. After being informed that my ticket could be collected at the main entrance to the stadium I was bidden an abrupt "goodbye". A neat example of the love-hate relationship that exists between football clubs and personalities from the media about whom they have no prior knowledge. Clubs need the coverage of games to boost sales of tickets, but they are prone to be distrustful, often with good reason.

I made contact with Sergio Triscardo, who agreed to meet me for an aperitif at six o'clock in the bar of the Excelsior Hotel. The local reporter for the Milan-based *La Gazzetta dello Sport*, one of the national dailies concerned exclusively with coverage of sporting events, he perhaps would provide me with up-to-date background material on some important aspects of the type of life Gary Byrne led: how well he trained, how easily he had fitted in with the other players, whether or not he had made any particular friendships and so on.

I arrived first at the lounge of the hotel, ordered a glass of Frascati and settled in a seat facing the door. Although it was not yet six o'clock the place was already full. Moments after the waiter had brought my drink, Triscardo entered the room and came across to my table only an instant after he had looked round the room. The English "cut" of my clothes, I supposed. A tall character in his early forties who wore on his features an expression of world-weary cynicism, he was becoming thin-haired and well-stomached. As he approached his walnut-coloured eyes looked furtively in every direction in the manner of a vigilante on patrol.

We shook hands, and having ordered a whisky and ginger ale from a passing waiter, he proclaimed, in kindly enough tones, "Please understand that in half an hour's time I'll be expected back at my paper."

"I'm grateful for your being prepared to spend the time."

He nodded. "How can I help?"

"I'm interested primarily in gathering information about Gary Byrne," I replied, carrying on to tell him that I was doing research for a profile of the player.

Triscardo gave a smile. "The latest idol of this city."

"Really?"

Triscardo nodded vigorously. "Certainly. You know about his career as a model?"

I shook my head.

"Ah. For the last few months he has been doing some modelling for the clothes manufacturing firm owned by the president of Fiorentina, Marcello Stirata."

"Tell me about him," I asked, sensing that an oblique approach towards Byrne might work best.

He scratched the hair behind his left ear, and started to look very solemn. "An interesting man. Fifty-eight years old. Some journalists don't much care for him, but I do. Whenever I have discussed footballing matters with him, he has provided realistic answers to my questions. Not like some I could mention, who are always full of fantasy. For his part Stirata sometimes offers me compliments on my pieces." He gave a small shrug. "But then, I always believe that honesty is the best policy. I work for a local paper which means that I don't have to spend my time inventing stories. And heaven knows, there's far too much of that around. Stirata became very religious about three years ago soon after his wife was taken away from him suddenly suffering from leukaemia. He was said to have rarely left her side during the last few weeks of her torment. She was several years younger than her husband, not yet forty-five and said to have been a very sophisticated woman who was much liked by everyone who came into contact with her."

"You didn't, I assume?"

"Afraid not. I only met her on two occasions at parties given by those who administer Fiorentina."

"So she didn't attend every match?"

Triscardo shook his head. "I gathered that she didn't like football overmuch, and mostly came to support her husband."

"Any children?" I asked.

"A son called Sandro, who must now be about twenty-five and works in Rome, and a daughter who still lives with her father and must now be about twenty-two. Giuliana. The death of his wife seems to have had a traumatising effect on Stirata. He suddenly locked himself away from the outside world and would see people only on rare occasions."

"Curious."

Triscardo gave a chuckle. "Agreed. Even more curious, however, is the most permanent legacy of her death: the fact that he has become fervently religious. Almost like a mania. He has been president of Fiorentina for nine years now, and gossip used to circulate around the playing-rooms that if a player wanted to join the club, the easiest way to do so was first to show himself to be a religious fanatic. Never mind about his skill as a footballer. It isn't difficult to imagine the jokes that were made by the opposing supporters."

That might be worth looking into. "And Stirata made use of Gary Byrne in his advertising?"

"Certainly. Gary is a very good-looking character. You see his features on billboards all over the place, there is always a posse of females waiting to collect his autograph after every match, and he is also very popular with his team-mates." He paused and shook his head slightly. "However I think that it is partly this adulation which is helping to cause his enormous gloom."

"Gloom?"

"Perhaps it is something more than that," Triscardo suggested. "His football in the last two or three matches has been truly forgettable. In the game last Sunday against Sampdoria at the Marassi Stadium in Genoa, he played at times like a sleep-walker. He made some exceptional passes in the first half, as well as committing himself one hundred and twenty per cent, but later entirely disappeared from the game. I wasn't the only one not the least surprised to see him being taken off midway during the second half." He paused and took a vast gulp of his drink. "Come to think of it, he was in pedestrian form when he played here the week before last in the match against Juventus and the Sunday before that at San Siro against Internazionale of Milan." Which only confirmed the information I'd received yesterday from Tom Kennart.

"Too many late nights?"

"Could be," said Triscardo, giving a nod. "Could be. He was given permission to move into his own apartment during the autumn – "

"Forgive me," I interrupted, "but I thought that throughout the season the freedoms given to players were strictly controlled."

"They normally are. Given the amount of money involved they have to be. But affairs at Fiorentina are comparatively lax when compared with those of the major clubs of Milan and Turin. Added to which, of course, is the fact that Gary has proved to be by far the best value for money of all the foreign players who have come to play in Italy." He gave a brief smile and tapped his fingers on the table-top. "From the moment he started with Fiorentina he was in the most inspirational form, appearing to possess endless stamina, making no mistakes and always threading together exquisite passes." Triscardo smiled, and summoned the waiter for another drink. "Indeed, in the way in which he attracted play around him he often appeared to be the most important player on the pitch, someone who had been performing with Fiorentina for several years, not merely several days. And all this for a fee that during the summer was considered derisory! By the way, you will probably hear the crowd chanting his nickname. In an interview with him published in September a printer's error had made his name 'Byron' throughout instead of the rightful 'Byrne', and that became renowned throughout the country overnight." He gave a chuckle. "Isn't it a name common in Wales, this Byron?"

"It certainly is," I replied, "it certainly is. But tell me, has he made close friendships with any of the Fiorentina players? People he makes a point of seeing after work, going to their homes, entertaining them – that type of thing."

Triscardo closed his eyes in concentration. "He seemed to form a close friendship with Roberto Cianfanelli, the youngster in the forward line, and others whom he gets on with very well include Franco Palmieri and Matteo Mandarini, the two colleagues who have regularly played alongside him in Fiorentina's midfield. In fact these four used to spend much of their spare time paying visits to the Viola Clubs in the region."

I interrupted. "Viola Clubs?"

Triscardo opened his eyes and gave a chuckle of apology. "Forgive me. Clubs that have been formed and are administered by supporters of all types – men, women and children, clubs that live in the hope that some of the players are able to call in and spend some time with them." He suddenly fixed me with a look. "However, that was all before Christmas when Byron and I used to be very friendly, and he would always be happy to be interviewed. But during these last few weeks he seems to have kept himself very much to himself. After each training-session he rushes away, and when you try to ring him you discover that his phone seems to be permanently engaged. He never appears in those bars and restaurants which he used to frequent, and those occasions on which I have been able to get some sort of quote from him he has been very terse."

"Has he made any enemies during his time here?"

Triscardo shook his head slightly, and gave a thoughtful frown. "I don't think so. When Byron first arrived he was given the welcome that is usually shown to foreign players, but in his case it was overshadowed by regret at the fact that he was a substitute for Pablo Cortes, the Argentinian player whom Fiorentina signed originally. One or two of his colleagues took a long time to accept him, particularly Mannie Haggan, the West German stopper of the team, but until the trouble of recent weeks he has been very popular."

"Could you tell me where he lives?" I asked.

Without having to consult a notebook, Triscardo gave me the player's address, an apartment in a house in the Piazza di Ognisanti.

"Thanks," I said, jotting down the information. "That type of behaviour isn't common, is it? Perhaps he's in some trouble that is making him increasingly restless."

"*Forse sì, forse no*. I do know that at a training-session last week he had to be held back from hitting one of the trainers."

"Good heavens! Held back by whom?"

"By Pietro Polacco, another trainer. A huge bear of a man, he stepped in between them and stopped it coming to anything." Triscardo gave a flash of a smile and shook his head. "Don't bother with that too much. Tensions often creep in to teams during the months of spring, although in this case it was all the more noticeable because up until then Byron had been a model of good humour. At any rate the player that you'll see now is a complete contrast from what you would have seen before Christmas." Triscardo finished off his drink. "Forgive me but I must go. Thank you for the drink, and I'll look out for you at the match tomorrow. *Arrivederci*."

I ordered another glass of white wine and considered what I had learned from Triscardo. The affairs of Byrne seemed to be in an extraordinarily muddled state, and the match against AC Milan would provide further valid information about his mental state.

Sunday, 18th February

I spent part of the following morning doing some homework on the game I'd be watching. Fiorentina lay fifth in the table and AC Milan just three points above at third, so the contest promised to be very close. Several players had won their place in national sides; and one of the foreign players whom AC Milan had signed was Julien Dubouis, a French forward who had already scored twelve goals although the season had only just passed its halfway point.

At breakfast, which I took at a bar along the Lungarno Corsini, I bought a copy of *La Gazzetta dello Sport* which provided a page that was replete with theorising about the game. The formations of both teams were dissected minutely, the manner in which the game should be played was hypothesised at length and finally a forecast for a result was offered which finished up by being an each-way bet between a draw and a victory for Fiorentina.

For his part Byrne saw his skills being compared with those of Istvan Bokor, Milan's experienced Hungarian mid-field player. Despite becoming less mobile (he had recently reached his thirty-third birthday) Bokor was still renowned throughout the Italian club game for the precision of his passing, whether over distances long or short. This comparison would indeed be most fascinating. The previous evening Triscardo had mentioned the player to me in terms of admiration. Although Bokor had been attached to Milan for several years he had suffered only minimally from injuries. During the seven seasons he had been playing in Italy he had missed just two games and, as Triscardo put it, "he never seems to get older". It was almost as though Gary Byrne had taken up the challenge and was saying to everyone "I may be here for only a short time but I'm determined to show you that I can compete with the best."

Amid the welter of copy, as though it could have any significance on the outcome of the match, was the information that Luigi Borro, Milan's highly respected central defender, would be celebrating his twenty-seventh birthday and was expected to perform well, thanks to his habit of drinking a glass of *grappa al limone* last thing at night. In addition was the news that his wife had given birth during the previous morning to a baby girl – who would surely bring Milan victory, wouldn't she? There were statistics concerning the private lives of the players of both teams. Listed were their names and ages together with their preferred make of motor car (Volvo most used), hobby (music), second favourite sport (tennis), reading (papers and magazines), person from the cinema (Dustin Hoffman by a neck from Robert De Niro) and favourite singer (Gianni Morandi from Elton John). Presumably this amount of flimflam would help to sell tickets in addition to those who had bought season-tickets, which explained the heading at the top of the page SEGRETO PER SEGRETO LA CARTA D'IDENTITA DELLE "GRANDI". The reader was given no option but to think that the game was of maximum importance.

I decided to go to the ground by car and was fortunate enough to find a place in which to park in the Via Frusa, one of the side-roads just to the north-west of the stadium. I collected my ticket for the press box from a steward at the main entrance, made my way up to the enclosure in the middle of the main stand and was well settled five minutes before the teams came out for their pre-match warm-up.

It was a cold but sunny day with only the faintest breeze blowing from the north. Most of my companions had their notebooks and other papers to hand so that they could be up-to-date with their statistics concerning the past results of the two teams. Soon after I took my place, both sets of players appeared – which appearance was immediately succeeded by a cacophony of noise as the crowd suddenly erupted.

The players created vibrant splashes of colour against the green of the pitch, those representing Fiorentina wearing a strip that was entirely violet while the players from Milan wore red and black striped shirts and white shorts. Emblazoned across the front of their shirts were the names of the relative sponsors, for Milan that of Mondadori, the publishing firm, and for Fiorentina that of Pallmark, a shoe-making firm partly owned by Marcello Stirata whose sales during the previous three years had started to soar.

As Triscardo had predicted, the Stadio Comunale was almost full. Ensignia commemorating the forthcoming World Cup finals were especially noticeable since the ground had been allotted three games from the First Round of that tournament, in addition to three further games in the later stages. Round the perimeter of the arena was a noticeable presence of carabinieri.

After both teams had come out I noticed that while most of the players of Fiorentina broke up into pairs in order to become warmed up for the match, Gary Byrne deliberately ignored his colleagues, preferring to remain by himself near the centre of the pitch practising his ball skills. Each to his own, it appeared.

It was Fiorentina who kicked off with that feckless breeze on their backs, but, in fact, it turned out to be a match very much of two halves. During the first half-hour or so the home team played some beautiful football, building up carefully from defence, doing their utmost to ensure that they remained in possession of the ball and didn't engage in moves that were too ambitious. Byron was especially noticeable for the ease with which he stroked the ball around, spotting unmarked players to whom he made telling passes, and linked up effectively with the central striker in the team, Roberto Cianfanelli. In fact it was the fresh-faced Cianfanelli who scored the first of Fiorentina's two goals before the interval, running on to a pass from Byron that caused the central defenders of Milan to be woefully out of position. I couldn't help thinking that Luigi Borro must have been thinking about his newly-arrived daughter, a feeling that was given added substance eight minutes later when he headed past his own goalkeeper a free-kick from the Welsh player that was curling towards the far corner of the net.

The theatrical quality of the game was increased by the way that the referee found himself being forced to argue whenever he made a decision. No players had their names taken but the official, a tall and straight-backed bank manager from Pescara, was frequently surrounded by two or three players who made a habit of questioning his decisions. This gave the first half the quality of a slow waltz, the rhythm of the play being interrupted frequently by stoppages.

Towards the end of the interval Triscardo was able to spare me a few moments after having phoned through his copy. "Yet another own goal," he remarked with a smile. "It's a strange statistic but during the past twenty seasons Fiorentina have led the table of clubs who have profited most by their opponents' mistakes. Many of those are scored here at the Comunale." He gestured towards the relevant goal. "They're playing very well and it'll be interesting to see what tactical ploys Milan change after half-time."

But what a contrast in the second forty-five minutes! As the match wore on Byron became increasingly leaden-footed and uninterested, giving the ball away on several occasions – one of which proved fatal. The outstanding Milan libero, Dino Lanati, intercepted one of his passes, strode forward into the Fiorentina half and stroked the ball in an aristocratic manner to Derek Juscikowskzi, the gifted Polish winger, whose shot from twenty metres away fairly screamed into the goal. As Istvan Bokor increasingly started to control the play for the visiting team, the pitiful form of Byron became even more noticeable. In the middle of the half a Fiorentina player jogged towards him after having received treatment from the trainer, and soon after I wasn't surprised to watch Byron making a four-course meal out of an innocuous tackle, rolling around on the pitch as though he'd received a ferocious assault. A stretcher was called for, which was followed by Byron being substituted by a defender who had started to change even before Byron had been tackled.

The last twenty minutes of the match, however, provided more action than had the previous seventy. The atmosphere was heightened appreciably when the referee awarded five free kicks in as many minutes to Milan, which saw him being surrounded by a posse of Fiorentina players gesticulating wildly. While Cianfanelli, who had always sought opportunities to make a decisive counter-attack, stood abandoned in the opposing half, the home defence was forced to resort to some scurrilous tackling to defend its goal as the Milan team threw forward several more players in an attempt to win the extra point required to gain a draw. Especially noticeable was the manner in which Haggan stuck magnetically close to Dubouis, bringing back memories of the harsh duel they'd experienced during the West Germany versus France semi-final match in the 1986 World Cup. Following the third foul in as many minutes on the part of the former, a chant went up from the Milan supporters of "*finocchio*", "*finocchio*", "*finocchio*" – and they weren't referring to fennel. After the Frenchman had slipped out of a challenge and flicked the ball just outside a post, the atmosphere started to crackle with tension and you could almost hear a collective sigh of relief pass round the ground as the referee blew the final whistle.

I went downstairs and joined the sizeable posse of reporters waiting to glean post-match comments from the two managers. Everyone agreed that it had been the right result to a game which most felt to have been lively and entertaining. Claudio Pandiani, the manager of AC Milan, made his appearance in front of the door to the changing-rooms after approximately five minutes stating that it had been a close contest between two sides very similar in strengths. In his opinion there should have been a penalty near the end of the game. He made it plain that referees were reluctant to give decisions against the home side, especially when they came so near the end of the match; and that if the game had been played in Milan he, as the home manager, would have been mightily relieved not to have a decision so harsh made against his team.

Soon after he had re-entered the dressing-room Fiorentina's manager, Sergio Taccone, came out, a tall thin man with a smile of contentment on his features. Several of the journalists immediately offered their congratulations, and when he came to speak about the game it was small surprise to find him taking a point of view opposite to that which had been expressed by the manager of AC Milan. No, he didn't think it had been a penalty but instead a fair challenge by a player who had only recently come on to the field. As for Byron, Taccone claimed that the player had been slightly injured in a tackle and might have played on, but in view of the fact that there was an important away game scheduled against Napoli the following Sunday, he didn't want to take any chances. He informed the press that the only other players who would be receiving treatment were the *libero*, Dobrilla, who had aggravated an injury to two of his ribs, and the half-Yugoslavian *tornante*, Giorgio Momcilovic, who had taken a knock on his left ankle when committing a tackle. Otherwise the slate was clean, and his disappearance back into the changing-rooms soon after was followed by a melting-away in the numbers of journalists.

I waited until the first three or four Fiorentina players started to leave before entering the dressing-rooms. The other members were in various stages of dressing, but the first object of my curiosity was Sergio Taccone, who was holding an animated conversation with the young star forward, Roberto Cianfanelli.

I waited for them to finish their conversation before begging Taccone for some of his time.

"Certainly." He spoke with all the contentment of a man who has just been victorious, and drew me aside until no one else was within earshot. When I informed him about the prime purpose of my visit, however, his benign expression vanished and his brow swiftly furrowed. "A shame you couldn't have come two months ago when he was in exquisite form. Now . . ." He gave a weary shrug. "No one knows how to make him recapture those moments during the autumn when he was unlocking every defence we played against. The players don't know and I don't know. Nobody knows." His voice sounded pained and acute. "*Nessuno*."

"I had a cocktail yesterday evening with Sergio Triscardo."

"And?"

"He doesn't know either." Not very amusing but at least it made him smile. "I liked him."

"He's very sharp and writes very truthfully as well as amusingly, but like us all is so frustrated at not being able to put the finger on what is distressing Gary Byrne." He paused. "Most upsetting is that some of our supporters have recently started to turn against him. Let me know if you come across anything interesting, won't you?" Taccone said before turning round to talk to reporters representing the German paper *Kicker* and the French paper *L'Equipe*.

I strode through to an area slightly beyond where my eye fell straightaway on the single person in that corner of the room, Gary Byrne, who was still in his football strip, making no attempt to get showered but instead, staring fixedly at the floor.

I passed benches which held muddied football strips, jockstraps, boots and stockings, walked up to him and said quietly in English, "Gary Byrne? My name is Ross Armstrong. May I have a few words?"

He looked up in my direction with a puzzled look on his face, his eyes a transfixing shade of light blue. "Of course," he said, a look of curiosity stamped upon his features since he obviously didn't recognise me as one of the journalists whom he saw on a regular basis. Lines of tension were etched across his forehead but still could not disguise the fact that his features were most striking.

"A pity about your injury," I said. "Will it keep you out for next Sunday?"

He shook his head and started to murmur in a soft voice, "That wasn't the reason . . ." before breaking off anxiously. He turned his head away and gave the floor another inspection. "It's nothing. I should be playing against Napoli next Sunday." He looked back at me.

I remained quiet in case he felt like continuing.

"I wasn't injured in that tackle. Everyone could see that I was going to be replaced minutes before the time when Luigi started to strip." Although there was a bitter edge to his voice, he was being very coherent. Astonishingly so.

"I understand, I understand," I murmured and held out my hand. "I'm here to gather details about you for a profile that is being planned by a television company. Could I take you out for a meal one evening sometime to have a talk?"

"How about tonight?" he said quickly, giving me a searching look.

"Name a time and place," I replied, surprised by the swiftness of his reply.

"You can make it? You really can make it?" His voice suddenly became sharp, excited, as though I was an angel from on high.

I nodded and gave him a smile. "Where and when?"

He thought for a short moment before naming a restaurant in the Via della Spada. "It's not really a restaurant but more a bistro very close to the station. Say about eight o'clock?"

"Does one need to book?"

He shook his head. "I eat there often but I'll give them a ring just to make sure."

"I'll see you there." I weaved my way to the door round sundry baskets and holdalls and turned back to give him a farewell wave. He had renewed the Rodinesque pose, however, staring glassily at the floor in front of him.

4

Sunday, 18th February

Just before I left for the evening meal I switched to a sports programme on television and caught the close of the discussion part of the show. The combatants involved were Rafaele Cozzato, a vituperative interviewer, together with the player whom he had chosen to eat alive, Gary Byrne. Underlining the point that against AC Milan Byrne had been substituted for the third successive occasion, Cozzato carried on to enquire whether the player expected to be chosen for the next game, in the Stadio Comunale in Naples against Napoli.

"You'd better ask the manager," Bryne snapped back.

The interviewer continued to probe aggressively, enquiring about Byrne's relationship with his team-mates, and moved on to ask about his private life, before finally putting the suggestion that it might have been distress in that specific area which was responsible for his loss of form. I was astonished at the impertinence of the questions being asked, and clearly so was Byrne. An enquiry concerning girlfriends was answered by an aggressive reply in which Byrne called into question the lineage of the Cozzato family – after which the player turned away most brusquely.

Whatever the provocation, interviewees simply do not behave in that manner, and the style of Byron's replies made me realise that the evening meal could turn out to be a disaster, despite his eagerness to attend. When I made my way there it turned out that the place in Via della Spada that Byron had mentioned was a bar with a restaurant section in the part of the establishment well away from the road. Presiding over the bar was an awesomely large Portorico coffee-machine that regularly emitted clouds of steam. Several slot-machines were noisily making their presence known while festooning the walls were ageing posters advertising Cinzano, Bitter Campari, Gancia, Stock Brandy, Martini, Fernet Branca and Cointreau among others. In a corner behind the door a trio of men were playing

Scala Quaranta, slapping their cards on to the table from a great height and shouting at each other with incredible vehemence. One of them, a pale-faced character in his mid-thirties who wore a brown suit, striped shirt and a black beard, was performing in such a frenzied manner I expected him at any moment to have a seizure.

I found a seat facing a mirror and was able to have a good look at Byrne when he came in. He ordered a whisky and dry ginger from the lean, young barman but when the latter asked him if he desired to go through to another room Byron gave a brief smile and shook his head. Which was when I turned to face him.

His eyes widened as he recognised me. "How long have you been here?" He glanced at his watch.

"About five minutes."

"Shall we eat straight away?" He answered his own question by finishing his drink in three enormous gulps, banging the glass down on the table-top and digging into his pocket for change.

"No, no," said the barman, waving his hand.

Byron murmured his thanks and, then, turning to me added, "Shall we have our meal?"

He led the way to the rear of the trattoria and sat down brusquely facing away from the two dozen or so other customers. I could hear whispers of his name and assumed that he didn't want to be pestered by autograph-hunters or the type of hassle that might come with being recognised. His features must now be among the best-known in Florence, given all the adulation he was receiving in the local paper and his face appearing nationwide on billboards, in papers and magazines and on television in the advertising campaign being put on by Giovanni Stirata.

He looked very smartly turned out. He was wearing a suit in light grey and a black cashmere polo-neck jumper. But if his accoutrements looked to be worth several million lire his expression looked totally bankrupt; one that was weighed down by worry.

The lines across his forehead seemed to be ingrained more deeply than they had seemed earlier in the day and the flesh around his eyes appeared more theatrical, as dark shadows circled them and lines of strain cut from the corners. His mouth was tight and the skin near his nose was white and pinched.

From ten metres away he appeared glamorous; from a distance of only one metre, however, he seemed to be in very bad shape — both mentally and physically. That must have been part of the reason for keeping his back to the crowd, loath to appear anywhere in public without being in absolute Alpha Plus condition.

As soon as I had sat down I asked the question that had recently puzzled me. "What was all that nonsense with the barman?"

He blushed slightly and turned away. "This is the first place I came to know well during my early days in Florence. That's all."

He had given only a vague answer to my question. "Is there another room behind my back?" I asked.

He nodded. "It's kept for use only by special guests."

"Thanks," I said drily.

Byron flashed a brief smile before saying, "We'd better order. I have a busy day tomorrow."

"Modelling in the morning, football during the afternoon."

"How did you know that?" he asked sharply.

I shook my head. "I just assumed it." I paused. "When did the modelling start?"

He gave me the whole story after we had placed our order. Interest had really begun at the start of the football season in the middle of September. The name Gary Byrne had been well-known in Florence ever since he had signed for Fiorentina in the summer and it had become known on a wider scale as teams began to play pre-season friendlies. But it had been Marcello Stirata who had been blessed with the astuteness to realise that Byron would make a marvellous model for clothing of style. In addition to being blessed with the wavy corn-coloured hair which lends itself emotionally to the sympathies of the Italian heart, he was very good-looking, with a full, firm mouth, delicate ears, a strong jawline and possessed the most mesmerising pair of pale blue eyes.

"What will you be modelling tomorrow?" I asked.

He looked puzzled as though his mind had been on other things.

"Remember? Earlier you said that you would be involved in doing some modelling in the morning."

"Oh, that," he said sharply. "Simply a new line in shirts that they want to promote before the summer starts."

43

"For a magazine?" I asked.

"They plan to put out a special brochure in early April so as to attract customers just before the summer season."

"And it pays well?" I asked.

"It can do," came the reply. "For this session tomorrow I could find myself earning roughly ten million lire." He paused. "Not all at the same time, naturally. Some in advance of the photographs being used and a percentage as and when the publication comes out."

"You must be a wealthy man." I gave a smile. "What with that money and your salary as a footballer, which can't be small."

He gave a bitter laugh and shook his head. "Small chance of that," he murmured. "My running costs are far too excessive."

"Girlfriends?" I asked.

"A few." He gave a nervous smile, and went on to offer the obvious appendix, "I like to treat them with style." Even a different girlfriend on each day of the week wouldn't use up more than a fraction of his earnings. He had answered my question, however, before giving me the opportunity to ask it. "Naturally, there's the money that I send back to my family in England."

In an attempt to further break the ice I played my trump card. "Actually, I talked about you with Eugenio Dal Bosco in London."

His eyes lit up immediately as though they had received a special charge. "Eugenio!" he exclaimed. "Such a marvellous person."

"Do you often hear from him?"

"Usually about once a week," came the reply. "Just to find out about my state of health, to ask if there are any favours I want doing. When I originally came to Florence he would telephone me almost every other day to see how I was settling in. You realise that in recommending me to the people at Fiorentina he was taking an enormous gamble. I'd played for only two clubs in England, and in addition had been loaned out as not having been able to fit in with a side; I had only won a few Under-21 caps for Wales and wasn't a name that would be of interest to some of the wealthier clubs such as AC Milan, Juventus, Internazionale, Roma or Napoli. I might not have been able to adapt to the special styles of football as played in this country; I might not have been able to find it easy to settle down in Italy – although the language wasn't completely strange to me." He was ticking off all these points on the fingers of his left hand, as though to show his gratitude to Dal Bosco. Again I found myself reflecting on what a fluent talker he was once he started.

It turned out that Byrne's early days in Florence could not have been more happy, principally thanks to his knowledge of Italian. Everywhere he went he was the undoubted centre of attention and his ability to make himself understood in the native tongue became crucial in speedily winning over the good wishes of the Florentines whom he met. But it also became crucial when talking to journalists who worked for newspapers outside Florence.

Foreign players had become catalysts within the Italian game and since Byrne was the sole entry that year to have come from abroad to join a side which had not been promoted he was of the utmost interest, particularly in view of the fact that a previous player to have been Welsh had been the legendary John Charles, who had spent several successful seasons playing for Juventus of Turin. Byrne could not have hoped to stand favourable comparison with "*Il Gigante Buono*" but it soon became apparent that some of the respect which the sporting press bore for the Gentle Giant was being accorded to his compatriot more than thirty years later.

"In fact," Byrne continued, "it could not have been much more soothing. There is a crucial difference between performing for a side which is struggling and one which is playing well. Almost from the first moment I started to play in Italy my form couldn't have been better and, in addition, there was the continuous interest being shown by Eugenio Dal Bosco."

He was obviously very drawn towards Eugenio. That was the third occasion he had mentioned his name without being prompted. "He's very much hoping that you'll get in touch with him soon."

Raising his eyebrows Byron pinkened slightly and gave a brief nod.

"Leaving him aside," I asked, "did you have much contact with other people who lived in England?"

He paused for a moment. "In my first weeks here I must have spent a fortune on telephone calls. Calls to friends who lived near Stoke, calls to other friends I had in the footballing world, calls to my family." He broke off and gave a smile. "One day I remember I felt so lonely that I spent almost two hours making long-distance calls to England! Still, I had little else to spend my money on." A pause. "Then."

"Now, it's different?"

He gave a brief nod but didn't elaborate. Not relaxed enough yet.

"Could you describe your average day – both before the season started and now that it is over half finished?" This struck me as a particularly typical journalist's question.

In the early days, just after his arrival in Italy, AC Fiorentina had been doing their pre-season training up in the hills to the north of the city, close to Modena. "That could be exhausting," Byrne explained. "I found the temperature a bit too much. One morning, when two of us were late for a training-session, the manager, Taccone, made us wait until last to board the coach that would take us back to the training-camp – and then drove off, ordering us to run back as a punishment! But mainly the drills were concerned with building up muscles that had been rested during the summer, of playing through a number of set-pieces that were new to the squad, of having brisk games of five- or six-a-side. When the season began we played fewer matches than they do in England but spent considerably more time on playing in small groups, practising our ball control. If the weather's warm we train outside on the training pitch; and when it's too cold we train inside. Tuesdays and Wednesdays tend to be our busiest days."

"How much time do you spend in training each week?"

"It varies as to whether we're playing a game in competition or not. But," he pinched his lower lip between thumb and forefinger as he paused, "I'd say roughly ten hours per week – not including the big match-day on Sunday."

I drew my eyebrows up. "So you have quite a lot of free time to do what you want?" Which had been the precise reason for my interest, but I was glad to see that Byron was becoming more relaxed.

"I suppose so," he said. "When I first arrived I found the other players were very considerate towards me. One of them, Roberto Cianfanelli, who spoke a few words and phrases in English, bought two Italian-English dictionaries, one for each of us so that we'd always be able to communicate. That was kind of him but after several days of living in Florence most of my knowledge of the language returned so that I started to *think* in Italian. I soon found myself being invited by some of the players to their homes to meet their families and occasionally their friends, and all told they couldn't have been more welcoming towards me."

"This popularity," I asked, "how long did it last?"

"It is present whenever I play at a level which approaches my true form." He paused. "Whenever. Whenever. Whenever." His voice slowly changed from outright speech to mumbling as he repeated the word several further times, almost as though he was drugged.

"When did your game start to be affected?" I asked gently.

He shrugged. "About six or seven weeks ago. At first it was really heartening that in Italy much more importance is attached to skill on the ball. If a player schemes out half-a-dozen brilliant openings then his value to his side will be considerable. The game here is like a giant game of chess with opposing teams trying to outwit each other. Consequently I spent a greater proportion of my time attempting to think out openings for the forwards, make passes that would split the opposition's defence. But suddenly just after the turn of the year I slowly began to go to pieces. Christ, I wish I could wind the clock back. Last year it was all smooth sailing: Byron this, Byron that, everywhere I moved and life was marvellous. But this year has been a total disaster for me."

"It might be a simple thing – such as losing form," I suggested.

"Possibly," Byrne murmured. He did not appear to be convinced, and looked away swiftly.

"I know that in Britain the programmes for the breaks at Christmas and Easter see clubs being made to play as many as four games in a ten-day period." I shook my head. "Complete madness, that. I can't believe that the Italians are such appalling masochists."

Byrne said slowly after a lengthy pause, "That was the start of my troubles. That Christmas break." He explained that Italian club football during that period of the year takes a weekend off, allowing the Italian players a few days' grace to rejoin their families as well as permitting foreign stars to return to their homelands for a short spell. "I was itching to tell my friends how much I had enjoyed the previous five months, so I took a short break."

"Maybe you're still suffering from a delayed reaction," I suggested. "Something like a footballing hangover."

He shook his head and gave a grim smile. "We were back in training on the day after our return. As for your footballing hangover, one week or two I could understand, perhaps, but not one which lasted for as long as six or seven weeks."

"But you can still perform outstandingly? That's the main thing."

"Sure I can. But there are one or two young players just itching to be given a chance. You can wager that when they are provided with one they'll go flat out to earn a regular place in the side." Ever since he had sat down at the table Byron had displayed signs of nervousness – brushing off his jacket non-existent pieces of fluff, easing his left forefinger round the collar of his cashmere sweater, incessantly pulling its sleeves down so that they covered his hands, shifting his glance from one side of his pale-blue eyes to the other as though he faced towards the restaurant.

He called a waiter and ordered a large Sambuca for himself together with a packet of Marlboro cigarettes. I kept silent until they had arrived, watched him take a few nervous puffs at a cigarette. "I didn't know you smoked."

"I don't," came the reply.

"You just started six or seven weeks ago?"

He gave a short nod and squashed out the cigarette viciously.

"How many a day?"

"It varies. Some days just two or three, some nine or ten." Suddenly he changed the subject entirely as though he knew I understood that the smoking was doing far more harm than good. "Do you ever play poker?"

"I have done," I replied, giving a quick smile. "I used to play regularly several years ago at gambling clubs such as Wickhams and – "

He interrupted me before I could finish. "Why don't you join me and some friends for a game at my apartment tomorrow evening?"

He must have assumed that I would still be in Florence, although I'd never said so. I nodded. "That would be nice. Thank you."

"Two local journalists, an American student and myself form a regular foursome, but the host of the evening is permitted to invite a guest."

"What sort of stakes do you play for?"

"Don't worry," Byron laughed. "They aren't too high. Anyhow, who knows – you might win." He failed to sound very convincing.

"I'm afraid that I'll be too rusty."

"Never you mind. It's only a game between friends, after all." He suddenly took a furtive look at his watch, pushed back his chair and leant across to shake hands. "I must leave and see someone else this evening." He stood up and walked speedily through the restaurant and out, on to the street. Strange, nervous behaviour that came close to being boorish.

I received a further surprise when I came to ask for the bill. The head waiter came over and told me there would be no charge: any friend of Byron was a friend of theirs.

The waiter, who was in his advanced middle-age, seemed happy enough to answer some of my questions. "Soon after he started to eat here regularly, Byron found himself totally unable to eat a meal in peace. Other customers used to pester him for his autograph, ask him for other mementoes which they could keep, write him poems and verses and on one occasion a man even turned up with a guitar to sing him a serenade. It all started to get out of control.

"Byron is a quiet and gentle person who was always polite on these occasions. He would often let his food go cold so that the *tifosi* of Fiorentina were kept content, and frequently would listen in silence while an ageing customer lectured him as to the demerits of the present team when compared with those that won the *scudetto* in 1955–56 and in 1968–69."

He paused and gave a brief smile. "After this became a feature of his visits back in the autumn I decided that he must be worn out by all the extra custom that he was attracting to the restaurant so I placed one of the tables out in the small room at the back of the trattoria. A place of quiet where Byron could eat in peace."

"He must have felt lonely on occasions," I suggested.

The waiter shook his head. "I don't think so. We are very close to his apartment; some of his close friends know about his liking for the place and would come and have a talk about life; and over the past few weeks there has been one girl in particular who has been a frequent visitor."

"Does she have a name?"

He gave me a flicker of a smile and blushed slightly. "*Scusi,*

49

but I'll leave that to Byron," he murmured before standing up and busily walking away.

I spent the rest of the evening in solitude in my hotel, hoping I could still play poker reasonably well, and watching a film on television which was full of atmosphere and suited my uncertain mood. *Indagine su un Cittadino al di Sopra di Ogni Sospetto* dealt with the machinations following a murder committed by a senior detective and the unwillingness of all his colleagues to believe that he had been the guilty party. Even though he'd placed all about the room straightforward clues as to the identity of the murderer, he remained the citizen above all suspicion. Trenchantly acted, it kept me enthralled until it finished just before eleven o'clock.

On an impulse I called Byron after having watched the film. Although I allowed the phone to ring more than twenty times there was no reply. He might have been having a bath, or might already have been asleep. I hoped so. Too much cavorting around town was the last thing he needed and might ruin his chances of being selected for the first team for the Sunday game against Napoli. I made a private prayer that things went well for him the following day. I'd seen nothing so far that had inclined me to give Tom Kennart a favourable report as to the wisdom of purchasing the player, and yet I was growing to like the young Welshman.

5

Monday, 19th February

At noon the following day I rang the bell alongside the wide front entrance of Stirata's villa which was set back a fair distance from the main road in the small village of Strada-in-Chianti, just to the south of Impruneta and approximately twenty kilometres away from Florence. It had been surprisingly easy to get him to see me. Such is the power of television.

I'd arrived in the area well before the agreed time for the meeting to reconnoitre the surrounding district and have a detailed look at the villa itself from the outside. It was a massive construction built in Tuscan limestone which looked as though it possessed approximately twelve rooms on three levels – plus an attic and cellar. Most eye-catching of all, however, was the exaggerated regard for security. A railing of wrought-iron circumvented the villa. One bodyguard stood permanently by the principal gate which was also made of wrought-iron and had been decorated with a purple fleur-de-lys, the motif used by Fiorentina as its emblem. A brace of guards sat behind a glass porch near the front door – glass which I assumed to be bullet-proof – and on my drive around the villa I had counted two further guards bearing guns whose mission clearly was to patrol the outside of the building. In addition I noticed that the chocolate-brown shutters had been drawn down over the windows even though it was a sunny, clear day in the second half of February.

I found myself being searched before being allowed inside the building and was relieved that I'd chosen not to wear any firearm. Who knows, I might have been presented to Stirata all neatly wrapped and packaged like a Christmas turkey? The interior of the villa was less fortified than its exterior but even so I noticed that all the windows had locks on them, each door an intricate network of chains and bolts in addition to safety-locks. On being told that Stirata himself had been unavoidably detained, I asked the maid for a glass of white wine and took the opportunity of her absence to take a walk round the sitting-room.

It was an area twelve metres by eight with dark blue chairs standing like sentries in the corners of the marbled floor. In its centre were a large rug, three small tables and a pair of matching armchairs in antique maroon. Expensive-looking prints of Florence adorned the walls, two of them from the eighteenth, and three from the nineteenth centuries. There was only one bookcase, but that ran along the entire length of one of the longer walls and contained books on Italian artistic life from the thirteenth century onwards. A writing-desk, a twenty-four inch colour television, an expensive phonogram together with a shelf stacked full of compact discs, two ornate standard lamps which both had a veneer of jade and a pair of stools covered with fine brocade completed the furnishings.

I'd just finished my drink when there was the noise of a car drawing up outside. There was much commotion as orders were issued before Marcello Stirata himself suddenly appeared at the door. Medium in height and wearing a shot-grey suit over a light blue shirt and an austere blue tie, he was a well-built man with hair that once had been black but was now touched with grey, a pallid parchment of a face that was heavily furrowed, a long spear of a nose, liquid black eyes of the type that always seem full of sadness and a jaw you could have broken rocks with.

I took to him from the moment he first spoke. "You'll have to forgive me for arriving late. The journey here was painfully drawn-out." He shook my hand with both of his.

"I'm very grateful for you seeing me at such short notice," I replied, and explained that I'd arrived a few minutes early. "Not knowing how long the journey would take, I wanted to give myself plenty of time."

"Of course, of course," he said and pressed a bell tucked away to one side of his armchair. When the maid arrived he said, pointing around with his forefinger, "Marianna, more wine for Signor Armstrong and for me, a gin-fizz."

"Sì, Dottore." The girl inclined her head and moved away to bring the drinks.

"Signore, as you know, I am researching a film about Byron, but naturally we intend to feature your great club, and therefore yourself. At the moment I'm completely in the dark about your background," I lied after the maid had disappeared. "I'd be very grateful if you could tell me some relevant facts concerning your past."

"*Certo, certo*." Stirata gave an understanding nod. "Although it's mainly due to you English," he continued, gesturing towards me quickly.

"I don't understand. What is?"

"My involvement in the world of clothes."

"But I always thought that the European cities most celebrated for their designs were Paris and Milan."

"They are, they are," he replied. "However, I became interested in art and design in the sixties when London was really the centre of the fashion world, with Mary Quant and Biba and Mr Freedom being the strong influences on me. I went over there for several weeks to stay with a friend who had a studio near Queen's Gate, studied some of the designs then in vogue and returned to Italy with real fire in my belly. I purchased a factory-site just outside Fadda, just to the south, which had formerly been used by a firm dealing in leather goods, and moved in with my own machines and staff." He gave a thin smile. "At the beginning times were hard, I had to look after a wife and two children, and there were several occasions when I thought I'd go broke. But no. I'm presently being quite successful."

"For sure," I replied. "But now you also have the pleasure of permanently living in a world of fear and of needing those characters outside."

"Plus three more who always travel with me wherever I move," he agreed, with a touch of desperation in his voice. He paused and then seemed to cheer up. "Let's have lunch."

The dining-room, across the corridor, was the size and height of a squash court. On its teak-panelled walls hung a collection of landscapes by artists from the secento and the settecento. Stirata motioned me to the far end of the long table some ten metres away, sat down and studiously placed a cream napkin across his thighs.

He ate the meal speedily in the manner of someone always keen to be punctual for appointments. A sizeable portion of *minestra di fagioli* was succeeded by *piccatina di vitello*, fruit and cheese but Stirata managed to talk at length about his business and the discovery of Byron as though he had been some type of saviour.

"For some months," he told me after the maid had brought

our soup, "I'd been looking into the value of launching a major promotion campaign for my business but whenever I was about to do so a minor matter would come along and prevent me. You know the sort of thing? Disputes on the shop floor of the factory, a model who had been signed up falling ill with chicken-pox and his possible replacement absent and doing other work; major and important figures at the business get flu. Those kind of things." Stirata broke off and took a noticeably long time to refill our glasses of wine.

"During last June I have seldom felt worse. There was a strike at my business, and as if that wasn't enough, Pablo Cortes, the Argentinian forward Fiorentina had purchased at vast expense, very severely broke his kneecap. The transfer season was almost finished, all the players of any reputation had already been signed by other clubs, so I asked our manager Sergio Taccone to discover from our agents abroad whether there remained any foreign players who might be worth purchasing.

"Only a few hours later Taccone was able to contact me with good news. He'd been told by an agent over in England, a Milanese called Eugenio Dal Bosco, that he knew of a player whose level of skill was right up to the standards which our fans would appreciate. Furthermore," he continued, his eyes starting to glisten with pride, "he was expected to be a marvellous cheap purchase because the transfer fee being demanded would be comparatively small.

"So I gave my blessing to Taccone, who'd seen the boy play, and when I first came to watch him train during our summer camp I realised what a useful purchase Taccone might have made. Byrne has all those attributes common to players in Britain – courage, enthusiasm, an appreciation of the value of teamwork – and although I was told that he is a marvellous player only for about an hour, I could appreciate that this might only apply in England where football is always played at a furious pace, and could understand how useful he could be for Fiorentina.

"Imagine our delight to discover that he had learnt Italian at school – which, naturally, meant that he wasn't starting 'from the cold'. Everybody liked him even more because he insisted on speaking Italian at all times – at first making the occasional mistake but always making a point of asking the person who he was talking to or by whom he was being interviewed to correct his faults in grammar.

"You can imagine how this display of humility endeared him to the reporters who covered footballing affairs and when a misprint in a paper put his name down as 'Byron' instead of 'Byrne' he became famous throughout the country overnight.

"The coverage of sporting matters in Italy, Mr Armstrong, has always been manic, so soon every newspaper dealing with sports news had adopted this new nickname." He tapped his left forefinger against his temple. "That was the moment when I realised that Byron was just the character to deal with all my problems. He was very popular here in Florence, and the attention he was receiving in the sporting papers was bound to rub off on the rest of the media."

"That misprint must have seemed like a stroke of good fortune," I remarked as Stirata finished his main course and pushed his plate away.

He gave a chuckle of satisfaction. "Yes. That could not have worked better since the name of the British poet is well known in this country, the sobriquet has a firm 'ring' to it, in addition to the fact that very soon our *tifosi* could observe that Gary Byrne was a true poet with the ball."

"Are most of the imported players re-christened by the fans?"

Stirata looked up at the ceiling and worried a lip in thought. After a pause, his head came level again. "It varies. Almost all are called familiar names by the fans, some of which make their way on to the sheets of the papers. Coloured players, especially, are ones who tend to benefit from those gifts. The first coloured footballer to play in our League was Luis Roberto la Paz, a Uruguayan centre-forward, who played several games during the 1947–48 season and who came to be widely known as '*Il Prete*' thanks to his looking uncommonly like a priest. Since that era noms de guerre have been terribly popular." He smiled. "After all, many of the *tifosi* do not read much except for the sports papers and comics."

"You were telling me about Byron."

Stirata nodded. "Most important for me, naturally, was the ease with which the nickname could be comfortably used in the world of modelling. One day when training was finished I invited him to my villa for dinner. When he arrived, he was nervous and acted as though he might have done something wrong and to start with he acted as though he was auditioning for an entry to a Trappist monastery." He gave a soft laugh. "However, he later started to relax and we had a lively discussion

55

in which he recounted to me some of the more bizarre events since he had moved to this country. When I sprang my surprise on him I found it was not difficult to get my way.

"The amount I promised to pay him for posing for some trial photographs must have seemed to him to be a nice sum; and when they had been developed, blown up and approved of by myself and two managers in the firm I intended to sign up the boy for a year's contract.

"As you can imagine I did that for considerably less than it would have cost to hire a top male model; added to which was the fact that I received an enormous amount of entirely free publicity whenever he got photographic coverage in the press or on TV." He suddenly raised his glass and finished his Chianti. "*Cin-cin*. Shall we move back for coffee and liqueurs?" He rang the bell for the maid to clear the table.

Once we were back in the lounge, and taking coffee, I asked Stirata how the morning session had progressed.

After looking puzzled for a moment (presumably due to my having such a close knowledge concerning his recent routine) he waved a hand in the air and said, "Not good, not bad. When Byron first turned up he looked as though he'd not seen sleep for a week. But the final result was very pleasing – once the photographs had been doctored. You don't have any idea what's troubling him?"

I was about to make some sort of reply when there was the sound of a car pulling up in front of the house, of someone slamming shut a car door and of voices in the corridor.

Stirata looked at his watch. "That must be my daughter, Giuliana," he said, starting to stand up. "She's home early." It had just turned half past two.

Giuliana opened the door noisily. She was dressed in a severe-looking black leather coat with a fur collar. She had nice legs. I had time to notice that she wore only a thin gold chain around her neck before she went over to Stirata and kissed him on each cheek.

"Giuliana," Stirata remarked sharply, "this is Ross Armstrong. He is making a film about the club. Mr Armstrong, my only daughter Giuliana." We greeted each other before he moved on to enquire why she had come home so early.

"Since I was given work only for this morning I remained in town for lunch and then came straight out." Her voice was a mixture of the polite and the brisk.

"Ah," murmured Stirata; then turning to me went on to explain, "Giuliana works as a model, Mr Armstrong."

I could understand why. Medium in height and slim as a flute she was blessed with the same firm jawline as her father, a wide and full mouth, creamy skin, cheekbones that were high and long, dark auburn hair which was swept up and partly held by a large-winged butterfly of black velvet. It was her green eyes, however, that straight away caught the attention. They should have been alive and sparkling; I saw them for only a few seconds before she walked out of the room but that brief glimpse was enough to tell me that they had completely lost their sheen and lay under her delicate eyebrows like pellets of jade, abject and flat.

"I'm afraid, Papa, that I shall be going out this evening," she informed him before swirling around and making her way upstairs.

After an embarrassing pause Stirata surprisingly seemed to take me into his confidence. "It's most disturbing, Mr Armstrong. Giuliana has been my constant companion ever since my wife died just over three years ago but recently she has taken to going out at all hours, refuses to have a bodyguard to accompany her and often fails to return to the villa until the early hours in the morning. I've offered to purchase her a new car which has an armoured body and bullet-proof windows but so far she has refused to be involved with any devices or services to do with security or protection. It worries me sick. But," he gave a mournful shrug, "what can I do?"

"Perhaps she doesn't approve of all this security," I suggested.

"I am only thinking of her." Stirata's voice sounded like a plain-chant.

"She looks very fetching," I said.

"*Certo, certo*," Stirata exclaimed. "Lord knows she's attractive enough to have the entire world eating out of her hand. I don't choose to pry into her affairs because I feel that might be the way to break apart the special relationship which we have built up recently, but I do pray for her at all times." He crossed himself reverentially. "But we have moved away from the point. You came here to discuss the affairs of Byron and here am I discussing the troubles I am having with my daughter." He gave a forced laugh. "What more can I tell you?"

"I don't know yet," I said. "I'm due to see Byron again in

order to find out his own opinion as to how well he has settled down, but can I come and see you on another occasion if I have to?"

"Sure, sure," he replied. "You had better telephone first to see whether or not I'm available."

"Of course I will," I replied. "Just in case you need to find me again here's where I am staying." I wrote down the address and telephone number on a piece of paper, gave it to him, made my farewells and was shown outside.

Out of the corner of my eye I noticed a powder-blue Alfasud which hadn't been there when I'd arrived.

6

Monday, 19th February

Mondays are traditionally a day of freedom for Italian players, a day when teams can count their assorted injuries, and start to plan for the following match.

Stirata had mentioned that Sergio Taccone was becoming increasingly concerned about the attitude of the team, and was holding a training-session that day, so I went to the training-pitch after lunch. Napoli were the opponents the following Sunday, a city where football had always been followed with intense fervour – a passion that had only been heightened ever since the coming of Diego Maradona in the June of 1984, and the triumph of winning its first *scudetto* three seasons later. It promised to be a tough challenge, but one that Taccone intended to meet with his players in a very fit state.

Marcello Stirata had promised each of them a substantial bonus if the match was won and Taccone had assembled the first team squad to make certain that his players realised the importance of the contest and were completely motivated. Muscle-building and other toning exercises had come first, followed by a session of ball control at which those present broke up into two groups of eight.

Byron performed well at certain stages but I detected a depressing casualness starting to creep in towards the end of the second half of the practice. Since Napoli favoured a system that used the old-fashioned deep-lying centre-forward, one player from the Blues had been asked to imitate this role, which meant that Byron had been forced to do much more marking, his defensive duties having been appreciably heightened.

During the training-session I noticed in front of the supporters numerous carabinieri, these being supplemented by several men in plain clothes. All appeared more interested in the movements among the assembled gathering than in those of the players. This attention to security was a natural corollary, given the increase in wanton vandalism and vicious crimes that had plagued a game which attracted vast amounts of money. I assumed that these few vigilantes belonged to a security firm regularly used by Fiorentina.

Byron saw me when the game had finished as the players started to return to the dressing-rooms. "Well," he said, "I hope they were pleased with that."

"I'm sure they were." I smiled at him. "I'm sure they were. I rang you last night but there was no reply."

A spot of colour entered his cheeks. "I had an early night," he replied. I didn't believe him. "Must have been asleep. How did you get on at lunch-time?" He turned his head away as though not interested in my reply.

"Absorbing," I replied. "I also took a nice drive around the area."

He grimaced. "All that security?"

I nodded.

"It must be some obsession," he said, shaking his head. "Anybody would think that the villa housed the crown jewels!" He broke off suddenly. "Though it can be lovely," he said morosely before he began to walk away. "See you this evening."

Byron had said "about eight", so I made my way towards his apartment approximately a quarter of an hour before and took a drink at a pavement café from where I could watch the arrival of the other players. One could never tell much from a brief examination but it might be of some use to have a preview of my poker opponents. You often anticipate cleverly after you learn three common facts: a person's age, their height and their weight. Those three statistics can so often influence the manner in which someone acts, and I wanted to gain some advance knowledge of the other players which would allow me to spend more time concentrating on the activities of Byron.

I ordered a glass of Orvieto Secco at the bar in the Piazza di Ognisanti, less than a stone's-throw away from Byron's apartment as well as the *Questura*, and sat facing the piazza. I waited for just under twenty minutes before sighting my first subject who must have been one of the local journalists.

Aged about thirty-five, medium in height and well-built, he had a face with dark pouches below tired eyes, a strawberry of a nose and fleshy lips. His features bore a perpetual look of disappointment, the expression of the archetypal also-ran.

It had long before started to run to blubber, in a way that made me assume he always drank a lot. He was also blessed with the double chin of someone who took no exercise, and was odds-on to die of a coronary. He was dressed in a dun-colour suit, a light cream shirt, dark red and white striped tie plus matching handkerchief and a pair of expensive-looking brogues.

Subject number two came along soon after – and imagine my surprise to see walking across the square none other than Sergio Triscardo, the reporter who worked in Florence for *La Gazzetta dello Sport*.

I could have no doubts whatever when it came to identifying the third man, who could only have been the American. Tall, thinnish and in his early twenties, he was dressed with the casualness of someone who habitually gets dressed quickly, one who never thinks about fashion. He walked with the loping stride of one who never has to hurry, and wore the type of blindly indifferent appearance seen on many students before they are turned cynical by the rough-and-tumble of the world and find their idealisms being swept away by the practicalities that come when forced to make ends meet.

I waited for about five minutes after the American student had passed by before paying for my drink, and making my way to Byron's apartment. It was on the fourth and top floor of a grandiose terrace in the Via Montebello which ran westwards straight from the piazza.

The fact that the building had no lift and two of the lights in the stairwell had fused made it a gloomy climb to the fourth floor. Byron answered the door when I rang the bell and showed me straight into the dining-room where the game was about to commence. All the other participants were seated round the circular dining-table which had its surface covered with an emerald-green rug.

Byron introduced the other players. "You know Sergio Triscardo who was in the press box on Sunday. This is Fulvio Bordi who writes on the political scene for the local paper *La Nazione*, and this" he indicated the American, "is Richard Scott Strickland the Third who is in Florence for a time writing a doctorate on a seventeenth-century humanist called Benedetto Accolti." The latter information he had clearly learned only a moment or two earlier. He paused and glanced over at the student. "Have I got that right, Richard?"

"Absolutely correct, Gary," the American replied and leant over to shake my hand. "Glad to meet you."

"Likewise," I replied. "So who and when were Richard Strickland the First and Second?"

They transpired to have been the father and grandfather of the Strickland whom I was facing, and men of a considerably less cultured turn of mind. Presumably there were still hopes that Strickland the Third would return to the family business in South Dakota after his period at Dartmouth, from where he had won an award to do a research degree in Florence.

Fulvio Bordi had already taken off his jacket and looked all set to start playing. There were four decks of new cards in the centre of the table and Bordi had put out in front of him his stack of money. I could see a pile of ten thousand lire notes together with some in higher denominations.

I looked towards Byron with some alarm. "You promised this game wouldn't be too serious."

Byron shook his head and spoke softly in English. "Don't worry too much. Fulvio often brings much money to the poker games to scare the rest of us rigid. No," he pointed towards Strickland, "no, that's where the money normally is. You'll soon see." He pulled out a chair. "Why don't you sit next to me?" I noticed that he had his back to the wall with the light from a standard lamp coming over his right shoulder.

When everyone had taken their places I found myself seated between Byron and Strickland with Bordi sitting next to the American and Sergio Triscardo placed between Bordi and Byron.

"We play a simple game. Second and fourth cards up, deuces wild and two hundred each in the pot for starters. That all right with you?" Byron's curt delivery, as well as heightening the atmosphere, underlined the degree of theatre in the occasion.

I played circumspectly for the initial dozen hands since I wanted to form some clear idea as to the manner in which the other people played. I was given an essential pointer towards the probable play of Bordi by the fact that, almost immediately after he had taken his seat, he lit up a cigarette and started to smoke in a hungry fashion, inhaling in a nervous manner and putting the cigarette out with savage stubs into the ashtray. It confirmed my impression that he was someone used to living on his nerves – a man who was highly-strung and who might very speedily lose his concentration.

In complete contrast was Sergio Triscardo. Throughout he displayed a considerable amount of élan and maintained at all times impassive features, the lizard-like calmness of an experienced poker player. He watched closely as the cards were being dealt to the others so that he might gain some tacit information concerning either the strengths or weaknesses of the hands he might have to control.

Richard Strickland seemed to be a very carefree player, one who had the fatal habit of looking forward to the following hand whenever he lost, one who possessed very little of the real application which underlies the poker of most skilful players. He perennially fiddled with his money, frequently looked at his thin gold watch, and as time wore on I noticed a factor which would be a direct give-away to his opponents: a slight tic which would show above his right eyebrow whenever he was dealt cards that were promising.

Byron, for his part, ingratiated himself skilfully with the other players – even with Triscardo who was also involved in the sports world. As far as Fulvio Bordi and Richard Strickland were concerned, it was exciting that he was a celebrity. In between hands Byron would seek to "bend" them towards him by asking searching questions concerning their work. Thus it was that when Bordi's supply of money noticeably dwindled, it was Byron he asked if he could cash his cheque – so giving the footballer a strong hold over him.

Bordi's problem occurred after we'd played approximately two dozen hands. I found that I was slightly down; that Richard Strickland had lost quite heavily and that Bordi had varied between some considerable losses and gains. He lost both his last vestige of patience was well as his funds when Triscardo forced him to bet substantial amounts. After being asked to show his hand, Triscardo had revealed a Full House of Queens over Sevens (one of the "wild" cards counting as a Queen) which had beaten Bordi's own Flush – Seven, Nine, Jack and King of Spades with the Two of Diamonds being used "wild".

I don't remember ever seeing anyone become enraged so speedily. Bordi's tie had long since been loosened and he'd been smoking Marlboro cigarettes as though there was no tomorrow but this defeat set him off swearing like a parade sergeant and promising bitter vengeance on the other journalist. Triscardo seemed to take it all in his stride, though, and after a while, having cashed his cheque, Bordi settled down. Intriguing stuff.

My interest in the game, however, had already been quickened when I had begun to suspect that the footballer was cheating.

7

Monday, 19th February

The canons of poker allow unlimited deception to win the amount being played for. That's an understood factor in the game. But when one player gives himself an advantage not being given to the others, that can only be assessed as bare-faced cheating.

Every player who stays alert to the patterns of a poker-session learns to "use" his opponents in ways that will be favourable to him: to watch scientifically as they handle their cards or lay their bets. That is a commonplace to an experienced player.

In the practice game I had watched, Byron had never displayed that intensity of feeling, that maniacally obsessional overdrive that belongs to those who possess the will to win at whatever the cost. Indeed, his performance during the football match had been far removed from that particular philosophy, almost as though winning was unimportant. His performance had been full of artistry and of delicate touches when with the ball, but that steely determination to win, that "*grinta*", had been manifestly lacking.

This game of poker, however, was different in a crucial way. It is a commonplace that the majority of the better players at the game always closely follow the hands of the dealer so as to watch those cards that are "flashed" during the deal, but it was only after we'd played several hands that I realised that Byron's main preoccupation during the deal lay not in watching the hands of the dealer but rather in looking down towards the table. His head would remain straight as though he was looking towards the centre of the table but his eyes would glance downwards. Resting on the table-top right in front of him was a silver cigarette case. It appeared to be well-worn and had initials engraved faintly on one side.

The previous evening Byron had claimed not to smoke when he had lit up a cigarette in the trattoria. While smoking he'd certainly not inhaled and had shown great nervousness, quite unlike someone well-used to smoking. So what was he doing today with a cigarette case in silver that must have set someone back a fair amount of money and which would only appeal to a regular smoker? I'd noticed that during the first three hours of play he'd only smoked one cigarette – and that during an interval when the players had taken a brief break in order to stretch their legs while Fulvio Bordi telephoned his office in order to make sure that his copy was being given maximum coverage.

After several hands during which my suspicions were turned to certainties concerning this cheating on Byron's part, I began to fathom his reasoning. I'd no idea how gifted had been the guest players, of course, but from past sessions of poker he might have surmised that the only regular opponent he had to watch carefully was Sergio Triscardo. Byron had made sure that the weaker players – Richard Strickland and Fulvio Bordi – were positioned at the far side of the table. Bordi he obviously dismissed as being a neurotic braggart, the self-effacing Strickland was very much someone who came to a session of poker looking for a good time, while, for my part, I'd informed him that I'd not played for years. Sergio Triscardo, however, was on his other side – and lying between them was that silver cigarette case.

Numerous gadgets have been used for helping a poker player to cheat without any form of collusion. Special contact lenses exist which allow a player to follow the colour as well as the inking of a card; there are cigarette packets and watches that have magnifying mirrors inside or on a face; various forms of trickery are possible such as dealing seconds, bottoms or middles as well as in cutting so that a skilled dealer can keep for himself those cards that are most useful. This cigarette case, however, possessed one unusual property: to all the other players it was just that, a handsome silver cigarette case that looked like a family heirloom. To Byron, however, it represented something else entirely: an amateur mirror that would allow him a secret glimpse at the hands being dealt to the person he thought of as the most accomplished poker player in the room.

It must have taken me about two hours to be entirely convinced. In that time Fulvio Bordi lost two large amounts while Richard Strickland kept on steadfastly losing largish sums and being comforted by winning several small hands, ones in which both Triscardo and Byron had chosen to opt out. Byron, however, showed his generosity of nature by allowing Strickland to take all the money on one occasion – although I noticed that his two Kings had beaten the pair of Queens which were shown by the American. The whole pot contained no more than ninety thousand lire but from the manner in which Richard Strickland carried on one would have thought that he had made a friend for life.

The footballer compounded his generosity by attempting to butter up Strickland. Initially, he made some favourable comments concerning the play of the young American; moved through discussing several of the previous hands; and finished up by talking about "luck" – as though that was a factor that played any significant part in a poker game.

First there had been the charity shown by Byron towards Fulvio Bordi in the cashing of the cheque and now there had been a strong attempt to curry favour with Richard Strickland. I began to wonder exactly when Byron would start to make use of this psychologically powerful piece of ammunition.

It occurred several hands later in the most bizarre of circumstances. It was my turn to deal and the "open" second cards I dealt were the following: to Richard Strickland a King, to Fulvio Bordi a Deuce, to Sergio Triscardo a Ten, to Byron a Jack and to myself a Nine. We all stayed in until the other "open" card had been dealt at the fourth round – to Richard Strickland a Queen, to Fulvio Bordi an Eight, to Sergio Triscardo a Seven, to Byron a five and to myself a Deuce.

"*Non posso crederlo*," whispered Bordi. I assumed that in addition to being surprised at seeing two Deuces dealt "open" in the first ten cards he was annoyed that there'd been one dealt to another player as well as to himself. It was at the next deal, however, that the game really took off, and the reactions were most illuminating. Richard Strickland's tic began jumping around after he received his card. Since his "open" cards had been the King and Queen of Spades I assumed that he must have a strong hand. Fulvio Bordi took his card, shook his head and then threw his hand on to the table. Sergio Triscardo shook his head "No" before I could deal to him. Byron took his fifth card and raised one eyebrow before fixing a stare on the ceiling. I dealt myself a fifth "single" card, but since my Deuce could have helped to make only one Pair I didn't show any further interest.

Richard Strickland had other things in mind. He reached inside his jacket and placed very close by him a black leather wallet edged with gold rims. After pausing for a moment he placed a bet of fifty thousand lire. Shaking his head sharply, Bordi confirmed the fact that his interest in the game was finished. After Byron laid his bet of fifty thousand lire I threw in my hand making it a two-player game. Byron matched each bid from the American. Two rounds of fifty thousand, then two of one hundred thousand. Suddenly Richard Strickland paused and carefully examined his cards – in such a manner as to suggest they had been changed. All of a sudden he reached into his wallet, produced another one hundred thousand lire note, laid it on the table and then looked away into the middle distance. The fingers of his right hand started to play on the tabletop.

Byron riffled through his cards as though they had only recently been dealt, steadily looked at each of us, and then gave a watery smile. "I suppose I'd better see them," he murmured to no one in particular.

Richard Strickland laid out his five cards most deliberately, with the expression of one who thought that he had to be the undisputed victor. The King and Queen of Spades, the King and Eight of Diamonds in addition to a crucial Deuce. That done, Strickland leant back in his chair and looked solemnly into the features of Byron.

As the Welshman stared at the cards fixedly Strickland remarked, "You can't possibly better those," and reached forward to take the money.

By way of an answer Byron gave a nod and revealed his hand in a theatrical manner placing each individually. To the "open" Five of Hearts and Jack of Clubs he added the Jack of Diamonds and the Jack of Hearts – a quartet that was laid on the table in the manner of someone performing a conjuring trick. He then took an agonisingly lengthy period to display his fifth card, which turned out to be the Two of Diamonds. While Strickland slumped against the back of his chair Byron painstakingly spooned up the notes displayed on the table, almost as though to prolong Strickland's agony.

Strickland shook his head, screwed up his features and he started to talk to himself. "Who was dealt a Deuce in the open?" He looked at me and then back in the direction of Byron. "What a goddamn fluke." He must have lost a few million during the game, but although he had a healthy disdain for money, he stood up swiftly and started to take his temper out on his chair, kicking it and wrestling with it before he got in control of his emotions. "Still, there's always the next hand. A good thing that last week I received some further monies from my folks." He slumped back on to his chair and with an apologetic smile reached for his wallet and produced a further cache of pink fifty thousand lire notes.

There followed a long pause which allowed our nerve-ends to regain their serenity and the succeeding twenty or so hands witnessed few large pots over and above the compulsory payments by each participant.

It was Triscardo who was involved in the next enormous hand; and his main opponent was – who else? – none other than Byron: a Byron, however, whose cheating went slightly, but critically, wrong. My interest was heightened by the fact that again, I was the dealer and that my cards would have a crucial bearing on the outcome. The first "open" cards in this hand showed up in this way: Richard Strickland was dealt the Five of Spades, Fulvio Bordi the Jack of Hearts, Sergio Triscardo the King of Diamonds, Byron the Ten of Clubs, and myself the Ace of Clubs.

We each stayed in until after the second "open" card had been dealt and the deal came this way: Richard Strickland was given the Eight of Clubs, which turned out to be his final card, Fulvio Bordi the Six of Diamonds, Sergio Triscardo the Nine of Diamonds, Byron the Eight of Spades and myself the Seven of Hearts. After a moment Bordi, having seen his card, threw his hand in disgust on the table.

When all the cards had been dealt I was left holding the Seven of Hearts and the Nine of Clubs as well as two Aces – those of Clubs, and Diamonds together with a Deuce. A strong hand that would undoubtedly be worth a bet or three.

Byron and Triscardo were up there alongside me as well. I guessed that the former might have a Straight and the latter a Flush in Diamonds; but I bet on the first three rounds in case their nerve failed, before deciding to throw in.

"Aces?" Byron spoke the question to himself and although I looked straight away he must have guessed that I had held more than one of them to carry on betting a few times.

The two of them continued to bet against each other for another couple of rounds before suddenly Byron took a steady look at his own cards, the backs of Triscardo's and said cheerfully, "It's all yours, Sergio. I only have a Straight."

Triscardo drew the money towards him, smiling faintly. "*Bene*," he whispered. "*Molto bene*."

"Sergio," I said calmly, "as a matter of interest what did you hold?"

He laid them on the table face up. The Nine, Jack, Four and King of Diamonds. "And this," he said laying down his last card – "the Ace of Hearts."

Byron's eyes narrowed. He was placed firmly on the spot. If he admitted having seen a reflection of any one card he would be branded for evermore as a cheat and most certainly would be barred from playing this select group of players at any time in the future. He'd obviously seen what he thought had been the Ace of Diamonds. He started to make a gesture of annoyance but I seized his arm and held him down. "Gary," I whispered quickly in English, "it's as Richard here is always saying: 'There's always the next game'."

He settled back in his chair and gave a vacant smile. When it was again my turn to deal I made a point of sliding out the Ace of Diamonds and the Ace of Hearts and of viewing them next to each other. They were so similar that I could appreciate how somebody intent on getting their image in a split-second might make a mistake.

But that particular hand was the turning-point in Byron's game. We only played five further hands but it was obvious that the concentration of the footballer had been seriously shaken, and he won no further amounts. When the telephone rang half an hour later he replied extremely tightly and it came as no surprise when soon after, at ten past one, he urged that we break up.

In those last few hands Richard Strickland experienced another sizeable loss, as had Fulvio Bordi – mainly in two hands which had been won by Sergio Triscardo. Byron had had that large win which managed to off-set several small losses while I'd won roughly the same amount as I'd lost. It had been Triscardo who turned out to be the largest winner, however, and he'd indeed been a delight to play against and to watch.

The evening's entertainment was far from being concluded, as it happened. I made my farewells to the other players before they left: Fulvio Bordi extremely briskly and Sergio Triscardo suavely urbane, while Richard Strickland seemed to be cheerfully resigned. Just before he left he passed across to Byron a small parcel.

For my part I promised Byron that I'd contact him during the following morning and made my way down the gloomy stairwell into the street outside. I had a sour taste in my mouth. Many factors simply didn't fall into place. Many, many factors. I couldn't see myself getting much sleep.

As I stepped on to the pavement, however, a set of further complications arose when my eye was caught by a car which pulled into a place some fifty metres down on the other side of the street. It was a powder-blue Alfasud, driven by Giuliana Stirata, that gleamed in the pale moonlight like a melancholic iceberg.

8

Tuesday, 20th February

I couldn't tell whether she'd noticed me but continued on my way as though I hadn't noticed her. I turned the corner and walked several steps before I heard the slam of a car door which was instantly followed by the pitter-patter clip of her heels on the pavement, and then by silence as she made her way to Byron's apartment.

Ten minutes passed before I retraced my steps up the gloomy staircase, moving as silently as possible. There was a lengthy pause after I'd sounded the bell, but just before I was about to ring for a second time, the door was slowly opened. Byron thrust his head out in turtle-fashion and peeked over my shoulder to make sure I was alone. As soon as he realised who it was, a look of relief washed across his features, followed at the next moment by one of anger: relief, I presumed, that the intruder was a person he knew, anger at having been so rudely interrupted.

"Sorry," I said and made a feeble excuse. "I forgot to take my cigarette case."

"But you —" he started, only to break off after I'd slid past him.

I shook my head. "No. I don't. Neither do you. But we'll come to that in a moment." I broke off sharply because I recognised the distinctive, musky smell of marijuana that clung round the room like a heady perfume.

Half of a joint that had almost died was still burning in the base of a glass ashtray. I took two steps and squashed it out ferociously before looking around the room. A small, black leather pouch was lying untied on the corner of the dining-room table, and alongside was a packet of cigarette papers and a small green plastic lighter.

I moved over, seized them all and put them into the pocket of my jacket.

"You bloody idiot!" I turned round and shouted at Byron. "How long have you been doing this?" I prevented my voice from sounding alarmingly hysterical. I'd not fully realised how involved I'd become with this young man, but there was something remarkably magnetic about him and the way he could draw you into his life.

He took some moments before he stammered, "My first time."

"I simply don't believe you."

"Promise." His eyes glazed suddenly and his voice leapt into a snarl. "Anyway, what the bloody fuck's it to you?"

"Gary, you're being a fool and an idiot." I pointed at the pocket which held the pouch. "This you need least of all. How did you come to start?"

He was quiet for a time, and gave an answer only after I repeated the question twice. Even then he had to take two steps back. "When we played last week it was Richard Strickland's apartment up in the Via della Pergola. He brought along a friend of his who's also studying for a post-graduate course at the university. The three of us had a drink after Bordi and Triscardo had left. This friend enquired whether football players relied on dope as much as basketball players did in the States. When I replied that I'd never come across it in the game and had never tried it, he suggested I had a smoke of something mild, such as grass."

"So that parcel I saw Strickland passing over to you contained this?" I reached into my left-hand pocket and produced the pouch.

Byron nodded. "Strickland's friend gets it from a contact in Morocco."

"Can't you see what a bloody fool you're being? As a player you must be very aware that twenty-one can become thirty-five before you know it. And even then you have to look after yourself properly. Messing around with drugs, however mild, is certainly no way to do *that*." I paused. "It's your life and you can ruin it any way you choose, but swear to me this is your only supply." I held the pouch up.

He waited for a moment before giving a forlorn nod. Then his voice became scathing. "Why the hell did you come back? Not because of that. You couldn't have known."

I shook my head. "Just as I was leaving," I replied, taking my time, "I saw Giuliana arriving in her Alfasud. Which helps explain why you suddenly lost interest in the game after her call. It was her, wasn't it?"

He nodded. "She was going out to dinner with some friends who live nearby, and hinted that she might call in here afterwards. Anyway," he became more aggressive. "What's that to you? I've to train tomorrow so I can't be late getting to bed." I assumed that even though he'd stopped being watched all the time by people associated with Fiorentina, he was still forced to be judicious.

"Of course, of course." I paused. "Right. Where is she?"

"Why do you want to know?" He came and stood close to me so that I could feel the anger burning in his eyes. Although his fists were clenched and he seemed ready to punch me, he'd find it impossible to convince me that he was mad, bad and dangerous to know.

"Look, Gary," I pushed against his chest with my right hand, "you may not believe this but I want to help you. You act as though you're in a hell of a mess, as if you've lost every friend you ever made, as if everyone is trying to do you down." I shook my head. "Wrong. Here's one that's not for a start. Right, where is she?"

He stared at me sullenly for a time before he turned on his heel and entered the bedroom. The sound of someone weeping came out as the door was opened.

While he was attending to Giuliana I used the opportunity to glance round the room. When I'd been playing cards most of my attention had been absorbed in noting the characteristics of my opponents, but the room struck me as being untypically spartan. Two colourful posters had been framed, and on the sideboard acting as book-frames squatted a pair of heavy ornate vases.

While the mantelpiece held only a bronze clock, travelling quickly round the room my eye fell instantly on a chair in a corner of the room that held a shiny leather training-bag into which had been stuffed all his winnings. I moved away speedily when I heard them talking just before they opened the door.

There was a brief pause but the two of them eventually appeared; Giuliana was clutching a pale-blue handkerchief and the skin round her eyes looked puffy. Byron was holding her close, one arm wrapped around the right shoulder of her cream long-sleeved dress.

"Do you want to tell me what's the trouble?" I asked. His one answer was to squeeze her more firmly. Neither of them seemed eager to talk. "You'd better stay the night, hadn't you?" I said to Giuliana. "You can't drive anywhere in this state, at least not now."

After she'd escaped from the dinner party in the Lungarno Amerigo Vespucci, Giuliana had toured round the neighbouring streets before telephoning to discover how much longer the session of poker was likely to continue. She'd subsequently driven round the block until we'd finished and had been desperately unlucky in that I had been the last person to leave.

Perhaps that might have been her stroke of good fortune. It certainly promised to be mine.

"I'll contact your father and explain that I bumped into you having trouble with your car, that I fixed a hotel room and that you'll return later in the morning." I walked across and held one of her elbows. "That's only being economical with the truth, isn't it?"

She gave a worried smile before allowing her shoulders to slump in relief.

"And when I return we can all have a talk." I couldn't help sounding slightly officious, but smiled warmly at both of them before making my way to the telephone.

It was answered after the first ring. A cast-iron voice only had time to grate "*Pronto*" before I asked to be put through to Stirata. "Tell him it concerns his daughter."

Moments later Stirata's voice came over the phone. "Who is this?" He sounded uneasy.

"Dottore, it's Ross Armstrong," I said soothingly. "Giuliana's fine. Her engine flooded when she left dinner and I met her as I was walking along the Lungarno Corsini back to my hotel. I've found a room for her and she'll be home later this morning. I was happy to help her." Not so far away from the truth.

There was silence at the other end. Relief, I presumed at discovering that his treasured daughter was all right; a relief I intended to use to my advantage.

"Let me talk to her," came the strained response. A brief pause was followed by a quiet, "Please."

I passed across the phone to the girl. "Papa – " she began, but before she could continue she was rudely interrupted by sounds of an excited voice that asked if she was all right, enquired whether she'd been harmed in any way, and promised that a car would be sent into town straight away to fetch her.

"*No, no, Papa. Calmati, calmati,*" she replied and stated that she'd see him later in the morning.

Further cries of "Are you sure?", "You're certain you'll be all right" and "I'll pray for you" could be faintly heard before he asked to speak to me again.

"Signor Armstrong," he said in very deferential tones, "I can't thank you enough."

I told him that I'd try to think of a way, informed him that his daughter would be with him a few hours later and hung up after he had offered still further chants of gratitude.

I turned round to discover that Byron had made some fresh coffee and was in the process of adding some Irish whiskey to his own mug.

Very wise, I thought, anticipating that he might soon require strong refreshment. I sat down and pushed my own mug over towards the bottle. "I'll also have some, please, but make sure you tell me *everything* that's on your mind. What's going on between you and Giuliana?"

His eyes glinted, almost as though something else had entered his mind, but he told me about their relationship in nervous tones. He'd met the girl when Stirata had used him as a model. "Since she already knew her way round that particular world, the president himself thought that she might be able to give me some advice that would be useful, some tips that might save both time and worries."

"When would that have been?"

"In late September. After we'd played our first three games in the League. It started when Stirata himself called me into his villa so that we could meet each other, Giuliana and I. What angles to avoid, how to display your strongest features in the best manner. And so on."

I turned towards the girl who had mercifully started to appear less distraught. "When did your interest in modelling start?"

She thought for a moment before whispering, "About twenty months ago."

"After your mother died?"

"Yes," she said, looking away. "A large agency had some work for me in Milan, and a friend of Papa's thought my face would be very suitable, so I went up there for a few weeks. I'd never been that interested in fashion but when not working I found that I'd spend large amounts of time wandering about the chic ghetto of the city just to the east of the Duomo." She threw back her head and gave a carefree laugh. "Merely looking at the new styles, the progressive designs, just having discussions with people. Now it's become almost an obsession with me. One night I had a dream that I'd be laid to rest in a grave within the area bounded by the Monte Napoleone, the Corso Vittorio, the Via della Sorga and the Via Manzoni!"

I smiled, and turned back to Byron.

He glanced towards Giuliana. "If you're married, or better if you're married and have children, then the club leaves you alone for most of the time. But if you're still single," he paused, "then the club does tend to become very paternal, seems to be concerned at every moment about the private lives of its players."

"But you were allowed to move into this place?"

"Mostly thanks to Eugenio Dal Bosco," he replied. "At the finish of every conversation with him I complained of being allowed so little freedom and wondered aloud when I would be permitted to find an apartment of my own."

"This one, or did you move somewhere else first?"

He nodded and looked around the room. "This place. The prompt for my move had come from Eugenio who suggested to Taccone that I might play even more relaxed football if I had an apartment I could call my own. That meant that I didn't have to be so watchful as to the company I kept." He glanced briefly at Giuliana.

"What do you mean exactly?"

He screwed up his face. "If you live in any type of hostel you find that every move you make is being watched and reported on. Players find themselves receiving favours and attention from fanatical supporters, and often find themselves being harassed by female hangers-on. Especially if you're not married. As my popularity grew I couldn't attend any function whatever without attracting immediate attention and though at first that encouraged me to feel more settled, very soon I found myself being denied any privacy." He gently pointed towards his companion. "Then Giuliana came along and my urge to move became more urgent." He took her hand and gave it a lingering caress, and looked into her eyes.

"When did she become someone special to you?" I asked.

"Almost from the day we met," he replied. "We were both keen to learn about fresh matters; I was eager to pick Giuliana's brain about modelling and she was keen to improve her command of English, to try and find work in Britain and the United States. Like so many of our age we find travel abroad always beguiling."

When they'd started to meet originally, however, Giuliana always suggested venues several kilometres away from Florence to avoid Byron being harassed by well-wishers. They paid visits to restaurants in Pistoia, Lucca, Arezzo – even travelling as far as Montepulciano – in their almost pathological desire to keep their friendship as secret as possible.

Once Byron moved into his flat, privacy was easier to obtain. "Things changed rapidly, as you'll imagine, after I found this place," he continued, pointing around the room, "so that finally I could have some time to myself. It was marvellous to see Giuliana in private, to be able to relax, and not have to keep vigil in case people spied on you. She made our relationship seem to be less important than it was by making sure that she went out with other men, but very soon after I moved here we started sleeping with each other. Giuliana started to lie to her father, telling him that she was going to be away on business or spending the night with another acquaintance from the modelling world. You know how possessive he can be?"

"When did this start?"

They looked at each other for a moment before she murmured "*Napoli*" almost under her breath. She then said firmly, "*il ventiduesimo d'Ottobre*," as though it was a date she would never forget.

He nodded. "I played my finest game to date with Fiorentina that day. We won 2–0 and the two of us went out to Fiesole for dinner."

"Then back here for the night?"

He nodded.

"And her father?"

"I invented a friend," she said and gave a guilty smile. "On the other side of the city entirely. It was the first occasion in months that I'd told a lie to him." She screwed up her face. "One part of me felt so squalid and cheap."

"And were you with this mythical friend last night?"

"I was simply being 'economical with the truth' again." She laughed and blushed prettily. "Ever since Mama died my father has held me in special affection and has always given me what I've asked for. That means that he's always watched my movements, since for the last few years he's had to combine the role of both parents. As you know he is very prosperous, but it's taken years and years of endeavour to become that wealthy, and lately he's become almost obsessive about security."

"I noticed," I said drily.

She nodded. "However when Byron here," she flashed him a look, "came into my life I was forced to choose to tell small lies as to my movements since I thought that Papa might become jealous."

I broke in, gave a look of horror and exclaimed, "His only and revered daughter becoming involved with a football player, one of his underlings. Never!"

She burst out laughing. "You're teasing, but it's quite true. When I first started to go out with boys, even when Mama was still alive, I discovered that they had all been carefully chosen and all came from respectable families, many of them titled." Her face suddenly became unexpectedly secretive, and her eyes lost their sparkle. "And then this."

I turned to Byron who gazed into her eyes for a long time before he gave an explanation in carefully measured tones. "What Giuliana means is that her period is more than seven weeks overdue. Naturally when she told me it was a couple of days late in not coming I tried to calm her down but as the time lengthened we both started to worry ourselves sick. You know."

I didn't, but much of the tension behind his recent behaviour started to make sense: his nervousness while playing football, his erratic behaviour when we'd had that meal together on Sunday night. The lines of worry around his eyes and mouth. It also helped to account for Giuliana's expression of misery, and explained her leaving the dinner party early, of needing to have the company of her soul-mate.

"You've not been feeling nauseous in the mornings?" I said, asking Giuliana an obvious question.

"Not yet," she murmured, shaking her head slightly.

I walked away from them over towards the window and addressed the curtain. I wasn't certain of my dates but felt that I had to make some points which couldn't help but sound outrageously forced. "The seventies witnessed some progressive times for women's rights under the law in Italy. Twenty-five years after having been given the vote and more than a decade after being permitted to enlist in the police force 1970 saw women being given the right to divorce, and it must be more than fifteen years since abortions were made legal." I turned round slowly.

"No, no, no," Gary exclaimed, rushing over to squeeze my shoulder as though we were about to start a fight. "Neither of us would even think of that. No." He shook his head several times.

"You don't want to consider marriage?" I enquired softly.

"Not at this time." Gary replied, with a sharp edge to his voice. "Not like this."

"Then what?" I asked.

A brief pause before he asked. "Do you live in London, Mr Armstrong?"

"Ross." I replied swiftly. "Yes I do."

"Earlier you said that you would like to help us." He gave a brief look across at the girl.

"Yes." I took his elbow and guided him back to his chair.

"Yesterday when we were discussing our futures," he continued, "we decided that one solution to this problem would be for Giuliana to go abroad for a time until after the child had been born. We thought of having the baby adopted, but as far as her friends in Florence are concerned it will very much have to be a case of 'out of sight, out of mind'. And," a swift look at Giuliana, "we thought of London as a possibility. Giuliana has never been there but the city has so much to see and do that she should easily discover things to keep herself occupied. In these last five months she has picked up some English." He paused and again looked across at Giuliana.

"How you might help us is this. Her father knows a number of people through his connections with the worlds of football and fashion. Obviously we can't get in contact with any of those in case he finds out what really is going on. This means that what we really want is a friend outside those two worlds who will help us and keep quiet."

"You said us," I remarked.

"Well." A strange, almost haunted, look entered his face, "I've been living in Florence for roughly seven months, and until the present situation began to affect us some weeks ago I can't remember a time when I've been happier. I'd have liked, if possible, to have remained in Italy when this contract expires, but Giuliana and the baby must come first. I will return to England at the end of the season." His tone of voice implied that he saw it as his duty to be similar to that of a buttress during those final tiring weeks of her pregnancy.

"When will that be?"

"Although the World Cup finals are guaranteed to dominate June, Fiorentina is still involved in the Coppa Italia so there'll be some important games taking place in May. I hope to be back in Britain soon after for the summer break so will be able to help Giuliana. I won't be around her for her first week or two in London, however."

Or longer, I wondered?

"So we need some person who'll be on hand and able to act as an adviser until I arrive."

I pointed at my chest. "Me?"

He nodded. "We'd be very grateful if you could find somewhere in London that Giuliana could live discreetly. When it comes to money . . ."

"Shall we worry about that when the time comes?"

His brow suddenly cleared and his eyes started to come alive. "You mean you'll help us?"

"I'll certainly think about it," I replied.

"Great." He gave a smile and looked towards Giuliana. "When we discussed this ourselves last night I realised how helpful to us you could be, knowing many people inside the world of the media. Great."

"And what would you have done if I had said no?"

His face suddenly fell. They obviously hadn't anticipated that outcome. "Thought of another way, I suppose," he said after giving me a worried look. I'd certainly taken the wind out of his sails, and his brow quickly reacquired its lines of worry.

"Added to which, how would you've coped if I'd not returned to your flat just now?"

"I'd have rung your hotel and asked to speak to you."

Giuliana nodded, as if showing that she was equally involved. "Do you know yet when you might leave the city?"

"Probably tomorrow." I shook my head before standing up. "I must get back to my hotel. You've given me a fair amount to think about but I promise to be in touch soon."

I moved across to shake Giuliana by the hand but for her that was being far too formal. She leant across and kissed both my cheeks, and held me close. I could feel how paper-thin she was. Or had become.

"*Grazie, grazie, grazie,*" she said, and stifled a sob which went straight through me. When she finally let go I saw that tears of gratitude had started to trickle from her eyes.

I shook my head. "For what? I've done nothing. Please don't cry. Just have a good night's rest. Remember, in the morning, your engine flooded, and since you didn't want to return to the dinner you booked into my hotel. Okay?"

Another unimportant inaccuracy that she'd have to tell her father.

"Okay." She gave a forlorn smile.

"See you soon." I blew her a farewell kiss.

Just before Gary let me out I thanked him and said, "I'll see what I can do, and on the principle that old jokes are often the best we must have a discussion sometime about cigarette cases and some of their more uncommon uses."

Part Two

During the spring of the previous year Domenico Mozzolino had been fortunate enough to take a place in a studio used by other avvocati. Only two hundred metres away from the Palazzo di Giustizia in the Porto Vittoria it was less than one kilometre away from the apartment which he had recently purchased in the Via Carlo Crivelli.

His life had taken a turn for the better two years previously when he'd started to act as a legal representative for Salvatore Brini, a very prosperous film and theatre agent who worked mostly in Milan. The advent of cable in Italy, alongside a flourishing television industry, had seen the rights of all those concerned with the stage become very important, and almost all involved made use of either an agent and/or a lawyer or both.

Domenico Mozzolino was making a considerable reputation as a lawyer guaranteed to draw up tight contracts in which the rights of thespians appeared paramount. Much of his work was involved negotiating the finer clauses of contracts with the television companies in Milan, but not infrequently he would have to fly down to Rome and see through a film deal for a personality from the stage who was a paid-up member of a powerful union such as Unione dei Lavoratori dello Spettacolo.

Salvatore Brini had approached him one day in a state of rare excitement. During his vacation the previous month in Sardinia on the Costa Smeralda he had hired a car and driven around the island looking for nuraghi, the massive and squat fortresses dotted round the island which each resembled a cone with its peak cut off, and were built from huge boulders. In particular he wanted to visit the Nuraghe Su Nuraxi, near Barumni some sixty kilometres north of the southern port of Cagliari, a nuragic castle with streets, homes and corridors, which dated from before the fourth century B.C. On his way southwards that evening he stopped for a drink at a hamlet called Villacidro, noted locally for its liqueur, and had watched a group performing in a village festa.

Once an agent, always an agent, and wherever he went Salvatore Brini sought out talent. One person who in particular caught his attention that evening was a striking girl of seventeen with strong olive-coloured features and flaxen hair bleached almost white by the strong Sardinian sun who danced and spoke with a rich, if raw talent. Astonished by coming across such promise, following the performance he'd approached her with his card, and encouraged her to contact him if she ever thought of coming to the mainland. She'd moved with such grace and eloquence and had thrown out her voice with such passion, he was sure that she would easily find work in the expanding world of television.

Time would tell, of course, he thought as he drove along the country road to Cagliari. Time would tell. She would have to lose that absurd epiglottal accent and certainly would have to change her name. Manuela Decchuras? That would never do. She'd require a much less awkward surname, and probably a stronger first name.

By the time Salvatore Brini reached Cagliari he was convinced he'd devised a winning combination. Donatella Spezia. Yes, that sounded right. Donatella Spezia. He repeated the name several times carefully, and, when he was sure, determined to save that name only for her. It could become a sort of personal patent if the girl ever thought of coming across the water.

Two years later she did.

9

Tuesday, 20th February

On the flight I drew up some notes about the player which were designed to give Tom Kennart a report that would be informative as well as unbiased. It was difficult, since on each occasion I'd met the footballer I'd liked him more, and in the early hours of the morning I'd been very touched by Giuliana's behaviour, and I hoped Gary knew how lucky he was.

I'd rung through to Giovanni Gallo earlier that morning. He was a small-time investigator based in Florence who carried out mundane clerical duties for a host of people, many of them larger operatives working for wealthy business concerns or small firms from other parts of Tuscany. He was also used by ordinary citizens who wanted certain information that tended to be difficult to obtain.

You know the form. An important fact concealed in a mass of other facts and the whole bundle wrapped in metres of red tape. Byron had opened an account at the Banca Nazionale del Lavoro in the Via Strozzi nearby, and I asked Gallo if he could procure copies of all the transactions carried out by Byron since he had come to live in Florence.

I reckoned that by this stage in the season the player should have managed to save a good amount. Whereas his expenses could not be crippling, his income must be extensive. He was being paid a nice starting salary, Fiorentina was having a successful season – which meant that the sums he received in bonus payments should be most healthy – and he had that additional sum of money coming in from his modelling.

But I needed details, to get some idea as to what extent worries concerning money were a thing of the past. Gallo promised to see to the matter right away and when the information arrived by messenger at half past eleven it proved to be absorbing. In addition to the sums Byron was paid by Fiorentina, and the salary he'd been receiving since September for his work as a model, other transfers had also been put through in no set order. Since these were variable, I assumed they reflected his success at poker.

However, there'd been regular withdrawals of huge amounts during the last week in each month that greatly interested me. Certainly Byron dressed smartly, but many of the clothes he wore would surely have been provided by Marcello Stirata's business, and he had no expensive vices. So where was all this money going to?

Giuliana? Surely not. She was very much her father's pet, came from a wealthy family, and had always wanted for nothing. When I'd talked to them the previous night, their relationship had struck me as being above all sympathetic and intelligent.

Who could say whether their affair would proceed for much longer? They'd known each other for just over five months, they came from totally different backgrounds and their attraction for each other had been nurtured by the fact that they had both been involved in the entertainment business; essentially a world of the present, one which tended to possess a very short memory, and one in which success could be based on suicidally slight values. In twenty years' time the godlike Byron might be a dipsomaniac like his father and Giuliana might be fighting a losing battle against the tape-measure and sagging bank accounts.

Speculating about their future occupied me until we were almost at Heathrow, and greeting me when I reached my flat I found a thick, hard-backed envelope that gave information I'd requested about his aunt and her second husband in Silkstone. In addition there was a slim buff-coloured envelope that held a photocopy of a document that gave details about an important event in Gary's life.

I gathered from reading the document, written by Maureen Kelly, his social worker, that on 22nd April, 1982 he had been placed on a Supervision Order, following the crime he'd committed in acting as a look-out when an old woman had been mugged. He was expected to be seen by a social worker on a regular basis, both on the treatment programme once a week, and at home, once a month.

His move from London had occurred almost immediately afterwards, and it was to Sheffield that he had been required to be taken by his aunt to take part in a treatment programme. Although Gary was released from the misery of having to attend in May 1984, his Supervision Order remained on the files and would be a permanent stain on his record.

I looked next at the material inside the thick envelope, the one which gave details about his guardians during those depressing years.

Details about Sian Wright were extremely sketchy. I gathered that she'd been born Sian Meredith in Oswestry on 8th January, 1951, was five years younger than her sister Gwyneth, had been to school "in North Wales" before moving to study at London University. From there she'd moved on to Milan in 1973. Soon after she had married *un avvocato*, who had been killed in a road accident slightly over three years after they had married. She'd returned to London in April 1978, had found work after some months as a translator of books and pieces from Italian.

Those about her husband Richard were much more extensive. Born in Harrogate on 9th November, 1937, the only son in a military family, he had lost his father during the war in North Africa. His mother had sent him to be educated at Ampleforth College from where he'd gained a scholarship in Classics to Pembroke College, Cambridge but when he arrived had chosen to read Modern History. He gained First Class Honours in both parts of his degree, but had again decided to change subjects and had opted to practise Law.

He'd then attended the Inner Temple until fully qualified, before going up north again in 1963 and working on the North-Eastern Circuit as a junior barrister in a set of chambers in the Headingley district of Leeds. He'd been made a Queen's Counsel in 1983, three years after becoming married for the first time. There were no children.

As I'd already gathered they owned a small house in Silkstone which dated from Georgian times and which Richard had purchased just before they married on 12th July, 1980. They owned two cars, a Mercedes Benz 525 and a Volvo 760. The snoop I'd gone to had provided glossy colour photographs of all that was informative.

It struck me as interesting that Sian had remarried within a comparatively short time after the death of her first husband, and to a Catholic who was more than thirteen years her elder. There was a copy of an old photograph of him wearing his graduation gown at Cambridge which, although browning with age, showed that he had dark, Latin features.

Another coincidence? No. The longer I thought about the people involved in this case the more convinced I became that I'd only seen a fraction of what might be disturbing Gary Byrne, and that I'd be a fool not to investigate further.

I rang Tom Kennart, and caught him just on the point of leaving the office.

"Good to hear you. When did you get back?"

"About an hour ago," I replied. "Is there any chance of seeing you tonight? I could get a cab and be with you in twenty minutes?"

"All right then. But it had better be worth it."

"Thank you. It is."

A lengthy pause was followed by a bark of a laugh. "It must be disappointing news, isn't it?"

"Can it wait until we meet?" I would prefer to give the bad news face-to-face. "See you soon."

I found a cab straight away, promised the driver a large tip if he made the journey in under fifteen minutes and was sitting in Tom Kennart's office eighteen minutes later, the poorer by twenty pounds.

When I told him he snapped a quick "Blast!" then lapsed into silence.

"Remembering what you said when we met, I thought you should hear the story as soon as possible. I'm afraid that soon the Italian papers will catch on to his story." I held up the folder in my hand. "Believe me, Gary's melodrama couldn't be bettered, so it could be no time at all before it's being spread across the papers in this country."

He gave a puzzled nod, so I passed across the notes I'd made. "If those don't strike you as a recipe for trouble, I don't know what will."

I could see the colour leaving Kennart's face the further into the story he read, so that by the time he'd finished he'd become completely blanched.

He laid down the folder on his desk before he looked up at me and muttered, "Why? Why do players destroy their careers so efficiently? They may be comparatively short, but while they're still active players can take home a nice amount of money." He pointed at the folder and shook his head. "If you can see any good in all this, please tell me, because I can't." He gave a snort of anger and started to pull at the skin on the back of his hands. "And there was I, almost congratulating myself for having pulled a fast one and beaten all my competitors!"

"Added to which," I said, "I think he's being blackmailed."

Kennart gave an unsympathetic growl of despair. "That's all I needed to hear!"

"I don't know who by, and I don't know whether it has anything to do with football, but that may help to explain his loss of form in the past two months and why Mick Knight came to you in the first place." I paused. "I never asked when we met for lunch. Why you in particular?"

Kennart threw back his head and laughed. That was more the spirit. "Journalists frequently do that. They hear some tittle-tattle in the changing-rooms, pursue it with the players and build it up into a story. That's why some football journalism stinks." All of a sudden he sounded angry. "I'm not saying it's written by people who know nothing about the game. They do. But the more primeval and subterranean papers always look for a drama to fill their pages and very often they bend the facts to suit the report."

It's lucky you don't work in Italy, Tom Kennart, I thought, or you'd have long since died of high blood pressure!

"But Mick Knight is not one of those, and he knew of my admiration for the player." There was a long pause while he looked away out of the window. "Each manager has his own way of running a team, and a few months spent maybe playing alongside David Connolly and mixing with the players would have made him used to my philosophy. But now . . ." He shrugged morosely.

"There must be other midfield talents," I remarked.

"Not like his, not like his." Kennart grimaced before glancing back at me. "We still owe you three thousand pounds." It sounded like a dismissal. "Plus expenses. I've not forgotten those."

"Of course not," I replied.

"Let me have your report and your invoice in the next two or three days," he said, and started to look through a clutch of papers on his desk.

"I'm sorry it's turned out like this. Very sorry indeed." I made my way to the door, turned round and saw that Kennart had stood up.

He gave a thin smile. "So am I."

*

The telephone rang roughly twenty minutes after I'd reached my flat. It was Keith Nightingale ringing from the office, and he was as brusque as usual.

"Armstrong?" He always referred to his staff by their surnames, even the man who held the post of vice-chairman of KRN Associates.

"I've just been called by Tom Kennart. He sounded very disappointed. Disappointed that you could bring no good news regarding Gary Byrne, but especially disappointed that the player himself seemed to be in such a distressed state."

"I'd say it was more than that. It saw him on several occasions, and was able to question him very closely. There's no escaping from the fact that he needs help very urgently." Maybe from a good psychiatrist, I thought.

Nightingale's Norfolk "burr" became more pronounced. "I agree, but when Kennart mentioned that he may be being blackmailed, my urge to discover his real problem rose to the top. I want you to make an investigation about the background of Byrne your top priority. Something in his past may be the cause of all this, something that may go back to his days at Stoke or at Sheffield Wednesday, or even when he was younger. Until we know exactly what it is it'll be like firing in the dark."

That would require a re-shuffle. "I'm due in Barcelona on Friday. The shipping fraud inside that firm of marine engineers."

"Cut that," he barked. "It can easily be carried out by someone else." He paused. "In fact I'll have Pedro Fuentes come up from Madrid and look into it. You stay with this case." There was a drilling sound as though he was drumming his fingers on the top of the desk.

"Why the particular interest, Mr Nightingale?"

"As you may have been told I was away when we thought of buying Byrne last summer, and when I came back to London I found that he'd been transferred to Fiorentina. I want to compensate for that." His voice sharpened. "Three years ago, when we were looking for a new manager, I recommended we appoint Tom Kennart. Since he arrived I've backed almost every one of his decisions. In early October I had to travel to our office in Milan and saw Byrne play for Fiorentina against AC Milan. Straight away I noticed what a gloriously gifted player he was, and determined to do my utmost to sign him when he returned to England."

"And you'd like me to return to Florence, Mr Nightingale?"

"That's it. I know the club still owes you some money, but you're not to worry about that. It'll be with you tomorrow, and if you need any more money get some wired through from our Milan branch. We'll discuss your fee when you return, but you'll find it won't be ungenerous. Okay?"

"Okay."

We'd always had a mutual respect for each other during the nine years since I'd joined KRN Associates, but I'd not fully realised how deep into their own pockets the people at the top in football were frequently required to dip. Nightingale seemed yet another of the hundreds involved in football who was eager to spend money helping his club.

"And make sure you report in as to how it's going."

"To you?"

"No. To Tom Kennart." There was a steely edge to Nightingale's voice. "Always to Tom. I want him to feel totally involved in this. He seemed so depressed when he rang through a few minutes ago. Although he's conscious that you did your best and no one could have done better, it appeared as though this news had blighted his life."

"He seemed terribly upset when I spoke to him."

"Yes. At our board meeting eight days ago he talked about Byrne as though he was the new Messiah, a star who could help the team win the championship next season." His voice suddenly became very effusive. "That's why I want you to give this all your attention." It sounded more like a request than an order.

"I'll start moving right away."

"Good man. And good luck."

"Thanks. I think I'll need it."

I now knew many factors which I'd not been aware of before, the most important of which was the possibility of blackmail. The more I thought about it the more convinced I became that the huge sums Gary withdrew each month were to pay a blackmailer.

Which event in Gary's recent past could have led to this blackmail – a blackmail that was helping to cripple his life?

10

Tuesday, 20th February

It was slightly after seven when I entered Park Mansions, the building which contained Dal Bosco's apartment, and Dal Bosco himself was there to meet me as I stepped out of the silent lift at the second floor.

A handsome and strongly-built man in his early sixties, he had a full mane of black hair and strong features that looked as though they'd only recently started to run to fat.

"I'm very grateful for you agreeing to see me at such notice, Signor Dal Bosco," I said after we'd shaken hands. "I know how busy you must be."

He shook his head and said expansively, "It's no trouble at all, no trouble at all. But please call me Eugenio. Just Eugenio." He gave a faintly conspiratorial nod and ushered me with a smile into his apartment, but I noticed that the smile was only around his mouth, not in his teak-brown eyes, and deep parallel furrows caused by worry leapt up on either side of his nose.

The apartment didn't succeed in making the Louvre seem like a slum, nothing ever can, but it was trying its damnedest. The walls were covered in a dark green paper with a matt finish that helped to make the place look austere, while the drawing-room seemed to be a display area for the costly pieces of bric-à-brac, the most ornate chairs and the most precious of small tables.

When placed against such a backdrop the figure of Dal Bosco himself seemed mundane. He was wearing a pin-stripe three-piece suit in charcoal grey, a dark blue shirt with a white collar and a tie which had red stripes running across a black background and was held down with a gold pin on which diamonds glittered. His shirt sleeves held a pair of gold cuff-links that were not in the featherweight class, and he wore an ostentatious watch chain that weighed down the front of his waistcoat in addition to gold buckles on his shiny black shoes.

In aggregate, you could have insured his personal effects for more than a few lire.

"What will you drink?" he asked, pointing in the direction of a showy drinks cupboard.

"A Campari soda," I replied. "Strong on the Campari but weak on the soda."

"I know, I know." He let out a laugh. "In too many restaurants they are utterly tasteless." He pointed in the direction of a maroon chair by the window. "Do make yourself comfortable."

While he mixed my drink and replenished his Scotch I took a glance round. Various prints of Italian landscapes gleamed down on the room, and the mantelpiece held a pair of cut glass vases that looked as though they could fetch the odd pound or five, but I noticed that the windows had been fitted with locking window-catches.

Dal Bosco brought the drinks across the room and placed mine on a small table beside my chair. He followed this by opening a box on the table almost full of cigarettes which had black paper and gold lettering. "Davidoff in Jermyn Street." He spoke the name with the spiritual tones of a priest at a confessional. The apotheosis of "*La Bella Figura*".

I shook my head. "I gave up several years ago."

Dal Bosco helped himself and lit it with a fetchingly thin lighter. In gold, naturally. "How can I help?" he asked, making himself comfortable on the chaise-longue.

"It concerns Gary Byrne, naturally."

"And how did you find him?" Dal Bosco enquired, but I couldn't avoid being sceptical about his interest. There remained a slight hint of resentment in his voice at having been ignored for so long. His pride must have taken a blow.

"Not very well, I have to say. Not very well." I'd steeled myself into saying the next few words. "And he's let it be known that he wants to return to England."

Dal Bosco's eyes widened in a spasm of surprise and shock. "When was this?" He didn't sound at all pleased, especially with me, and he rose to his feet. "Last Friday you informed me that you were involved in securing information for people who were doing a documentary about him." His voice had started to rise, and his eyes to harden. "What is this story you are giving me now? When I last spoke to Gary he seemed to be perfectly content."

"When would that have been?"

"A few days before the Christmas break." Dal Bosco towered above my chair. "Answer my question, please."

I answered it by handing over one of my cards. "Forgive me for lying, but in this job you sometimes have to."

Dal Bosco made no comment.

"As you know, over the weekend I spent some time with Gary. Now I'm doing some background work about his past life before returning to Italy. I must contact him again and find out precisely the reasons for his decision. In the past the lure of the lire has frequently led to it being one-way traffic, so it must be bizarre for a player to want to return to England." I'd tell him about Giuliana's pregnancy at another stage.

Dal Bosco had received no news of this decision and shook his head slowly several times. His eyes remained fixed on mine like those of a fish.

"I apologise again for not having been truthful with you. Please forgive me."

I fully expected him to ask me to leave, but instead he shook his head. "But why?" he asked in a strained tone. "But why? Reports I've received suggest that he's been one of the successes of the season."

I nodded. "That's what everyone says. Or said." I didn't want to give much away at this stage. "Before I start to follow Byrne's wanderings around this country, however, I'd like to know exactly what happened last summer when he moved to Italy."

Dal Bosco, still in a state of shock, took some time to answer, but finally pointed towards the phone. "We could try ringing him, but each evening I've tried to make contact since the New Year, there's been no reply." He gave me a searching look. "I made certain with the operator that I had his correct number, so can only assume that he's been enjoying himself around Florence. To tell the truth at present I'm having to spend too much of my time worrying about my business but I'll do anything I can to help you find out exactly what has happened to him. Anything." His voice sounded like that of a father searching for a prodigal son.

"As a result of the success he's experienced in Italy, have other people been in touch with you to ask advice about transfer negotiations?" I asked.

"Several," Dal Bosco said. "Clubs in France, in Spain, in

West Germany and in Portugal have been in touch with me concerning his contractual position, and on Sunday I got a call from George Hughes, the manager of Celtic." He gave a resigned shake of the head. "Naturally, I've had to stall them. But at this moment the news about Gary is far more pressing. I would desperately like to hear from him. How he is, what he's been up to and so on." His voice sounded heavy-hearted.

"I'll tell you everything I know," I said, interested by his reply since I knew that Hughes was praised all over the Continent for his coaching, "but I'm still not completely clear about the events of last summer."

Dal Bosco nodded slowly, and pointed towards the television set in one corner of the room. "It all began with that," he explained. "When he was down here performing in London, on loan to Chelsea. One night, it must have been two years ago, a game in which he was playing appeared on the screen, and though I'd heard rumours about how skilful he was I'd not seen him play before." He raised his eyebrows and briefly shook his head from side to side. "It was extraordinary the things he did with the ball: the pinpoint passes, his awareness of what was happening all around him, his knowledge of where players were running when they were off the ball. You can never fully judge the skills of any player until you see him play live, so in the succeeding two weeks I went to see him in the flesh and witness for myself his elegant brand of skills.

"Any good player, indeed all good players, have one very rare commodity. They can appear as though they are playing in an entirely different match to that one's watching. The sudden spurt of acceleration that leaves opponents floundering, the far-seeing vision of what is going on around them, that split-second timing in their passing that swings every factor on to their side and leaves none on that of the opposition – all these plus that certain disdain, that certain arrogance which makes the truly gifted player appear as though he was performing among novices, or a collection of fools."

"And Byrne possessed all those?"

"He stood out head and shoulders above his team-mates on the day. He put through several exquisite passes, only one of which, alas, proved fruitful." He stood up, took my glass along with his over to the drinks cabinet and talked while replenishing both of them. "I couldn't help but think of his prowess being used inside the Italian game. He was comparatively unknown over here so his transfer fee couldn't be a high one, he had the type of skills that are very rare in this country, added to which he possessed a vicious shot when he came close to goal. I made some notes concerning him and sent them to a friend in Italy."

"Does he have a name?" I asked, giving him a querulous smile.

"Which I am about to tell you." Dal Bosco chuckled and took a lengthy sip at his drink. "It was Sergio Taccone, currently manager of Fiorentina. He'd just accepted a contract to remain in Florence for a second year and was keen to keep in touch with football all over the world." He paused, then held up one finger. "You know that now each club is allowed to play three *stranieri*, foreign players."

"Yes," I nodded.

"I maintained my interest in Gary Byrne, and went up twice to watch him play for Stoke City last season. I felt that he could become a sort of bargain purchase, someone who possessed rare skill whom everyone appeared to undervalue, and thus on my third trip to see Stoke play an important match I arranged to take Taccone with me."

"Sorry to interrupt, but why Fiorentina?"

"My parents-in-law used to live in Pistoia," he explained.

"Please continue."

He gave a quick nod. "It was fairly easy. Since it coincided with the Italian team playing in a friendly international, there were no club games that particular weekend. Taccone was able to fly over from the new airport in Florence on the Friday, spend the night here," he waved his arms around, "so we were able to travel up to Stoke during the Saturday by car."

"And he liked what he saw?"

He smiled briefly. "You must remember that nowhere else but in this country are games played with so much running – "

"And so little thinking?" I finished his sentence.

"*Precisamente*," he said, pointing a finger at me. "You said it, I didn't. Taccone was much less concerned with his stamina than with his vision of play: and he completely agreed with my assessment that maybe the name of Byrne was one to put on a short-list of possible players to get in touch with in due course."

"And that's what happened?" I enquired.

He shook his head. "*No*." His brow started to furrow. "It was the other way round. About this time last year I received a letter from Gary asking me the possibilities of playing in Italy and wondering whether I could be of any assistance.''

"Did he already know about your thoughts?"

"Not from me, he didn't." Dal Bosco shrugged. "Another player probably told him who knew I might be a useful person to get in touch with." He paused. "However, I'd already looked into his past record with clubs in this country, discussed him with several journalist friends and, most important, noticed that he'd missed only one or two games through injury. This aspect is crucial. Gary Byrne, happily, is one of those who seldom gets injured, and this aspect interested Fiorentina considerably. One celebrated Brazilian international who went to play in Italy was fit to perform in only approximately half the matches that took place during his time with the club – so you can appreciate that if a club spends millions of lire on a player it doesn't want to watch him missing lengthy periods of a season sitting in the stands nursing an injury." He leaned forward in his chair suddenly as if he'd received an electric shock. "Ironic that it was an injury to another player which eventually led to Byrne coming to Italy last summer." Dal Bosco made his way over to an eighteenth-century kneehole desk made in satin-wood, drew out a drawer and from a generous number of cardboard files deftly flicked out one which had "Fiorentina" written across its front.

"In Italy," he continued, "the cost of transfer is always crippling, but Fiorentina had spent a massive amount of money purchasing Pablo Cortes, an Argentinian star forward. Riches down," Dal Bosco tapped the file to emphasise the point, "in addition to a salary that was truly astonishing. On paper he was a good investment, primarily thanks to his being a household name, one who was guaranteed to attract column inch after column inch in the papers in addition to creating a wave of interest before the season started: one which induced supporters to purchase *abbonamenti*, or subscriptions, for the season."

I was surprised. "Surely, just one player could not have such a great effect?"

Dal Bosco pointed towards the floor. "True. As I am standing here. In the first few days after his transfer was confirmed, the club sold over four thousand extra season-tickets compared to the previous year. And that in a city not notorious for its footballing mania."

"What has all this to do with Byrne?" I enquired.

Dal Bosco took two clippings from the file and passed them across.

They came from a sporting paper, *Tuttosport*, and the first set the scene for a match that had taken place on 3rd June of the previous year in Buenos Aires between Argentina and Colombia. I turned to the page from the edition for the following day. Leaping out at me in huge capital letters were the words: GRAVE INCIDENTE PER CORTES.

There were two photographs below, one showing the player lying on the ground, clasping his left leg with both hands, and the other which showed him being taken off the field of play on a stretcher with agony stamped across his face. Needless to say the match-report of the contest, which was a "friendly" (Argentina won by three goals to two), was dwarfed by a report concerning the injury received by Pablo Cortes. It transpired that he had broken his left kneecap when he had been tackled by a Colombia midfield player, Rafael Marqua, known locally as "El Toro". The incident had occurred in the last five minutes of the contest when the visiting side was attacking in numbers, attempting to force a draw, and during which Cortes had retreated in order to give help to defence.

"Although the match had taken place several weeks after the finish of the season and was only related to Italian football in a secondary sense, many people in Florence were deeply upset by this. Expressions of gloom and doom were heard in many places."

"Except from you," I pointed out.

He gave a thin smile and tapped his waistcoat. "Correct – except from me. As soon as I was made aware of this information, I contacted Taccone at Fiorentina to discover how serious the injury was. He couldn't have been more depressed. It was thought that Cortes would be out of the game for anything up to nine months, perhaps longer – which enforced pause would have meant that the player *might*" he stressed the word, "only have started training some weeks ago and *might* only have been fit to resume his place in the first team during the coming months.

"Call it second sight, call it a hunch, but the following moment I found myself telling Taccone that I would be with him that afternoon." He made a dramatic pause before wrinkling his forehead and uttering a short laugh. "Hindsight helps, naturally, but at that moment I knew precisely what to do."

"Gary Byrne – the missing piece of the jigsaw?" I queried.

"Exactly, my friend, exactly." Dal Bosco returned to his chair and sat down. "When I read reports of that accident to Pablo Cortes I sprang into action."

"I thought you told me that Pablo Cortes is a forward?"

"Quite correct," Dal Bosco replied, "and you're wondering how that affects Gary Byrne, who is a midfield player?"

"Tell me."

He'd flown to Florence that afternoon and was able to see Taccone that evening. It was only the first week in June, and the great bulk of transfer movements which applied only to Italian players had to be finalised before the end of the month, but Dal Bosco had carried out his research most thoroughly.

Although Taccone was still numb with shock Dal Bosco pointed out to the manager of Fiorentina that several seasons previously a foreign player had been permitted to join a lowly club solely for the second half of the season. In these circumstances might it not be worth bringing to the attention of the appropriate authorities the reports concerning the injury received by Cortes?

"I've always believed that certain rules and regulations were made to be broken," Dal Bosco exclaimed, giving a mischievous grin. And this was precisely what took place. During the next few days, after Taccone had regained his composure, Fiorentina indeed approached the League Council with an appeal – one in which they were successful.

The match in which Cortes had received his injury had occurred thousands of kilometres away from Italy and, more important, had taken place "out" of the period given over to home-based football. This meant, of course, that the injury was deemed to be "special" in a legal sense, outside the laws and codicils that applied to the Italian club game. On being informed of the serious nature of the injury, and the lengthy period Cortes might be out of the game, the council created a special ruling for the case. This allowed the Tuscan club permission to purchase another foreign player – the only demarcation being the factor that the potential graduate to the Italian game would have to be warned that after a year the Tuscan club could be free to restate its interest in Pablo Cortes.

"The amount of money which Fiorentina were paying over to Independiente was so vast that it was agreed that the Tuscan club could divide it into two amounts – half on signature and half to be paid a year later. Which vital date just happened to fall on the 1st of June last year." Dal Bosco speared his right forefinger towards me, and gave a weighty nod. Always a master of the dramatic, Dal Bosco, but it turned out to be worth waiting for.

As one who followed the world of Italian football closely, he was very aware that over many years the Squadra "Primavera", Fiorentina's youth team, had been one of the most successful academies for young players in the country. In that year's crop of youngsters was one Roberto Cianfanelli, an eighteen-year-old forward of prodigious talents who was certain of being launched soon into the First team. Would not this be a perfect occasion on which to promote him? Added to which was the killer argument, namely that Fiorentina couldn't possibly afford to hire another expensive player, thanks to being almost bankrupted by the arrival of Cortes.

The purchase of Byrne, however, would truly be at peppercorn terms when compared to all the enormous monies which had been spent on foreign imports the previous summer and overnight, Taccone arrived at the conviction that these two debutants in the Serie A might make a neat cocktail of skills, the precision passing of Byrne combining perfectly with the opportunism of Cianfanelli.

"The following day Taccone set into motion the purchase of Byrne. He'd been asked to set out his arguments for and against the signing to the directors but they were still in such a state of frozen lethargy following the reports about Cortes." Dal Bosco broke off in order to light a cigarette.

"Wouldn't the club have received something from the insurance firm?" I interjected.

"Some of the money, yes," Dal Bosco agreed. "But naturally the insurance firm claimed that since the assault had taken place outside Italy, it wasn't liable. In the end, as you can imagine, the whole affair grew into a most unsavoury business with various firms of *avvocati* behaving in a very squalid manner." Dal Bosco here pointed to me in a despondent manner. "Added to that loss must be gauged the amount of money Fiorentina might fail to acquire from the *abbonamenti*, the season subscriptions for the coming year."

"But what amount of monies were Fiorentina forced to lay out to acquire Gary's signature?"

"The sums were these." Dal Bosco took a sheet of paper from

the folder and read through the details. "For the acquisition of Byrne, Fiorentina paid Stoke City the equivalent of five hundred thousand pounds in sterling. Two: the signing-on fee was one of ninety million lire, and three: his monthly salary was one of just over twenty million lire before taxes, the pension scheme that exists to aid retired players and other sundries are taken off."

So Byrne wouldn't be short of the odd penny or two to spend on himself, I reflected. Agreed that footballers have a very short time in which to accumulate sufficient money to see them comfortably through the rest of their lives but still . . .

At that moment the telephone rang. Dal Bosco quickly looked at his watch. "That could be someone ringing from Milan." He slipped a magazine out of his briefcase. "While I'm occupied, why not have a look through this feature which will give you a good idea about the numbers of foreign players in Italy during the last few seasons. I shall take the call in the study." He gestured towards the wooden door.

The magazine that Dal Bosco had handed to me was *Guerin Sportivo*, a weekly that appeared to be principally concerned with reporting affairs from the world of football. This particular number served as a distillation of facts which had occurred during the transfer season and also gave a detailed run-down of exactly which overseas stars were going to be performing for which clubs. Every fact about which anyone could have wanted to be informed was provided, right through from the physical characteristics to the style of play preferred by each player, from their previous careers to their expectations. Tables abounded which laid out national identities, tastes in music and films and reading matter, whether or not players were married and particular hobbies. Almost every international star of any worth was named on the list, making the Italian club game appear to be the most richly-jewelled in the world, a positive Mecca of club football. Many of these players had been acquired for sums that seemed to be outrageous.

I was still engrossed in reading that article when Dal Bosco returned to the living-room, sat down and lit up yet another cigarette.

"Very interesting," I tapped the magazine. "There can be few well-known football players in the world not playing in Italy."

Dal Bosco shrugged. "Agreed. But they certainly earn their

payments. Football in Italy is treated like a form of theatre, and as you must have noticed, our friend must be a wealthy young man." His eyes narrowed slightly as he looked up towards me. "Very curious therefore that he should have transferred a good part of his fee for signing-on into an English bank soon after the money was paid."

"He might have left some debts in this country when he left for Italy," I said slowly, "and wanted to settle up on those. I have this curious suspicion, however, that his main point of trouble is closer to home, and," I made my words weighty, "he is being blackmailed by someone in Italy."

"Blackmailed!" exclaimed Dal Bosco. "Of course. I'll make enquiries. That would explain why he has been withdrawing a fair proportion of his salary. That can be very high when topped up with bonuses which stand to be gained by the winning of points in the *campionato*." He paused and spread out his arms in explanation. "Especially in the games played away from home."

If Byrne really had a plump nest-egg secreted somewhere in Britain, I hoped he'd found good, sound financial advice. There are any number of professional "wide boys" prepared to get to work when a nice, juicy, ingenuous player trusts them with his money. One of the most unfortunate facts of life concerning professional football is the possibility that many of the star players who've left school when they were not more than fifteen or sixteen can be ripped off in some way if they aren't careful.

"Forgive my asking, Eugenio, but how do you know about his channelling his money into a bank in England?"

"I was told by a friend who works as a financial journalist in Florence and has his ear close to the ground," Dal Bosco confided. "In fact the money was transferred to a bank in Stoke."

Interesting. Would that be the most profitable first point of call in my investigation, I wondered?

Dal Bosco suddenly put out his cigarette after having taken only a handful of puffs and picked up my glass in order to give it a refill.

"*No, grazie*," I said, shaking my head. "I must be on my way, but could I ring and see when we can continue our talk?"

He held out the palm of his left hand towards me and nodded vigorously. "Of course."

11

Wednesday, 21st February

I'd already a clue as to how Byrne might have played as a youngster for Sheffield Wednesday, but only when I got in touch with Mike Townson, Gary's last manager in England, did I learn vital facts about his career as a player in England.

I'd telephoned Townson the previous evening, explained that I was working on a profile of Gary Byrne and was attempting to gather some background information about the player. On asking whether he could spare me some time, I was lucky enough to be given an appointment to see him the following day.

"You'd better come in the afternoon," he said in a quiet voice. "During the morning I'll be busy at the club." There followed a brief pause. "Say about one o'clock?"

"I'm very grateful."

He then gave me directions. "My place is on the outskirts of Barlaston just to the east of the A34 and about six miles south of Stoke."

After I'd put down the phone it struck me that there was absolutely no need for Townson to have accommodated me so swiftly.

I might have been imagining it but when I'd mentioned the name of Gary Byrne, Townson's voice became less resentful at having a complete stranger eat into his time. It hinted that Byrne and his former manager were on the same emotional wave length, that Townson had the type of personality to bring the best out of the player. The talk with Townson might provide useful answers.

Townson lived in a converted farmhouse which still possessed its thatched roof. When I arrived he was still quite tense after a busy morning at the office. A medium-sized character with a thatch of auburn hair (was that what attracted him to the house, I wondered?), he was dressed in a dark blue pair of corduroy trousers and a light blue jacket over a light blue shirt and dark blue tie with white polka dots.

"Come in, come in," he said gruffly when he answered my knock at the door – and I could sense his bad humour. "You don't find me in the best of tempers, I'm afraid. On my desk this morning was a transfer request from one of our players who thinks that he's good enough for one of the more lucrative clubs in the First Division. Not by a mile, he's not. International football. That's part of the trouble. You've players who go off to represent their countries, have a drink or two after the match with team-mates who play for wealthier clubs and when they return they think they've suddenly become worth about ten times more than they're being paid." His voice had taken a sharp edge.

"On my desk at work I've always a sheaf of circulars from other clubs offering players for sale. In fact, one or two of the poor clubs often have to tout *all* their players for sale, they're so broke. But it's always in the wealthier clubs that you get the sort of nonsense I was just talking about. Pah!" He ran his right hand across his face and briefly shook his head. "Please forgive me for sounding off. How can I help?"

I sat down in an armchair by the window, and got back to the point of my visit. Gary Byrne. "I notice that neither of Gary's managers in this country have been Englishmen."

He looked across at me and murmured, "Charlie Taylor comes from Ireland and I was born in Stirling. You certainly have done your homework."

"That's what I'm being paid for."

He gave a quick smile. "Something you may not know is that Charlie and I used to play against each other before we both came south to get into coaching and managing, he for Rangers and I for Celtic."

"Was there much bitterness in those games?" I asked.

"On occasions anyone would think that it was the start of World War III! I played in only three Glasgow derbies in the midfield, and on each occasion was marked by a tall, hatchet-faced character called Jock Jardine who tackled as if he'd already booked me a place in the morgue." He suddenly stood up. "Let's see if lunch is ready."

We walked through to the dining-room next door where we were greeted by a handsome woman with one of those wise faces that seemed as if it had been always middle-aged.

"My wife Jean," said Townson, introducing me. "Sorry, but Mr Armstrong must be in a hurry." I hadn't actually said that, but he was right, and he'd told me he was.

"So you want to know all the facts about Gary Byrne?" He smiled grimly. "You'd better ask the good Lord because I think He's the only person who can help you. Gary certainly couldn't. That boy got himself into so many fixes you simply couldn't believe. And he was at the club less than a year! Certainly something was troubling him, but we never discovered what."

"Girlfriends or . . ." I left the query deliberately unfinished.

"No, no," Townson started to laugh. "He wasn't a jessie-boy. He did like the girls all right, though. Several times after he'd just joined us he would report late for training with some feeble excuse or other. 'Please, boss, I just missed the bus,' or 'Please, boss, I couldn't find my shoes; they were caught under the bed.' Something or other very trivial. I knew they couldn't be true, however, and on occasions used to fine him for being late."

"He never complained?"

Townson shook his head. "Never. Several clubs have on their books silly buggers who love acting as barrack-room lawyers and are always looking for trouble. Thank heavens, Gary had more sense than to pick a quarrel where none existed."

I enquired about the circumstances when he'd been able to purchase Byrne from Sheffield Wednesday.

"I'll explain in a roundabout way," he replied, piling a mountain of potatoes on his plate with the finesse of a weight-lifter. "Whenever people compare the majority of our players to those who come from the Latin countries or from South America, the most noticeable difference is always stated to be in technique. British players compensate for lack of this by being full of spirit, full of stamina and full of adventure. While on the Continent spectators often pay astronomical prices for a ticket and frequently finish by watching a match that is stupefyingly turgid, very few of the games in our league are dull, so the crowd usually gets good value for money."

Townson held up his hand, as though to explain why he hadn't answered my question. "My point is that, although Gary Byrne developed inside our game, and therefore could appreciate its strengths, he has also been blessed with extraordinary talent.

Wednesday were the first team shrewd enough to spot these gifts early on, and tried to bring the best out of the boy. When Byrne was still eighteen, he was an automatic choice in midfield. During the summer break, though, there was a change of manager. Maybe the new man didn't value Byrne's skills so highly – "

"The new man?"

Townson gave a quick smile. "Forgive me. Kevin Smith took over from Charlie Taylor but I'm really emphasising my earlier point. While in England, less in Scotland, many teams favour a long-ball game – transferring the ball as quickly as possible from defence into attack and using as few passes as necessary – we have a few managers and players who prefer to work the ball through the midfield with elegant short passes, like a geometrician using his slide-rule."

"And Gary was one of the latter?"

Townson nodded. "Decidedly. Maybe Charlie's successor didn't like his style of play, or maybe there was another reason that might explain it, but whatever, Gary was no longer a regular first-team choice."

"You've no idea why?"

Townson shook his head. "Afraid not. And as if being dropped from the team wasn't enough," Townson continued, "he became involved in some troubles in his family, as a result of which his form fell right away. When I phoned one afternoon, I was astonished to discover that his transfer cost would be absurdly low, and quickly received permission from the board to buy him for a relatively giveaway price."

"Family troubles? Do you know what these could have been?"

He shook his head. "Afraid not. When I later mentioned it to Gary, he was very uncommunicative."

Townson carried on to explain how he himself had arrived at Stoke. "I've been around a fair time and have had to deal with a crisis more than once. The unfriendliest reception I ever got was at a team in Lancashire where it was always like trying to ski uphill. To save on the overheads I had only a part-time secretary and took a licence to use a Public Service Vehicle so I could drive the team bus to away matches." His accent was becoming more pronounced. "My reward was having a self-promoting chairman, one of those who has a photograph and piece in each programme, and a thoroughly constipated board of directors, many of whom didn't know much about football and didn't give a shit about the club. That was terrible, and this sense of failure comes across strongly to the supporters. When you manage a club that's going through a lean time you become accustomed to such vile language that shouts of 'Bloody Rubbish' at the end of a home defeat appear a compliment. Pah!" He sounded angry.

"It must be soul-destroying," I said sympathetically.

Townson gave a determined nod. "It is, but you just need the will to survive, and then the will to conquer. That's why I was brought here, being the type of person who could bring back memories of former times." He paused. "When the club was demoted to the Second Division a few seasons back and affairs appeared bleak, the attitude in the city became so fraught that frequently prayers used to be said by the city council. Memories among the supporters always harked back to famous internationals such as Stanley Matthews and Gordon Banks, but nowadays, names such as those seem to have performed a million years ago." He chuckled. "The sure fact about Gary Byrne was that he had similar talent to those two. When I came here, I brought with me Gerry Foley, the coach from my previous club." He pointed out Foley on a photograph of the current team which hung on the wall. I remembered having seen Foley play for Everton more than ten years earlier, an Irish terrier of a midfield player who always loved to pass the ball right up his team-mates' nostrils, according to his outrageous imagery. "He's been acknowledged as one of the most demanding coaches in the country, and you can understand how the laid-back attitude of Byrne took some getting used to."

"A few moments ago you were talking about Gary feeling low. Was he still depressed when he came here?"

"Christ, no. Although he was gifted with enormous talent, his move here seemed to provide him with an extra zest for the game. During the first few months with us he used to perform with all the confidence of someone who'd matured over several seasons, and would always demand the ball in an imperious manner. His colleagues, however, never resented this since he often appeared to be several seconds faster in thought than them. Many games took place when I felt positively privileged to be his manager, and watch him playing at close quarters. In fact I wasn't surprised when I started receiving several calls asking whether I would be prepared to transfer him. He'd work himself to the bone to keep up with the other lads, although during pre-season training his basic sense of casualness often came through. I was always afraid that he'd pull a hamstring or injure a groin – the two areas which are the most vulnerable after an off-season rest. But we were lucky, and he was able to appear in almost every game while he was with us."

The telephone sprang to life in one corner of the room. "You'll have to excuse me." Townson sounded apologetic. "That will probably be the Watford manager, John Gill, who promised to ring at two o'clock. Sorry, but it's quite urgent."

I stood up and stretched my legs while Townson and Gill had a very intense discussion concerning a player from Stoke whose contract was due to expire at the end of the season.

When he put the phone down, Townson was full of praise for John Gill. "There's someone I like doing business with. We've always seen eye-to-eye. He's no bullshitter. Many of the managers of larger clubs who spend millions of pounds each season have no real concept of what it's like administering a club on a fraction of their turnover, of not being allowed to make too many false judgments when acquiring a player. John and I both have to organise a fruitful youth policy and also have to filch players from the bargain basements, bringing the best out of young and skilful talents in the lower divisions."

"To return to the events of last summer, Mr Townson," I said.

"Gary had expressed an interest in playing in Italy and asked me what I thought of the idea."

"I presume that you warned him that the chances of his being signed up by an Italian team were remote," I interjected.

Townson gave me a steely look, and raised his eyebrows. "You read in the papers or see on the television that club X has bought player Y from club Z, and you think that it has been so simple. Not at all. Because there can be a fair amount of money involved, some clubs have a player watched by specific scouts on up to ten different occasions before they make up their minds. At almost every top game that's played in this country there'll be a number of scouts whose job is to provide reports about various players to clubs which are more wealthy," he explained. "So you can be sure that on several occasions we played there would be present someone who had links with football in Italy."

"Money isn't everything," I remarked, offering the cliché.

Townson sat down. "You know that and I know that, but to someone of Byrne's age, who has yet to accept the responsibilities of being married, it seems to be enormously vital. Although you always have to find some balance in your life, as I reminded him when he came to ask for a transfer at the end of last season. He was the best paid of our players, even though he was one of the youngest, because he'd interested a company that makes cereals and had picked up a cheque for several thousand pounds for allowing his name to be used by that particular sponsor. I explained that he would be allowed to keep a much higher percentage of the money he earned by playing abroad, but stressed to him some of the difficulties involved and pointed out that whatever he would gain in terms of wages he might lose in terms of peace of mind. But no matter. He seemed determined to go and see for himself."

"At the end of last season?"

A sad expression came over Townson's face, and he shook his head sorrowfully. "Before, I think. A few months before. Gary had kept his ties with Sheffield, and was in the habit of driving over there of a Sunday if we'd been playing away the day before. The reason for this was a girl called Andrea Cornelius, who'd frequently come over to watch him play when we were at home."

"You didn't happen to talk to her?"

"Certainly. We held a small party the Christmas before last, and encouraged the players to bring along their families." He paused. "Very attractive, she had strong features and wavy hair the colour of burnished copper. She was quietly spoken, with only a trace of a Yorkshire accent. I was very busy that evening, so only had time for a few words, but she struck me as being just immensely likeable." He gave a meaningful shrug.

"Gary didn't invite anyone else?" I interrupted.

Townson's brow furrowed in concentration. "I don't think so," he replied.

"Forgive me. Please carry on."

"About this time last year, I received a call from Gary explaining that he had to take a short break. He sounded terribly distressed. Naturally I gave him permission to be away for several days, but only on condition that he came to see me when he returned so that we could have a talk." The punctuation was a soulful smile. "I didn't hear from him for five days."

111

"Where had he been?"

"He refused to talk about it, however, and for several days wandered around the place staring and hardly saying a word. I never saw the girl again, and at first presumed that the two of them must have had some sort of row."

"Had they?"

He shook his head. "A couple of days later a friend at Sheffield Wednesday, where her father is a director, told me that she'd just died as a result of a brain haemorrhage. Berry's Aneurism, I think they call it. The result of having high blood pressure. Apparently she became very distressed when her parents divorced." He shook his head slowly. "As you can imagine, it was a great effort to steer Gary's mind back on to the basics, to make him realise that all the mourning he felt couldn't resurrect Andrea."

Townson halted his speech for a moment. "In this business there are a very small number of players in whom you have total confidence. For me Gary was one of those, and many was the time after a training-session or a match when I would find him and have a chat. During those next few weeks, though, he refused to discuss anything with anyone. In training-sessions Gerry was really good about always taking him on one side, well away from the other players, and soon found this the most fruitful way of getting him to work.

"The two of us were eventually successful, but it must have taken us about a month to make him realise that the best way to get over her death might be by doing what he could do best – and that was to play superb football. We had a young team, and eventually Gary made it his aim to act as one of its leaders and to channel his whole energy into football."

Townson paused and looked up at the ceiling, then continued, "I'll give you a specific example. At that time we had on our books a young winger of immense talent called Kikis who was experiencing a miserable loss of form."

"Kikis?" I queried.

Townson nodded. "Kikis. He'd been christened Kyriacos Achilleos Poliviou, but we suggested he shorten it when we'd completed his purchase from the Larnaka club, ETA. It would have been a commentator's nightmare." Townson gave a quick smile. "I'd seen the boy play in a tournament in Cyprus the summer before we signed Gary, and he'd struck me as having an exciting amount of talent. He spoke some English and settled in well, but it took some time before he became used to playing entirely as a professional. He performed mostly for our reserve side during his first year with us.

"During the following autumn he was put into our first team and became very prolific, scoring fifteen goals in twenty matches in all competitions, some of them with explosive free-kicks that were still accelerating when they hit the net. Then he struck a very sad patch, scoring only one goal in the following three months. Since we were playing to a formula with four men in midfield and only Kikis and the central striker Mike Drew in the attack, his entering this fallow period placed more stress on Mike, but Kikis himself became very upset and increasingly withdrawn.

"Maybe because he'd recently experienced a profound tragedy, Gary Byrne took it upon himself to steer Kikis through his lean patch and bring him out the other side. He became the great unifier, making Kikis and Mike Drew play for each other. Any team that loses its sense of unity becomes desperately fragmented and very volatile. Little jealousies start to creep in that can affect the team's form critically, and Gary recognised this.

"This worked like a treat, and there were several matches in which young Drew displayed the most incredible stamina, would run himself tireless, at one moment falling back to help out the defence, only for the next to be up in the attack. Enormous energy and an endless will to play. I was very grateful for this because it saw Stoke going through a successful patch." Townson paused. "I also became very impressed with Gary during those weeks, and felt that he'd matured to a great extent, had channelled a lot of the energy that had been spent in sorrow into acting as a mediator between Kikis and Mike Drew. In fact this came to work in our favour in that it helped to increase the valuation the club came to put on him when it received an enquiry about him. The character of a player remains so, so important."

Which strength of character would be critical in dealing with the problem of supporting Giuliana, I thought.

"Did Kikis continue to perform well again?"

Townson gave a brief shake of the head. "We were forced to cancel his contract in November. One morning while training he went totally berserk and starting laying into Mike Drew. It took three men to pull him off. No good reason that we could

113

discover. Jealousy was the obvious reason since Mike had started to strike a rich vein of form, and began to receive acres of space in the press that suggested he could soon become a member of the England squad. We later learnt that Kikis had flown back from Manchester to Nicosia without telling anyone."

"Reaction at there being no Gary Byrne to help him piece his life together?" I asked.

Townson gave a sorrowful shrug. "Who can say?"

"A pity that," I remarked, but the incident when Gary had recently attacked a trainer at Fiorentina leapt into my mind. He must have been in touch with his former colleagues during his Christmas break.

Townson nodded. "He was a delight to watch but," he tapped his temple, "trouble like him I can do without."

I'd noticed from my watch that it was late, but hadn't wanted to interrupt his flow. This tragic tale was telling me, I felt instinctively, a great deal about Gary Byrne. Still I had to get back to my original question. "Can you tell me more about Gary's transfer?"

"Certainly," replied Townson, frowning. "I think it was at the beginning of April that Gary told me he had an ambition to play in Italy some time but it wasn't until one morning in early June I received a telephone call from Eugenio Dal Bosco who'd enquired after several key players on a regular basis. One of whom was Gary Byrne."

"But I thought you said it was Byrne himself who came and asked for a transfer, and mentioned the possibility of going to play abroad?"

He nodded, "It was."

"Curious," I murmured softly.

"Curious that the suggestion came from him, you mean?"

"And not from you," I said.

Townson gave a shrug. "In these times it seems that anything goes." He didn't sound particularly bitter. "Especially when agents are involved."

"Sorry. Go on."

"Gary may have had a talk with Eugenio Dal Bosco sometime or other. Although their clubs can start negotiations concerning major players throughout the year, the Italians must have fixed all their transfers by a certain fortnight, normally in July. They have a minor type of market in the autumn, a kind of postscript to the main market in the summer which only applies to either players who can be transferred from one division into another, or to those who have not yet played for any team. As you will know, it is very unlike our own system in which a wealthy club can purchase a player at any time of the year; indeed, purchase certain players who can see the side through a rough period or make it highly successful." Townson spoke with the scepticism of one who'd recently seen another team purchase a player he had been watching.

"Dal Bosco had already gained some knowledge as to the particular strengths and weaknesses of Byrne's style of play from television film-clips, gossip in footballing circles, discussions with journalists and so on. But was there some other reason away from the footballing world that would explain why Gary wanted the transfer?

"That's what interested me, and it took a totally different type of phone call to make me realise why he might have started to perform below his best in the last few months with us."

"Different in what way?" I asked sharply.

"This call was not from someone inside the game but from his bank manager, who told me that the lad was about five thousand pounds overdrawn."

I whistled. "Car, house, clothes, records?"

Townson ticked them off briskly on the fingers of his left hand. "Didn't drive, didn't own a house, didn't dress that well, records don't cost that much . . ."

"So what did you do?"

He shook his head sadly. "Well, the bank manager suggested in his call that we could make a loan without Gary knowing, and could then deduct the money from his wages for the following year."

"That was thoughtful of him."

It was Townson's turn to interrupt. "Very thoughtful," he said, and gave a bitter laugh. "Very thoughtful indeed. The only trouble was that we'd transferred Byrne three days before we received that call, and he'd already left for Italy!"

So the wheel had gone full circle. Being in debt might well have been the reason for Byrne to mention a transfer, since Italian clubs were reputed to have paid enormous signing-on fees to their players.

"A very strange boy," said Townson. "He had this fantastic amount of charisma, of charm that was simply magnetic and he

115

was always popular with his team-mates. As far as the girls were concerned he possessed an enormous amount of personality, and, to use an old-fashioned word," Townson broke into a smile, "of chivalry. But always at the back of his eyes was this enormous sadness, this look that at all times said, 'You can never give me what I'm after,' and the feeling that he was just using us.

"And the overdraft? How do you explain that? We made a tour of all the bookies in the area, but the managers of the shops denied ever having seen him." He stopped and shook his head.

"May I use your phone?" I asked suddenly, after having looked at my watch. It was just past three o'clock.

"Use the one in the hall on your left," he said.

A calm and measured female voice answered after the third ring. "Silkstone 8576."

"Mrs Wright?" I asked.

"Speaking."

"My name is Ross Armstrong."

"Ah, yes. You rang last night."

"Yes. I wonder if I could come and have a talk about your nephew Gary Byrne." I made my voice sound mild.

"Why?" she asked sharply.

I stuck to the same story. "Well, a television company is planning to do a profile on him. I've already been to Florence and have met some contacts, but now am back speaking to people who knew him well before he left."

There followed a long pause – so lengthy that I began to think she'd hung up the phone. Finally she asked in guarded tones, "And you want to come and see me?"

"If I could."

"Are you calling from London?"

"At the moment I'm near Stoke-on-Trent. Would it be possible to come over and see you later this afternoon? If so, I'd be very grateful."

Several moments passed before she said in a quieter voice, "It's the first house you get to beyond the slight hill in the village. See you in about two hours' time."

I returned to the dining-room, told Townson the whereabouts of my next port of call, and made my thanks and farewells.

"Get in touch again if I can be helpful," he said as I started my car.

"The odds are more than even," I said before driving away. However, I doubted it, although he'd made many percipient observations. There was something more to be discovered about Gary Byrne, but I didn't think Townson was the answer. And I wanted to find out the answer. Not for Tom Kennart, not for Keith Nightingale. But for myself. And maybe for Gary Byrne as well.

A mile north of Stoke on my way towards Yorkshire, I stopped for petrol – and in addition received an earful of recollections from the blue-suited cashier when I casually mentioned the football team, echoes of the remarks which had been made an hour earlier by Mike Townson.

One year away from retirement, he had been a regular visitor to the Victoria Ground, Stoke-on-Trent, since just after the end of the war. The most treasured moments, he informed me proudly, had come in the early sixties, when the club had been near to the top of the Second Division. Jackie Mudie, Jimmy McIlroy and Dennis Viollet – they had been three inside forwards who had possessed magical qualities, renowned throughout the country for their skills on the ball. The magician who had been primarily responsible, however, for breathing new life into the club had been the immortal Stanley Matthews.

"'e were forty-six year old, he were, when he came to 'The Potters' in the summer of '61," the attendant enthused, "and even at that age he could show most players a thing or two." He stared up in the direction of the ceiling, as though reciting a vesper. "The gates went to over 30,000 and the club soon got promotion. Mark you, we've had several good players since then, like George Eastham, Gordon Banks, Peter Shilton and Alan Hudson – but it were our Stanley who first lit the flame."

His eyes came down to meet mine and he pulled a face. "I still went up in the 'ard years five or six seasons ago, tho' it were nivver what it used to be. Thousands of people in the area without work, crowds down under 10,000 and the club forced to sell all their best players in order to pay the bills. What a disgrace for a team that's second oldest int' country!" He leant forward slightly, as though to see if I'd been aware of that fact. "Let's have your money then."

While I was waiting for change from a twenty pound note, I mentioned the name of Gary Byrne. "He was here last season."

"I know he was, I know he was." The cashier held my change in his hand while he treated me to another of his homilies. "Just now," he speculated, "I mentioned the name of Jimmy McIlroy. But, you know, the player whom Byrne reminded me of most was the man who partnered McIlroy for Northern Ireland. And that were Danny Blanchflower."

Danny Blanchflower. I'd seen *him* play, both live as well as on television, when I'd been a youngster and had always been astonished by the manner in which he appeared to think out moves several seconds before his team-mates and therefore had been able to make the most shrewd of passes. Not strong, not fast, but a player who was full of guile and always a supreme strategist.

"It often made you wish he were playing for a more successful side, that boy Byrne." The attendant looked past my left shoulder as he gave me the notes. "Hope to see you again."

12

Wednesday, 21st February

I travelled north-westwards along the snake of a road that curled its way across the Peak District and cut to Glossop through Leek, Buxton and Hayfield. The traffic wasn't dense, and I was able to give thanks for not being in any hurry since Sian Wright hadn't been precise about time, but it was only when I turned eastwards just to the north of Glossop that I was able to relax and to appreciate the beautiful moorlands of the southern part of Yorkshire which offered up a pageant of memorable colours – russets, greens and yellows all toned down by the falling light – which served to make my Mercedes Benz seem like a ghost car travelling on a vital mission.

When I stopped at the local newsagent to ask for directions to Hilldrop House I was told that it was just to the north of the main road and set back from that thoroughfare by some distance. I drove up the gravel driveway past a tennis court and parked in front of an emerald-green Volvo 766 that was three years old.

Only a very small number of people have faces which can be thought of as being striking, but Sian Wright was decidedly one of that number. Tall and slender, she had jet-black hair faintly streaked with grey that fell in languid waves down to her shoulders, a wide and full mouth, and a delicate nose that looked as if it had once been broken. But it was her eyes that hypnotised my attention for they were the colour of water-sapphire, pools of pale blue that completely transfixed me. She wore little make-up, merely a tinge of eye-shadow and a hint of crimson lipstick, and was dressed in a beige suit, with a short jacket, over a blouse in washed-out cream which was decorated with a paisley pattern. In addition to a flat garnet engagement ring above a thin band of gold, round her neck was a two-stranded gold chain and I caught a glimpse of earclips made of ivory set into gold.

"Mr Armstrong?" she asked in an assured voice after she had

fully opened the teak door. For a moment those eyes widened, as though I reminded her of someone else.

I nodded and pulled myself together as she showed me the way through to the sitting-room. She walked with a slight limp. On the air hung a scent of perfume that was either very strong or had only been recently put on.

"A charming place you have here, Mrs Wright," I said as I looked around. The large sitting-room held three armchairs as well as a chaise-longue, all covered in material which was heavily patterned. There was a dark grey carpet on the floor, several rugs strewn on top of it and the wallpaper was a light pattern. A fire in the corner had recently been lit and the dark green velvet curtains had been drawn. In one corner stood a rosewood desk on which sat a green telephone and which was covered with a typescript in addition to various papers, on top of which lay a fountain-pen. In emerald green, of course. That was obviously the colour of the year.

"I'm very fond of it," she said, giving a brief nod. "It was built in 1745 and for over two centuries belonged to a family who were concerned with the keeping of sheep. My husband bought it roughly ten years ago when we were married, and we've spent a bit of money on it since."

"It's good of you to see me," I said. "Especially at such short notice."

She gave a smile, but her eyes remained ice-cold. "I don't know to what extent I can help you but I'm certainly willing to try. Why don't you sit over there," she pointed towards a large armchair wearing a dark green antimacassar with a Gothic pattern, "while I get some tea?"

There was a withdrawn quality to her voice, which was an intriguing amalgam of dialects, part-English and with the very noticeable musical resonance of Italian, but I could just trace fragments of the Welsh. While she was away in the kitchen I took the opportunity to wander round the room. It might have seemed comforting during the day-time but at this late hour it gave off a scream of gloominess. On the walls hung a series of prints which showed an Italian city during the eighteenth century, as well as many decorative pieces in silver and bronze such as daggers, shields and as other memorabilia of the period.

There were three bookcases full to the top of novels by Italian and South American writers and some standard works of non-fiction, such as an atlas, a *Brewer's Dictionary of Phrase and*

Fable, books of quotations and numerous encyclopaedias. An expensive radiogram sat in one corner, the other commanded by a television with a large screen. Sian Wright was in the middle of reading *The Heart of the Matter* by Graham Greene and I noticed that the bookshelves were plentifully supplied with works by Greene, by Evelyn Waugh, by Norman Douglas and those British poets who had been famous in the years before the war such as Auden, Spender and Macneice.

"His most moving book," I said pointing to the Greene novel when she reappeared from the kitchen wheeling in a tea-trolley. "Scobie remains in the mind for a long time. One of his best-drawn characters."

"I can't stop reading it. It must be about my fifteenth time through." She smiled quickly, but I noticed the coldness in those bewitching eyes that seemed as soft as silk at one moment but could become as hard as ice at the next. "How do you like the car? My husband drives a similar model."

"Thoroughly patrician and terrifyingly fierce." I gave a laugh, before pointing towards the desk. "What are you working on at the moment?"

Her eyes brightened for a second. "Some short stories by an Italian writer called Tommaso Landolfi that were found recently which I'm translating for a firm in New York. Several firms over there have done translations of his work. You've not read him?"

I shook my head. "Afraid not."

"You should. He was an original. He lived from 1908 to 1979, mainly in Florence and Rome, and first made his name with distinguished translations of works by Russian authors like Tolstoy, Pushkin and Dostoevsky. He has also written several collections of short stories which have been much admired. Not dissimilar to the work of Borges and Calvino."

"He sounds interesting."

"He is. I think you'd like him." Dabs of colour entered her cheeks. "You were telling me that you'd just visited Florence."

"Only for the weekend."

"And how did you find Gary?" She poured out the tea and after passing me a plate holding some sandwiches, sat down in one of the other armchairs. She was wearing tights in black lace which had a diamond pattern, and a pair of leather shoes which looked handmade and might have been imported from Italy.

"Extremely well-liked, and during the autumn he was

playing some of the best football of his career. As I told you, while I was there I saw Fiorentina play, and was able to speak to several people about him. However, at the moment I am pursuing my enquiries in England."

She glanced away from me for a second and pretended to be concerned with the tea-trolley before she looked back towards me. "Perhaps it'll be easier if you think of some questions to ask." She stood up looking around her for the box holding some cigarettes, which turned out to be on the desk in the corner of the room.

While she was involved in finding and lighting one for herself I remarked, "My principal requirement is to research into the past, since so far I don't know much about the history of Gary when he was still a child and young man. For example, how did he come to play first for a Yorkshire club? And secondly, after he began playing football why did he change clubs?"

"To answer your first question first," she said after she had resumed her seat. A tight edge had entered her voice. "You know his father's English? Well, when Gary was little more than five years old my sister Gwyneth was forced to ask for advice from a doctor in London because she was just about to give birth to her fourth child." She stopped and looked across at me as I began to look puzzled. "She had had a grave time with the birth of her previous child two years earlier, so the family doctor in Liverpool advised her to go to see a specialist in London . . ." A lengthy pause followed. "I can't tell you how worried she was when she found out about the new pregnancy. She had three children already, including Gary, and at the back of her mind was always the memory of having come close to death two years before."

"No particular problems?" I asked.

She shook her head. "No, but the next few years took a great amount out of her." Her voice suddenly became savage. "Although we had few interests in common I used to go and stay with her from time to time and saw at first hand how the bastard she was married to carried on leading a life that was totally self-centred, causing her to become increasingly down-trodden and subservient. The inevitable, of course, happened and by the time Gary was twelve or thirteen he was completely out of control, mixing with a rough crowd and staying up until all hours."

"But his father?" I asked.

"*Ma che stronzo!*" Her mouth pursed itself, and she shook her head abruptly. "He was quickly turning into an alcoholic." Although Sian was clearly not used to talking about other people in such hostile terms, she spat the words out angrily. "When Gwyneth was advised to put herself in the care of a specialist in London, he at least left his job as a local government officer in Liverpool and began working in Ealing. But not surprisingly he found it difficult to make friends in London, and after he'd bought a house near his place of work, he seemed to think of a bottle of Scotch as being his best friend."

Given this lack of control, Gary often failed to report at school and became a member of a gang of juvenile delinquents. Just after his fourteenth birthday he took part in a crime of a more serious nature. Together with the younger brother of one of the participants he agreed to be a "look-out" while the two older boys mugged an old lady in her apartment, and soon after was taken into police custody.

Gary had been involved in a crime that would warrant at least a Supervision Order by the local branch of the social services, but suddenly his mother's younger sister volunteered to care for him. Gary learned that his aunt would be prepared to start looking after him when he accompanied his mother to court, and heard her make a plea that her sister might be given permission to look after him. Sian had spoken to her sister, and had then been contacted by the social services department in her area suggesting that if he was allowed into her care he would participate in an intermediate treatment programme, which although voluntary, would include many tasks that would keep him out of mischief.

She gave a nervous flick of her hair. "A vital witness was Gary's headmaster who confirmed that until about twelve months before Gary had been a model pupil, cheerful and hard-working and successful both at work and at games. Thank heavens, the judge sitting that day was a humanitarian who could understand that the boy might be far better behaved removed from all his so-called friends. Added to which was the important fact that my husband is a very successful barrister," she gave a faint smile, "and therefore considered to be a trustworthy character."

"His parents couldn't cope?"

Sian shook her head. Gary's father had been well on the way to spending a sizeable proportion of the family income on spirits, while her sister found her life full coping with the children as well as with him, and was gradually going to pieces.

"The previous occasion I'd seen Gary was at our wedding," Sian continued. "Although he must only have been twelve he'd been very well-behaved and displayed interest in what was being discussed. Two years older, however, and he seemed to have changed considerably for the worse. In this new set of circumstances it was little surprise that matters were extremely difficult for the first few months."

She stopped suddenly and looked past my right shoulder in the direction of the television. "It took a fair time before Gary completely trusted me, but I was enormously helped by the fact that soon after he came to live with us the finals of the 1982 World Cup took place.

"Gary, however, simply became mesmerised by the whole event. That made for a smooth start to his stay, and I was certainly one of that small number who wished that the World Cup finals lasted four months instead of four weeks!" She smiled a thin grin. "Although when that entertainment was over trouble came in leaps and bounds. There were the inevitable arguments as well as fights and sometimes the tension was so sharp you really wondered why on earth you were doing this." Sian gave a humourless laugh. "Then I thought of my sister with all her troubles and thought to myself, come on, Sian, there are millions out there with problems worse than yours." She looked into the fire that was starting to blaze away. "Anyway, there was the fact that I couldn't have any children myself." Said in almost a whisper.

It was easy to imagine what it might mean to a woman unable to give birth to children, to have a fourteen-year-old rascal suddenly thrown at her; and not difficult to visualise all the psychological and philosophical changes which it might bring.

"Do you want to talk about it?" I said after a long pause.

For several moments Sian looked searchingly into my eyes, before she nodded, but inevitably there was a staccato rhythm to her speech. "Several years ago, in Milan, I had a miscarriage. I was four and a half months pregnant. I'd been feeling unwell many mornings after I'd got up, but the cramps gradually became much fiercer and finally I was forced to call the doctor. I began bleeding in the ambulance, and eventually they had to remove the foetus with forceps." Her voice had become deathly soft. "My husband was involved in an important case down in Rome. Something to do with the contractual rights of people involved in the theatre. I can't think of a time when I've ever felt more dejected or more alone."

She looked towards the fire. "At the hospital they told me it was a boy. Every year I remember his birth-date." Her voice started to become much more strong, and she held her head up. "A few months later I was involved in an accident while pregnant for the second time. I had another miscarriage, and later discovered I couldn't bear any further children." There followed a gloomy silence before she returned to the present and gave an ambiguous smile. "You're the first person in this country I've told about this."

I assumed that meant that she'd not told her husband, but wondered why she was telling me. "That must have been a most traumatic moment," I said sympathetically.

"It was," she said, standing up sharply. "However; what's past is past." She looked down at her expensive gold watch. "What would you say, Mr Armstrong, to a drink?"

The time had really flown. "I ought to be going soon," I said, looking at my watch, "but would love a glass of white wine to see me on my way."

"Easy," she said and drifted over to the drinks cupboard before turning back to face me. "Couldn't you stay and have some supper?"

It would take three hours to drive back to London. As long as I was in bed by midnight.

"That would be very pleasant," I replied. "By the way, where's your husband?"

She frowned quickly, an expression of surprise starting to drift over her face. "Didn't I tell you?" Her voice sounded annoyed.

I shook my head.

"Please forgive me. I'm very sorry. Since Monday he's been involved with a case up in Newcastle."

"Concerned with what?"

She looked into the fireplace while trying to remember. "I think it's to do with fraud, but I'm not sure. He takes cases in both civil and the criminal list, and rushes round the practice like a whirlwind. Whenever he does come back he frequently doesn't return home until late."

I wasn't to realise the precise relevance of that remark for several more days.

I watched as she returned from the drinks cupboard, her expression full of thought. She put my drink on a nearby table and said, in a quiet voice, "For supper, I think I have some veal which I could very quickly cook up?" She made it into a question.

"That would be marvellous. Thank you." I waited for her to settle down before continuing. "Now tell me a bit about yourself."

She smiled and smoothed a hand across her skirt. "Nothing much to tell," she said in a matter-of-fact voice, before offering a "really" that couldn't help sounding very Welsh. "I was born in Oswestry, five years younger than my sister, and gained a scholarship to Bedford College, London to read modern languages. I went there when I was eighteen to read Italian." She paused. "Those were some of the happiest days of my life. We held our studies in a stylish Regency building designed by John Nash which overlooked the lake in Regent's Park – so there was no excuse ever to feel depressed. And I was fortunate enough to be taught by a tutor who was deeply inspiring."

"What was her name?" I interrupted.

"Male, not female," she replied. She coloured slightly and gave an elusive smile. "And he's far from dead. Penry Davies."

"Did you live in a hall of residence?"

"Yes and no," she replied. "I stayed in one for my first two terms, but found it very restricting and moved to a flat in St John's Wood."

"You weren't interested in doing research?"

She shook her head. "No. I won a research scholarship and my tutor fully encouraged me to stay. I preferred to spread my wings, however, and went to Italy straight after I'd taken my degree . . ."

"Doing what?"

She shrugged. "Oh, teaching English here and there to make ends meet, but I benefited most from being among Italians." She gave a flicker of a smile.

"And that's when you met your first husband?"

She nodded serenely. "Yes. Domenico Mozzolino was his name, and he was a very gifted lawyer. We first met at a party thrown by an Italian friend of mine who was a journalist on the Milan paper *Corriere della Sera*."

"Milan's not exactly a peaceful place," I put in.

"It certainly isn't," she agreed, and gave a fleeting smile. "At least not the way Domenico and I used to run our lives. He used to have to work on his papers most nights but when he could spare a free evening we normally made a point of going out to enjoy ourselves."

"Tell me," I enquired, "during your time in Milan you didn't happen to meet someone called Dal Bosco, Eugenio Dal Bosco?"

She looked away for several moments and frowned briefly. "I don't think so. Eugenio Dal Bosco," she repeated the name slowly before shaking her head. "No, I'm afraid it means nothing to me. Why do you ask? Is he a friend of yours? A doctor, maybe, or a lawyer."

"No one so specifically trained, as far as I know. He's just an ordinary businessman like millions of others." I was sure, however, that she must have come across his name in England – if at no other time than when Gary was being transferred to Fiorentina.

She nodded, stood up and excused herself before making her way through to the kitchen. That gave me another chance to look round the room. In addition to its collection of modern English novels and books of reference, there were celebrated South American classics such as several titles by the Argentinian novelists Julio Cortazar and Ernesto Sabato, *One Hundred Years of Solitude* by the Colombian Gabriel Garcia Marquez and *The War of the End of the World* by the Peruvian Mario Vargas Llosa, as well as several shelves of Italian books among which were works by Italo Calvino, Cesare Pavese, Italo Svevo and Luigi Pirandello. There was a voluminous collection of records and tape-recordings. Works by Verdi, Rossini, Donizetti, Vivaldi and Monteverdi featured prominently while albums by Adriano Celentano and Gianni Morandi showed that she was determined not to be thought of as being entirely classical. While I waited for her I dipped into a book by Italo Calvino.

Twenty minutes later she returned to announce that supper was ready and set two places at the small oak table. We ate our way through veal served with a sauce of mushrooms in cream with a touch of parsley, fresh fruit and Italian cheeses all accompanied by some fragrant red wine, a Barbaresco 1983. As we ate she continued with the biography of her nephew.

For the month or two after moving to live with his aunt and

127

her husband (Sian never referred to him as anything else, which made me wonder about their relationship), Gary had been surly, unco-operative and at times downright vicious, threatening each of them with attack while wielding a bottle or knife. Gradually he'd calmed down, especially after he'd been threatened with a swift return to the reform school, and in time had made some friends in the district. It was through football, however, that he gained a new sense of freedom. Very skilful at the game, he'd soon won his place in the appropriate school side as well as in a side that played on the occasional Sunday morning made up of people from local pubs and clubs — enthusiasts who were eager when playing to use all their brawn to compensate for their lack of brain. Playing against this type of fanatic ensured that Gary had a chance to develop his talent in the harsher world of the men's game, skill being by far the most effective method of keeping out of harm's way. At home he spent long hours practising and although he wasn't well known enough to win his place in the Yorkshire Under-16s he was seen one Sunday playing for the pub side by a scout from Sheffield Wednesday who the following week wrote and asked him to come to the club for a trial.

"The trouble was, in his first trial game Gary twisted his right ankle halfway through the first half."

"That must have been a bitter disappointment."

She nodded. "But they must already have seen enough of his talent since they asked him to report back to the club's training round each Thursday afternoon for the following three or four weeks."

"And they signed him up?" I asked.

"Well, the club took him on as a junior, but since he was doing very well at school I persuaded him to stay on and have a try at his O and A levels instead of becoming an apprentice. Since thousands of boys never make the grade at football, good results at school are always a safe investment for the future."

"How well did he do?" I asked.

"Not bad at all," she replied with a smile of pride. "Not bad at all. He took three subjects for A level, and got a Grade A for Italian, Grade B for French and Grade B for English."

"He didn't want to pursue his studies any further?"

"Afraid not," she said in tones of disappointment. "I attempted to persuade him, but . . ." she shrugged.

"He equated the riches coming from inside the football world with another sign of freedom?"

"Yes. During the previous two years he had been pursued by scouts from other clubs as well as Sheffield Wednesday."

"Still, you must have been very close to him at this stage."

She paused as a smile came over her features. "I got to know his life quite well during that period. He was very fond at that time of pop music and it seemed that at all times the house used to resound to numbers by Dire Straits, Genesis and Culture Club. But I used to drive him over frequently to the Wednesday training ground at Bolderstone, just to the west of Sheffield and then go on to do some shopping. In the end, though, Gary remained with Wednesday for only two seasons before moving to Stoke City. Something to do with his style not suiting that of the team. 'A glorious player when his team is a goal ahead, disappointing when it's a goal behind.' That's what they used to say, and they lent him for short spells to Chelsea, as well as to Barnsley just down the road." She gestured briefly.

"Forgive me for breaking in," I interrupted, "but when I mentioned this period to the manager of Stoke City just now, he thought Gary's lack of form might have been caused by some family troubles." I let my statement linger in the air like a question.

Sian shook her head. "Family troubles, did he say? I've no idea what he might have meant."

"Did he live here when he played for Sheffield Wednesday?"

She shook her head. After he had chosen to become a full-time professional Gary had found digs in Sheffield. In fact after he moved there he seemed to become more remote from her. He would come over every now and then on a Sunday, driving up in his brand-new Volvo, but increasingly she felt his sympathies being pulled in other directions.

"Girls?" I asked.

"Naturally." In her voice I noticed a tightness that had not existed before. All of a sudden she reached for a cigarette and took a fair amount of time to light it.

"Did he bring any of them here with him?"

"Yes."

"And . . ." I prompted.

"In general he could play the field, and since he was tall and good-looking he usually found himself faced with a large field to play." She looked away from me and blew smoke through her nostrils, as though signifying that she had finished with the topic.

"But was there anyone in particular?" I pressed.

Sian gave me a withering look and then shook her head. "Just the usual rabble you see at any game. The perpetual 'hangers-on'." Her voice had become as hard as a piece of ice.

"Gary must have been earning a nice wage to afford to run a Volvo," I remarked casually, to change the subject.

"No," she said, shaking her head after a brief pause. "The club made a deal with the car firm for some advertising and were given ten models for the players to drive around as a promotion device. Gary apparently was lucky in the draw between the full-time professionals and gained the use of one."

"Very fortunate. Although I suppose he must have had a number of friends who were quite rich."

"Or expected to be." She laughed unexpectedly.

I glanced at my watch and saw that it was just before ten, more than time for me to make for the main road.

"I must be going," I said, standing. "Thank you for so many things. First of all for agreeing to see me. Then for giving me so much useful information about your nephew. And finally, for a most memorable meal."

"Do you have to go?" she asked, standing up and walking across to me. Her voice had sunk, had become almost a whisper. "We must have much more that we ought to discuss."

"Sorry," I said. "I have someone coming to see me first thing tomorrow." A pure invention.

"You could stay the night and drive down before breakfast-time," she suggested, fixing me intensely with sapphire-blue eyes which suddenly had become very hard-edged.

I slowly brushed away her left hand moments after it had been placed on my chest to inject some form of physical emphasis behind her pleadings. "I could talk for many more hours about Gary, but ought to return to London." I suddenly found it difficult to speak.

She took a step away, and her eyes sparked with venom.

"And since I didn't expect to stay overnight," I continued lamely, "I've brought nothing with me."

She raised her head and gave me a penetrating look, but a smile lay behind those fierce eyes. "It will take me just a few moments to make the bed in the spare room, I can find a spare pair of pyjamas easily, and an electric razor is inside the bathroom cupboard."

That was that, it appeared. "I feel like a grappa if you have one," I replied as I sat down.

"Nothing could be easier," she replied, and the smile had moved down to her mouth. She opened the walnut drinks cabinet and poured a generous quantity of grappa into a cut glass, which she handed to me. "Excuse me for a moment while I make up your bed."

Before I could reply I heard her running upstairs, and the rest of the evening was taken up with a discussion regarding Gary. When she'd returned to the ground floor Sian had poured herself a fair measure of sambuca, taken off her shoes and sat on the rug by the fireplace. She said how disappointed she had been that Gary had not pursued the academic career that could have been his for the asking.

Gary had gained a place to read modern languages at a college in London University, and it came as little surprise to learn that the college in question was that at which Sian had studied some years earlier, Bedford College.

"Don't tell me," I interjected, making a guess, "the head of the Italian department wouldn't have been Penry Davies."

Sian gave a faint blush. "Yes."

Eventually Sian showed me up to a small room on the first floor, along the passage from the bedroom in which she slept, and next door to the spacious bathroom. It possessed that eerie dampness of a room that has not been used for some time. Magenta curtains had been drawn across the wide window, and the furniture consisted of a cupboard, a chest of drawers and a marble fireplace together with a pair of tables on each side of the bed that was at the centre of the inside wall.

On top of the bed were a pair of midnight-blue pyjamas with gold piping which bore the label of Roberto Brai, Via della Spiga, Milano, which I presumed had belonged to Sian's first husband, Domenico. Mercifully, since it was a frosty night, she had made up the bed with many blankets, and soon after my head touched the pillow I was asleep.

I've always been a light sleeper, and woke up when I heard the noise of the door being opened. A quick glance down at the luminous face of my watch on the bedside table to my right told me that it was half past two.

At first I thought that she might have been sleep-walking,

131

until I realised that the pattern of her footsteps was far too irregular. I tried to keep my breathing regular, determined not to show that I had heard her, while I waited to see what she would do.

I received an answer soon enough when I felt a rush of cold air on my back, followed an instant later by Sian snuggling in behind me. She smelt of fresh perfume and her animal scent. Despite the biting temperature she was entirely naked, and her firm breasts with their raised nipples were pressed relentlessly into my back. Her breathing was heavy while she stroked the small hairs on the back of my neck, but after a few minutes I felt her left arm angle across and her fingers start to play awkwardly at the front of my chest, making featherlight circles, delicate meanderings that were intended to be suggestive. I kept my breathing steady, needing desperately to stay in charge of the proceedings.

She next threw her left leg across my thigh and pressed herself closer to the small of my back. Gradually her fingers unbuttoned my pyjamas and brushed lightly against my chest. When they started their inevitable descent, and reached my groin, I suddenly grasped her arm tight, moved to my right and switched on the bedside light. I then sat up, held up the bedclothes on her side of the bed, and shook my head.

"Stop there, Sian," I said in a controlled voice. "That isn't a very good idea."

Although her body was still curved like a spoon, her head instantly jerked up. Her ghostly blue eyes had opened in shock, but the shock quickly turned to rage as she realised the finality of my words.

"You bastard," she cried. "You complete bastard." She spat into my face.

She shook her arm free, climbed swiftly out of the bed and walked towards the door – her head uptilted. Before the door was slammed shut I was able to notice a pale shaft of a scar that ran down below her right breast which I assumed must have been a legacy of her accident.

It wasn't easy to find sleep. There had been a quality about her effort to seduce me that had appeared artificially awkward.

Complete silence reigned in the house when I woke the following morning at twenty to seven. I got straight out of bed, dressed quickly and didn't bother to shave, but in the kitchen I did snatch a breakfast of a piece of toast and a cup of Nescafé.

I left a note thanking Sian for her hospitality – but as I drove away towards the motorway couldn't help wondering whether I had made a vindictive enemy. Hell hath few furies like a woman spurned.

The thought that accompanied me on the drive south lay in wondering the precise reason why Sian had wanted to climb naked into my bed, and the manner in which that might be linked to the threat of blackmail.

13

Thursday, 22nd February

On reaching London I booked a flight to Milan for the following day, telephoned Dal Bosco and arranged to see him during the evening, took a shower and had some brunch. I also ran through my notebook and marked off some events and names that still puzzled me, although my mind kept reaching back to Andrea Cornelius, the girl with the long copper-coloured hair with whom Gary had been involved. Gary had obviously been very fond of her. Sian had obviously despised her.

I spent a few minutes before my visit to Dal Bosco browsing through a street map of Florence. My bank sent me traveller's cheques and crisp ten thousand lire notes. I telephoned the Hertz agency to arrange for an Alfa to be brought round at a suitable time to the main entrance of Linate Airport.

I'd been in touch with an estate agent who handled properties in the north-eastern district of London and carried with me some of the brochures that had been sent. I took out an extra insurance policy and, since both my parents were already dead, filled in the name of Cecelia Alexander as the person who should be given all my worldly possessions in the event of a tragedy. The daughter of an English father and Italian mother who came from near Bologna, she read Italian at Oxford and now taught the language to members of the Foreign Office at Palace Chambers in Bridge Street. During the past two years we'd become very close whenever I'd been in the country.

At seven o'clock Dal Bosco met me on his landing looking every bit as ornate as when we'd met initially. He was dressed this time in a three-piece suit in light grey, together with a dark blue shirt which had white collar and cuffs. On this occasion he was wearing a pair of dark brown shoes in calf, but they didn't look to be worth any less than two hundred thousand lire. Each, that is.

He grasped me close to him, and sang out "*Ciao*, Ross, *ciao*, *ciao*" in a friendly manner, before showing the way through the salon de luxe. He poured me a glass of chilled Frascati without waiting for me to ask for one and brought it across.

I wondered what all this display of friendliness presaged, but he merely gave a relieved smile. "*Bene, bene*," he said, almost to himself in a tone which suggested he was surprised to see me, before he sat down weightily. "I've been busy on the phone," he continued, after having poured himself a glass of wine. "I couldn't get hold of Taccone yesterday but I did talk to the club secretary about Byrne."

"You know that he has a place in the central part of the city where he seems to have settled in very easily?"

Dal Bosco nodded.

"Have you been there?"

He shook his head sadly. "He telephoned me soon after he had moved in. But as I told you the other day, he's been strangely quiet of late."

So. I wasn't going to hear any news directly from Gary. If I was to learn anything more at all, I was going to let the Italian talk on in his own sweet way.

I was in for a surprise, however. There was a brief pause before Dal Bosco rose, walked over to his desk, dug inside for a few moments and then strode back towards me clutching a blood-red folder.

When he was comfortably seated he took out of it a xerox copy of a formal document. "Yesterday morning I telephoned some journalist friends who put me in contact with someone who is familiar with the intricacies of your particular world." He paused. "I found part of the information they gave me most interesting – let us discuss it now." He looked at me.

"There's not much point in my saying 'no'. Is there?"

Colouring noticeably, Dal Bosco began to read. "You were born as Ross Merric Armstrong in Edinburgh, son of a Scottish father called Graham and an English mother called Jennifer. You will, begin your thirty-third year on the seventeenth of July." (I liked the Italianate way of putting that.) "Your height is one metre and eighty-five centimetres; and you weigh thirteen stone two pounds or eighty-five kilograms. Your passport number is N441943A and you have scars on your forehead and above your right eyebrow." He looked up at me in a form of questioning.

"I fell forward into a fire when I was ten months old," I explained.

He nodded. "When you were still young your parents moved south to Somerset where your father continued his work as an architect in Taunton. When you were thirteen he sent you to be schooled at Millfield College near Glastonbury, which has a first-class record at producing games players."

"It took me some time to settle down to bookwork," I interrupted.

Dal Bosco continued as though he'd not heard me. "You left when you were eighteen, spent the next few months travelling round Europe, and later were given a job aboard a surveying ship named *The Corell Beach* when you were involved in several scrapes along with a South African colleague, Chris Kuhn . . ."

"That period toughened me up a great deal," I butted in to throw him off his stride. No one likes being dissected in such a thorough manner, but I was thankful he made no mention of a fight in a bar in Barcelona where Chris and I had to flee after being set upon by some Filipino sailors armed with knives.

"Then you took a course in economics held in the University of Perugia." I nodded but Dal Bosco held up a hand, pleading for silence. "You were then taken on by the Nightingale Insurance Agency as an investigator. During the past decade you have been involved in cases in all parts of the world, have taught yourself German to add to your use of French, Italian and Spanish." He stopped and looked up at me. He gave an owl-like nod.

"Eugenio," I said, "now it's my turn. Could you give me a brief curriculum vitae of your own career and tell me how and when you came to live in London." I paused and gave a smile. "Please."

Born in the town of Trento, just to the north of Lake Como, in a family who had Hungarian ancestors, Dal Bosco found himself being snapped up at an early age by Internazionale of Milan, for whom he'd performed at fullback for several years, despite being twice lent to sides in the Serie B. That had been succeeded by a period playing for Bologna, and he'd seen out the twilight of his career playing for Torino. A dependable player who'd made merely two international appearances, he'd managed to keep most of his wealth, which he invested in a travel business in the early sixties.

That had been very astute since the sixties had witnessed a real explosion in travelling to other countries, aided and abetted by the formation of the Common Market, which helped to "dissolve" all national barriers. During his spell with his final club, Torino, Dal Bosco taught himself English (playing alongside Denis Law and Joe Baker had provided the initial impetus), so that when his playing days were over, he'd borrowed some money and came to London to open and run a branch of his firm.

During the first summer or two it was very difficult getting Dal Bosco Tours functioning properly – "and this was not entirely due to the fact that my English came with an accent that was a mixture of Northern Italian and Northern Scottish," Dal Bosco chuckled. He'd been required to charter planes that flew from Luton Airport: four a week during the first year, eight a week the year after, flying to resorts in Italy such as Brindisi, Cagliari and Catania along routes that hitherto had remained little used. "I had my share of pilots complaining of exhaustion, but I knew that a too heavy workload – four hours' sleep a night and companions who've barely learned to fly adequately – could lead to cases of nervous exhaustion or even of suicide, so I always took care not to overwork my staff."

However, his love of football was a constant companion and during the winter months, when business was less strained, he managed to make contact with two or three clubs, volunteering to act as a spy on those English teams which might provide opposition in the three European Cup competitions. Presidents came and went in addition to coaches being hired and fired, but one person who would forever be a permanent fixture was Eugenio Dal Bosco, an experienced scout who kept his ear to the ground. Since 1980 when Italy re-opened its doors to foreign players, Eugenio had found himself increasingly in demand and now received retainers from these leading clubs to carry out for them the task of attending matches and providing dossiers on outstanding players.

"Doesn't that lead to bad feeling?" I'd have been surprised if the answer had been in the negative.

"You refer to my having divided loyalties?" Dal Bosco asked, and then explained. "On occasions the line is very thin but," he tapped the table in front of him, "I make it my business to know the strengths and weaknesses of those teams for whom I scout, and am always very careful to keep in touch with them regarding certain players. Added to that, there's the benefit of modern technology." He gave a smile and pointed to his video machine.

"You mean that you were able to keep in contact with the coach of Fiorentina, whom you informed about Gary Byrne several weeks before he moved there?"

Dal Bosco gave a nod and a weak smile drifted across his face.

"A perfect example of being in the right place at the right time," I pointed out. "It must be primarily thanks to a man called Eugenio Dal Bosco that Fiorentina have made such a wise and profitable purchase. *Complimenti.*"

After nodding his thanks Dal Bosco told me about the crucial dinner that had occurred towards the end of June in the previous year. Those present had included, apart from himself and Byrne, Sergio Taccone and the current president of AC Fiorentina, Marcello Stirata, together with two representatives from City, Mike Townson and the chief shareholder, Ken Pritchard, a very wealthy engineer from the area. Both sets of men were highly satisfied: those from Stoke because they were acquiring a good price for a player who would be only twenty-one, while those representing Fiorentina had reasons for much optimism since the reports from Dal Bosco had always suggested that Gary Byrne might be a player in whose talents the Tuscan club might invest.

Dal Bosco gave a quick smile. "Before you return, please promise me that you'll allow yourself to adjust to the tempo of the local life, and won't put up the backs of some important people, especially not that of Stirata."

"When we met on Monday, we got along very well."

"Good, but this trip could be very different. Very different and more than a bit dangerous." He paused for a moment. "Where do you plan to stay?"

"The Excelsior is very well appointed."

"Naturally." He reached into his pocket, took out his diary and quickly wrote on a page of it. He tore off the relevant sheet and slipped it towards me. "However, here's the address and phone number of a very good friend of mine who has an apartment on the Lungarno Corsini and who can put you up for a few days."

The name and address Dal Bosco gave me was

> Francesco Barberini,
> Lungarno Corsini 21,
> Tel. 85.82.28.

I began to thank him. "Eugenio – "

"*Ma no, ma no,*" Dal Bosco interrupted. "*Niente.* Houses were made to be lived in, weren't they? In fact Francesco travels so much he should be keen to have you there just for the sake of having his place spared from a visit by *i ladri*, who might rob it clean." His eyebrows rose dramatically, as if to emphasise his point. "Moreover, you must find somewhere such as that, much more calm and relaxing than a hotel which can seem to be highly cold and impersonal. And to put you in the mood for Italy, my fatherland," he said very sombrely, "let's have some more wine."

"Tell me something, please, Eugenio," I said quietly, after he'd sat down.

"Francesco is very trustworthy," Dal Bosco quickly replied. "I've known him for these past twenty years and he – "

"No, no," I broke in. "It's not concerned with that. I've enjoyed your company on two of these past three evenings but I wondered whether you live alone while your wife is in Italy or . . ."

Dal Bosco gave a sorrowful shake of his head. "My wife died a few months before I left Italy, Mr Armstrong. She was visiting her parents in their apartment on the Via Puccini in Pistoia, and on her way back after doing some shopping she was caught in crossfire between a young terrorist and a detachment of the carabinieri. She was hit in the neck and the chest, and died on her way to hospital."

"I'm sorry."

"We had a boy and a girl. They've grown up and have left their grandparents now. I didn't like to bring them with me," he said in a firm tone and looked me firmly in the eye. "He's now an engineer and she a dentist. I used to send money across to pay for their education, and they visited me here several times." He paused and then smiled. "Shall we return to this business?"

"Please." I nodded.

"What time does your plane leave?" His eyes had taken on a melancholic sorrow.

"Eleven o'clock. I should arrive in Florence tomorrow evening."

"You might see the game next Sunday between Fiorentina and AC Napoli," Dal Bosco enthused unexpectedly, as though relieved to get away from talking about subjects that discomforted him. "I envy you, my friend, I envy you. That'll be one of the matches of the season, you mark my words."

"Maybe," I replied, "maybe. A few minutes ago you said that my trip might be dangerous."

Dal Bosco nodded gravely. "I followed up that suspicion you had on Tuesday about Gary being blackmailed, and can confirm that he has been having an interesting time with his finances. Much money going into and out of his various accounts."

This was new. "Accounts? I've only been told about his account at the Banca del Lavoro in the Via Strozzi. You mean he has others?"

Dal Bosco nodded, and reached for a folder. "Just along from there is a branch of the Banca Commerciale Italiana, where he has another account in the name of Tim Lacklove, and yet another round the corner at the Banco di Roma in the Via Vecchietti in the name of John Savage." He passed across a slip of paper. Followers of Dr Freud might have been interested in those names.

"How come you know so much about his money matters? Surely not all from your journalist friends?" I enquired.

He gave an enigmatic smile. "Friends in high places in the banks of Firenze." He paused for a moment before he explained. "It's all kept very secret but in fact many clubs carry out this type of investigative procedure, especially in Italy."

Dal Bosco seemed to sense that he had been indiscreet and set about changing the subject. "Does the name of Richard Stokes mean anything to you?"

"I don't think so," I replied after a pause, but it did. Stokes was a cold-eyed trouble-shooter based in Nottingham. "In what connection?"

"He got in touch with me yesterday morning, wanting to talk about Gary Byrne."

My heart went cold. I genuinely hadn't expected anyone else to be walking along the paths which I had to follow. Even a cretin could guess which club Stokes might be working for.

"He spoke with the type of accent they have in the Midlands. It was very difficult to understand." Dal Bosco gave a chuckle. "As difficult, I suspect, as my accent was when I told him that I could not help with his enquiries."

I gave a smile. "Thank you, Eugenio. Thank you." That would give me a useful start. But why had he helped me?

"Don't thank me. Thank Gary Byrne. It's a simple truth that everyone who's ever been in contact with him has become in some way involved in his problems. You like him. I can tell you want to help him." Dal Bosco glanced at his watch and said, "It's already time for my dinner at Montpeliano's. Forgive me."

He shepherded me to the door, which he systematically double-locked before he guided me to the lift. He then led the way outside, and, after shaking my hand, strode down in the direction of Montpellier Street.

After I'd reached my flat I made a call to Pino Cardone, who kept a small shop in the Via Maffia, just to the eastern side of the Piazza Santo Spirito on the southern bank of the Arno. I'd been given his name by a friend in the Special Branch who seemed to be familiar with small gun shops in most of the major cities of Europe.

The phone was answered on the ninth ring.

"*Pronto*." A gruff voice in a bass-baritone.

"*Posso parlare con Signor Cardone?*" I enquired quietly.

A brief pause. Then, "*Chi è questo?*"

"*Uno scozzese chiamato Ross Armstrong.*" I allowed that to sink in before continuing, "*Sono un amico di Harry Tattersall.*" I omitted the first letter from the Christian name, but was to feel a fool only moments later.

"*Ah!*" Another pause, followed by "*un momento,*" and I heard the phone being put down and being followed by the riffling of some papers. Suddenly someone came on speaking in English. "Yes. What do you want?" It was the same voice I had heard a moment before. The accent was a northern one.

I explained that I'd be arriving during the evening and would like to collect a handgun soon.

"What make and calibre?" asked the voice.

"I'm fairly used to a Beretta 92E," I replied. I had become accustomed to wearing a gun in a shoulder-holster, and, although there were pistols which were more lethal, the Beretta suited me and it was light.

"Ring me after you've arrived in Florence and I'll have something for you." A brief pause. "Where are you staying?"

I told him.

"Perfect. No more than five minutes' walk away. I'll see you in a few hours' time."

"I might arrive quite late," I said. "What time do you close?"

He gave a growl of a laugh. "Don't worry. My apartment is right over the shop." The phone went dead.

14

Friday, 23rd February

I travelled Alitalia in the hope of gaining further practice of speaking Italian while en route to Milan and was fortunate enough to find myself sitting next to Norberto Lanceni, a well-known tenor who was returning home after having sung several performances at Covent Garden in the part of Manrico in Verdi's *Il Trovatore*. We chatted amiably about his recent roles in Paris, Vienna, Madrid, Copenhagen and Buenos Aires but eventually, unprompted by me, the conversation came round to football. Like the majority of Italians he had a favourite team which, although he lived in Lonate Pozzolo, a village just thirty kilometres or so to the west of Milan, was Torino, primarily due to a family connection, an aunt of his having been married to a close friend of Valentin Mazzola, one of those who perished on the mountaintop of Superga just outside Torino on the 4th May, 1949, an event that everyone in Italy remembers.

Wherever he was performing he always made it of prime importance to catch up on the league results from a Sunday, and always carried with him a league fixture list of games being played. When I informed him that I was on my way to Florence, he immediately reached for his wallet so as to let me know who they were playing.

I'd allowed myself to be so caught up in this conversation that it came as a complete shock to realise that the Boeing 737 was descending on to the tarmac of Linate Airport, and I felt impelled to return my thoughts to the matter in hand.

I was once given by an Italian friend an acronym I could never forget. The letters ALITALIA stand for "Aircraft Landed In Turkey All Luggage In Albania". But on this occasion all went well, and very soon I was on the road.

It was a cold but bright day for the drive down south. There had obviously been a heavy fall of snow during the past week and the fields on either side were carpeted with whiteness, but a thaw was in process and the gutters along the sides of the autostrada carried flowing streams of water.

Arriving at Bologna at just before one o'clock I had a glass of white wine before ordering a veal *piccatina* with a side salad of mushrooms, tomato and lettuce at a friendly restaurant in the area reserved for pedestrians. Serving at my table was an elderly character with little hair, an aggressive paunch and a mightily cavalier attitude to his profession. He would ask people for their orders and punctuate this with vociferous greetings to anyone he knew who was passing by. Every now and then he would steal outside and throw a finished bottle of wine deep into the heart of one of the half-dozen clumps of privet that formed a boundary outside.

The centre of the town was full of short streets, closely packed together and that period of the day, just before the citizenry returned to work, made them comparatively free from traffic. I spent anything up to an hour learning how to handle the car in tight situations and by the time I set off for Florence, which lay slightly above a hundred kilometres away, I had become very used to the character of the car.

So keen was I to reach my destination that I rejected the opportunity of travelling south on the small roads through the marvellous countryside of the hinterlands of Bologna and Florence, and instead chose to travel all the way on the autostrada with its tunnels and sweeping curves.

I left the autostrada at the north-west corner of the city and made my way into the centre before ringing Barberini, explaining who I was and what I wanted.

"Of course, of course," he broke in before I could finish. "Any friend of Eugenio's is a friend of mine." He went on to explain that he had an appointment with someone which should have started five minutes previously, that it would last for a very short time and that he expected to be back at his apartment in the Lungarno Corsini in about twenty minutes' time.

"Don't hurry on my account," I said. I would use the time to get to know the city better. My previous visit had provided too little of this, so it was after driving around the city streets for forty minutes, reacquainting myself with their idiosyncrasies, that I found my way to the Lungarno Corsini. Francesco Barberini lived on the third floor of a tall, thin, terraced house made of local stone. He himself was in complete contrast to the building, being short, plump and having a relaxed, brown face.

143

He greeted me in a friendly manner, handled my case as though it merely weighed a few kilos and led the way upstairs, ignoring the lift. At the top he turned round to face me as I made my way up the last step or two, patted his ample stomach and said, "If it wasn't for doing that I'd be even fatter than I am." He must have drunk wine by the litre every evening and eaten everything put before him.

It was a pleasant apartment with a front room which looked out across the river. Lights were beginning to come on, causing grim shadows to appear which threw into relief the bridges to my left and right.

Barberini pointed eastwards. "That is the Ponte Santa Trinità and beyond that is the Ponte Vecchio and the Uffizzi and – "

I stopped him before he could describe more landmarks. "All in good time, Francesco, all in good time. I know this city well enough from a tourist point of view. The well-known sights won't have changed. But restaurants, garages, hotels . . . you can help me a great deal with the practical side of life, and save me a lot of time by showing me the good places on the map."

I didn't plan on visiting Cardone until well into the evening; which gave us enough time to go through lists of useful places in Florence with my being kept busy marking the relevant details on my map. After approximately two hours I knew my way round the local streets and when I left to visit Cardone at about half past eight I felt I knew the city as though I'd lived there for a long time.

Barberini and I arranged to go out later for an evening meal, then I left the apartment, moving slowly westwards along the street, turning to cross the Arno over the Ponte alla Carraia.

Cardone's quarters in the Via Maffia were in local stone which had been stained dark brown by the elements. A sign saying "*Chiuso*" in large black letters hung on the front of the glass-panelled door but I remembered his telling me that he lived on the premises and pushed the bell. There followed a brief pause before the door was opened.

Cardone – I assumed it was he – was a medium-sized character of approximately sixty with an open face but hard black eyes. I supposed that their bleakness was to do with his having dealt for the past thirty-odd years with a few customers who could not afford to be honest.

"Mr Armstrong?" he said in English.

I nodded.

"You'd better come in."

I followed him upstairs, turning right on the first landing to enter what I assumed to be the sitting-room. It was furnished comfortably with three armchairs and a chaise-longue finished in dun-coloured leather but my eyes instantly travelled round the four walls which were decorated with ebony cases that held dozens of antique guns.

"What will you drink?" Cardone asked, again in English.

"Before I reply," I said, "please tell me when you learned to speak such good English."

He gave a brief smile and shook his head. "It's very rusty nowadays, although I still read English books and journals. Many years ago I spent time at the Bela River Camp for prisoners of war at Milnthorpe, about ten kilometres south of Kendal at the foot of your English Lake District.

"After I'd recovered from the shock of being captured I decided to make the best of my life, and when I gave help on local farms I always made a point of asking questions in English. Naturally I was accused at first of planning an escape to my home in Piedmont, but after several weeks of working alongside them the local people began to treat me generously. I was able to remain in the region long after we were released." He paused and waved an arm around him. "And if you wonder why I now live in Florence the reason is simple: my wife comes from a small village in the Val di Pesa and had become so attached to this area that she wouldn't move." He shrugged and shook his head. "*Le donne.*" He tapped his temple. "*Pazze.*"

"Another case of love conquering all."

He repeated his question.

I asked for a glass of white vermouth, and while he was pouring the drinks remarked that his collection must be worth millions of lire.

He gave a smile. "Many of them I have put together from parts of broken guns . . ."

"Fakes?" I asked him.

His voice sharpened. "Of course. They wouldn't fool an expert for one-tenth of a second. In my display-room downstairs I find there are many *turisti*," he almost spat the word, "who don't care what they are buying so long as it reminds them of Florence." He rubbed his right earlobe between his thumb and forefinger. "This business in buying antique pistols has rocketed since we came to live here, and I find it makes very good business to use my knowledge of how guns work to assemble pieces which were originally of totally different origin." He gave an impish grin.

"But you must know many real collectors," I remarked. "Harry Tattersall knows a great deal about handguns and he wouldn't have given me your name unless he'd been convinced."

Cardone gave an impatient shrug. "Of course, of course, of course. But when I know that an enquiry is genuine I often send the gun out of Florence so that what I refer to as my *perfetti* may be examined minutely by the prospective purchaser."

"Isn't that highly risky?" I asked.

"I've never been double-crossed." He held his thumb up. "I can always get into contact with the purchaser." A forefinger. "The world in real antique arms is very, very small and word can get round so swiftly causing the weapon to be positively the last that character can ever purchase. Or else." A middle finger, and a pause while his eyes glinted. "There are not a few people around who can ensure that no funny business gets played. If you know what I mean?"

"*Gambizzare*," I said. "Blowing kneecaps off."

"And much worse."

I shook my head. "Silly men."

"And women," Cardone said. "More than a few of those."

I expressed surprise.

"Why certainly," he explained. "On average once a month I am telephoned from New York by a wealthy heiress; and there is a clutch of three or four women in Europe who have collections of antique guns." He strode over to a cabinet. "Here, I'll show you." He pressed in a switch on its side and opened one of its doors to take out a handsome-looking pistol, barely a third of a metre long.

"This is an eighteenth-century pistol which was produced in this part of the country by a craftsman who called himself," Cardone gave a smile, "Il Fenomeno. I'm sure that the American heiress will be most interested in making a purchase when she's informed about it. Look at it while I collect your gun from downstairs."

It was a beautiful thing to examine but must have weighed approximately three or four times as much as a contemporary handgun. When I looked around I noticed that a fair part of his collection was of a Latin nature being of Italian, Portuguese or Spanish origin. Standing close to the cabinet I could see the names of some of the craftsmen written on the barrels. Gaspar Fernandez, Lazzarino Cominazzo, Geronimo Fernandez. As these weapons had been mounted on green velveteen I assumed that they represented the cream of his collection – an opinion Cardone confirmed when he returned upstairs.

"There," he said, handing me a brown paper parcel. "One Beretta and a hundred 9-millimetre shells." When I reached my hand for my wallet he shook his head. "Not so soon, my friend. Why not pay when you let me have it back?"

I murmured my thanks to him before returning the ornate pistol. "Like many people I have my ration of likes and dislikes. I wonder whether you could attach these," from my jacket pocket I brought out two strips of suede, "to the stock." Harry Mann had given me that tip some time ago.

"But – "

I cut him off before he could start. "It's just a personal foible," I said. "Nothing more, nothing less."

Cardone gave an emphatic shrug, took the gun and the suede strips over to a bureau and began sticking them down. "A fast-drying glue," he explained, "but I wouldn't do any shooting tonight."

I told him that I didn't plan to.

I thanked him again and made my way out of the building and street. After enjoying a relaxed meal with Francesco Barberini at a restaurant where the menu was written on a blackboard, each table being provided with opera glasses to read the alternatives clearly, I was in bed by eleven o'clock accompanied by the latest edition of the *Almanacco Illustrato del Calcio* and a history of Italian football. My last memory before falling asleep was reading of the sense of disappointment being expressed in a description of the Italian 4–3 victory over West Germany in the 1970 World Cup final competition. Disappointment, because the two defences were accused of being too weak!

Part Three

For Donatella Spezia fame occurred most dramatically. Three months earlier she'd been hailed as a star of the future in an edition of the Corriere della Sera *after her triumph at the Piccolo Teatro in a production of* Iphigénie en Aulide *which had been acclaimed throughout Italy as marking the birth of an actress who possessed a true dramatic talent. It had been announced that the production would go on tour to other Italian cities, and soon after had come the declaration by her agent that she was being considered for a part in a film to be directed in the forthcoming spring by a leading Italian director.*

For a youngster who hailed from the village of Villacidro in Sardinia to break into the sophisticated world of Italian films would indeed be a rare triumph. After he'd first seen her acting in Sardinia the agent Salvatore Brini had made sure to keep in regular contact. Twenty-four months later, after the girl had been ordered by her blind father to leave and search for fame on the mainland, she'd flown to Linate Airport from Cagliari. It wasn't until the plane had flown for half an hour that she discovered in her handbag an envelope that contained most of the family's money.

With the advice of Brini she'd stopped using her given name of Manuela Decchuras and spent many long, painful hours at stage school learning how to shed the strong Sardinian dialect with which she'd grown up. Very cryptic, with its many vowel sounds, it was almost impossible to understand for anyone not accustomed to the cadence and rhythms of its sound. She'd persevered with dedication in the task of teaching herself to speak pure Italian, and had been given inspiration by looking back to the example of Sophia Loren, another actress from a poor background who had found success, both on stage as well as in films.

Now, almost five years after her arrival at Linate Airport, people had started to see her as another star of the future. Where next, they had wondered? Where next?

15

Saturday, 24th February
The following morning I attended a practice-session of the
Fiorentina players on the training-pitch which was an adjunct
of the Stadio Comunale. Despite the presence of several
lead-coloured clouds and a chill wind that blew from the north,
several hundred supporters were in attendance. A clutch of
players had been drawn up into two teams: the Reds versus the
Blacks. It was knock-about stuff, practising both attacking and
defensive moves; and Byron was particularly noticeable – but
for entirely the wrong reasons.

From the start he made mistake after mistake, displaying no
true sense of purpose nor providing any hint of intelligence. He
failed disastrously to integrate with his team-mates, several of
whom would have been used to his style of play. At half-time
Taccone, wearing a pale blue tracksuit and overseeing the
session at close quarters, drew him well away from the rest of
the players and started to harangue him fiercely. Byron
attempted to utter some words but found himself unable to cut
through the assault from the manager who shook his head
angrily and briskly led him back to join the other players. It
came as small surprise to find Gary being asked to change his
colour with a player from the other side.

This relegation into the reserves, however, did little to
strengthen his determination. Although the standard of his
passing slowly improved and there seemed to be much more
resolve to his play, I wasn't surprised at the end of the game to
overhear one journalist discussing with another the possibility
that Byron had every chance of not being chosen for the game
against Napoli. His place might be given to Dario Bellone, a
fresh-faced twenty-year old who had been displaying the most
exciting form in practice matches.

As they left the pitch, the expressions of both Byron and
Taccone were revealing. Roberto Cianfanelli had caused havoc
whenever he appeared in the opposing box, but he'd been the

only attacking player to perform with any incisiveness. This could prove to be of the utmost importance since, although Napoli would be deprived of the majestic skills of Diego Maradona, who had pulled a hamstring, it was still a most difficult team to play against in its own stadium, having won nine out of ten matches that had been played there during the season. To make any attack incisive, however, a team requires an inspirational midfield, and with Byron showing such wayward form, inspirational the Fiorentina midfield decidedly was not.

This was an opinion obviously shared by Taccone, who walked straight past me without saying a word. On his features was a mask of frustration which suggested that while the gifted Welshman might not have been the only player to have displayed mediocre form, his lack of touch resembled a cancer which had eaten away at the confidence of his team-mates.

I waited until Gary himself was on the point of passing before I took a pace forward. "Can you spare a moment?" I asked.

Far from expressing any surprise he looked at me with porcelain-blue eyes that were painfully tired.

"I rang your number last night as well as this morning," I continued after he'd made no reply. "How I dislike answering-machines."

"Why did you return?" he asked in apathetic tones. "And when?"

"Yesterday evening. I'm staying with Francesco Barberini, a friend of Eugenio Dal Bosco." I paused and noticed that the name meant nothing to him. "To answer your first question, during the last few days I've been travelling around England, talking to people who have given me useful information."

His eyes suddenly became alive, but they narrowed. "Who else – apart from Eugenio?"

I was just on the point of speaking when Taccone came back and hurried Byron away in the direction of the changing-rooms. "I thought that you had left," said Taccone after he'd swiftly returned to me. The remark seemed to imply that I, and I alone, was responsible for the loss of form by one of his star players.

"I did," I replied, giving him a smile which did nothing to lighten his countenance. "But now I'm back."

"So I can see." He gave me an uncharacteristically chilly look. "In two hours' time we're flying down to Napoli from Peretola.

I'd be grateful if you would keep yourself to yourself for the next twenty-four hours, and not start taking the minds of any of the Fiorentina players away from the most important task in hand. That of taking one, if not two points from tomorrow's game.

"Especially not Byrne. I'm not sure yet whether I'll select him, but if I do I want him to concentrate his mind fully on the match. All right?" Pointing a finger at me, he nodded and strode away.

I waited a few minutes longer. The majority of the enthusiasts had drifted away, leaving only a small clutch of fanatics remaining in the cold. My perseverance was rewarded soon after by the appearance of the player whom I had been hoping to talk to, Roberto Cianfanelli. I was forced to wait while he signed a handful of autographs but eventually we were alone.

He looked towards me bemused. I was manifestly not seeking his autograph, and although earlier that week he'd gained his first selection for the national squad, he clearly didn't recognise my face as being that of a member of the press corps hoping for an interview.

I introduced myself and gave him my cover-story. Although, as his closest friend in the team, Cianfanelli probably knew of the importance of Giuliana in Byron's life, I thought it best not to mention her name. I did, however, decide to take a small risk and informed him about the possibility of blackmail.

"You have no ideas about this?" I said, pressing him for an answer by standing close to him.

"Blackmail!" He was obviously astounded and took some moments to answer. "Blackmail! I can't think of *anyone* who'd want to blackmail him. As far as I know he's always led a most respectable life here in Florence." There followed a long silence during which he looked solemnly into my eyes. "I'm sorry."

"Never mind." I gave a weak smile. "Do me a favour, and don't mention this to any of the other players. We both know that Byron's football is going through an especially bleak period. We don't want this news to make it any worse."

"Of course not," he replied and shook his head. "Of course not!" He looked at me as if I was an idiot to have thought that he would.

"Thanks. All the best for tomorrow."

"I think we'll need it." He smiled.

"Maradona's not playing."

"No, but Gregorio Stabile is." I hadn't heard of him. "A

155

young midfield player who's recently come into the side and is sending their fans wild. May see you again." Cianfanelli held out his hand before striding away briskly in the direction of his car.

I returned to the apartment in a disconsolate mood. Dropping Byron from the first team might reduce his price in the market, which would make him better value for money, but surely no one would want to purchase any player who was in such a pitiful state – and certainly not Tom Kennart, for all his admiration of the player from times past.

Nevertheless, intending to travel to Naples on the following day, I made contact with the president of Fiorentina.

"You've returned to Florence?" It was a question rather than a statement.

"I've visited some people in England," I replied, "and now intend to continue my research in Italy."

"Ah."

Before he could say anything else I reminded him of the promise he'd given during the early hours of Tuesday morning. "I'd like to attend the game tomorrow afternoon. I'll use my press pass but would like a ticket to take me to and from Naples."

"Nothing could be easier." His voice sounded as cordial as though we'd been close friends all our lives. "It happens that I'll be unable to go to the match myself, the first match for several months that I've not been able to watch live. Representatives from a large chain of Brazilian shops will be in Florence, and I must see them. But you can certainly make use of my plane to take you to Naples and bring you back."

I started to protest but he cut me off. "It'll be so easy," he continued. "In addition, I will ensure that you are collected from Capodichino Airport, taken to the stadium and brought back to it in one of my cars."

I started to remonstrate again, but to no avail. "*No. No. No.*" Stirata said, and again thanked me profusely for having looked after his daughter on that Monday night.

Sunday, 25th February
I was woken by the telephone ringing. It was still pitch dark; but turning on the bedside lamp I saw it was five minutes to four.

"Ross?" enquired a feminine voice before I could speak. "I'm sorry to wake you, but you're the only person in the world – the only *other* person in the world – I can talk to, and I just can't keep it a secret any longer. My period has started."

Which news woke me fast. "When?"

"About three hours ago."

"That must be a great relief," I said rhetorically while I swung my legs over the side of the bed.

"I must have missed two times." She couldn't contain her happiness. "I've not told Byron yet. I didn't want to disturb his sleep. Taccone telephoned Papa during the evening and explained that another player had recently been affected by a stomach virus which meant that he'd been forced at the last minute to call in Gary."

"First thing in the morning, then," I said sternly. "I'm sure that Byron needs to hear your news, but do try and get some sleep, *cara*. It may be difficult but please try. I'll be in touch in a few hours' time."

I put down the phone and climbed back into bed. I assumed that she'd got my phone number from Byron before he'd gone south to Naples. However, my thoughts had been given a sharp twist by the news I'd just received.

I certainly had to travel down to Naples to attend the match between Napoli and Fiorentina. It would be interesting to observe at close quarters the manner in which Byron performed having been freed from all the concerns over the condition of Giuliana.

Although there had now been introduced another cause for concern: surmising the extent to which Byron had been affected by that, or by differing factors. During the afternoon I had received copies of his bank statements at the Banca Nazionale del Lavoro. There had been, naturally, a considerable increase in the sums which he had invested after he had started to pursue his career as a model. However, I also noticed that large sums had been paid into the account each week but that in addition a lump sum of a thousand million lire had been withdrawn each month. Whatever monies were paid in, irrespective of whether these were accrued by the week or by the month, it made no difference: once in each month since his arrival in Florence there had been that regular withdrawal of one thousand million lire.

The telephone rang again at twenty-five minutes past nine.

"I fell asleep as ordered, but when I tried to contact Byron in Naples just now his telephone was engaged." The voice of Giuliana sounded flooded with anxiety. "What shall I do?"

"First of all," I said in comforting fashion, "calm down before you make yourself ill." I waited until she had stopped breathing heavily. "He is probably preparing for this important match and may not want to be disturbed. He might be trying to have a lengthy rest before a game which is doubly important for him, since he is playing merely thanks to injury to one of his team-mates. You don't know. I don't know. The most useful thing, I should think, is to send him a telegram at the San Paolo Stadium. That can be guaranteed to make him play the game of his life-time." After that thought had been given an opportunity to sink in, I put the phone down, leaving her sounding almost deliriously happy.

Giuliana's news made my mind race. What would Byron do now? He had hinted to me that his preference might be to remain in Italy, preferably in Florence with Giuliana, but it had been an English club that had involved me in this case, and naturally I owed it to them to play fair. If Giuliana's good news had an effect on the morale of Byron, a recording of the match could be most revealing to Kennart.

I then made contact with Eugenio Dal Bosco, who was already up and breakfasting. "Gary Byrne is playing this afternoon against Napoli," I informed him. "Do you think it will be shown on television?" He'd informed me that he possessed a television dish that was able to receive programmes from Italy, Germany, France and Spain.

Dal Bosco had his doubts. "There's a derby match scheduled between Internazionale and AC Milan which should be the game to be followed by the television people. There'll probably be only highlights of the game between Napoli and Fiorentina."

"Leave it with me, Eugenio, leave it with me."

I rang back to Stirata's villa and got through to him after the foreseeable security check. When he came on I asked for another favour, a copy of the film he would be making of the game that afternoon.

"Nothing could be easier," replied Stirata. "Nothing could be easier. But for both our sakes I hope Byron performs better than he's been doing recently."

That took me by surprise. "Both?"

"Why, you with your profile on the player, and me with

158

my added interest in him as a model," he explained after a moment.

"Of course." I let out a long breath. "I see what you mean."

"You'll have to excuse me, but a car will be with you shortly. *Arrivederci.*"

He was as good as his word, as I'd expected, and it was close to eleven o'clock when the bell sounded. Soon after I was accompanying a slim chauffeur along the Lungarno Corsini to where the dove-grey Ferrari 412 gleamed in the morning sunlight.

When we arrived at Peretola Airport, this engaging aura of efficiency was continued and I soon found myself flying southwards in a Piper Cheyenne II. On the journey, which lasted five minutes over the hour, I glanced at some articles concerning those mercenaries who had been attracted into Italian football from abroad and who were being dismissed as failures.

These unfortunates had come from all over the world – where they normally returned one or two seasons later complaining either of having been ignored by the manager or of having been unable to adapt to the particular strictures of the Italian game. Not a few had been treated with some contempt by their team-mates, thanks to their being paid higher salaries in the expectation that their performances might help swell the crowds and thus increase the monies being taken by the club. Alas for all of these, that had not been the case. I was still wondering whether or not Byron might qualify for entry into the catalogue of imported players who'd failed in the long term, when the plane approached the runway at Naples Airport and the smooth running of my journey continued.

The car to which I was shown was a twin of that which had driven me to Pisa, the colour on this occasion being metallic silver.

"Does it spend its whole time on club business?" I asked the chauffeur, a handsome character in his thirties who had brooding dark brown eyes and a trim figure.

"It's like this, Signore," he explained formally, while he eased into top gear and travelled towards Naples along the Tangenziale. "Just over five years ago Dottore Stirata discovered that the agent of Ferrari in Tuscany on some occasions used to take guests to games at the Stadio Comunale in order to watch Fiorentina play. He got in touch with the man soon

159

after and informed him that, in future, he would be most delighted to help if he was able. The following month we were asked to travel north to the Ferrari Headquarters in Modena and collect not one, but two, models of the Ferrari 412." He looked across at me. "Just like that. Still, I suppose it makes for good advertising."

"Riveting," I said drily, "but you haven't answered my question."

"The cars spend all their time on club business," he answered quickly. "I spent all this morning driving down the autostrada specifically to meet you. And after I return to Florence I will be given other trips which have to be made during the coming week. So . . ."

"I gather that Dottore Stirata is not coming down to watch the game."

"Something important came up yesterday with this party of Brazilian businessmen I was told. I gather that they could give the firm much good business and Il Dottore says he can't afford to waste time hanging around in airports waiting for service. So . . ." Again he failed to finish the sentence.

"So," I said, leaning back in my seat next to him, "who's going to win today and why?"

"The papers say it is going to be a close-run thing but me," he took his left hand off the steering wheel and tapped his chest, "I disagree. I think Napoli will win easily. Easily," he repeated sombrely. "It could be by a clear two or three goals. You want to know why? Why in a word has been the recent performance of Byron. During the past few weeks he's almost stopped having useful ideas, ceased to play with other members of the team and is in the very worst form physically. Last Sunday in that game against Milan it showed very clearly." His voice had taken a higher pitch.

"What showed?"

"Whenever a player's sent off the field or comes off due to some kind of injury you can normally get a clue to his feelings by looking at his eyes. They can show anger or pain or disappointment or . . ." he broke off and paused. "You know what I mean, don't you? Last Sunday when I watched Byron coming off the field his eyes wore a blank look as though all the events of the preceding hour had been meaningless. He's gone completely to pieces and today he's only playing as a substitute." News travels fast in footballing circles. "No. Some friends of mine were filling in their slips for the Totocalcio and put down all three possibilities for this game but me, I said all along that only one result would be possible. A home win." He gave a quick shrug of disappointment as he reached the point where we had to leave the Tangenziale.

"You might not be right," I said. "In fact, I'll take you on a bet myself. I give you ten thousand lire if Fiorentina lose; you give me ten thousand if they win. A draw and no one pays. Okay?"

"You must be joking," he said and gave a boisterous laugh. "Of course, it's okay."

"This saloon should really be painted in violet, Signore," the driver stated after a minute's silence. "It was felt by those in authority, however, that it would only look cheap and maybe gaudy. So this . . ." he didn't bother to finish the sentence but simply gave a shrug of disappointment.

We found ourselves caught up in a small traffic jam just as we were on the point of reaching the vast San Paolo stadium in the western part of the city.

"What's the delay?" I asked trying to see far ahead.

The driver shook his head and we both got out of the Ferrari. Some way ahead three police cars were drawn up with their lights still flashing while some members of the carabinieri formed a ring.

"It's probably another killing. The Camorra," the driver explained with a shrug, after he'd been to take a look. "In these times it's very rare to read a daily paper and notice a report of some unpleasant atrocity or other, but they still occur. Sawn-off shotguns, bodies being dismembered, people being hung – " he gave a shake of the head. "Neapolitans are so colourful and have a warm-hearted attitude to life but the area in and around Napoli has often been a notorious locale for this sort of activity, its overcrowded housing being some of the worst in the country."

Colourful indeed!

While plain-clothes officers of the Squadra Mobile were busy carrying out detailed measurements around the locale of the murder, members of the carabinieri placed on a stretcher the body of a glaze-eyed and blood-spattered youngster in a once-white sweat-shirt and faded jeans. As soon as the area was cleared of traffic we were allowed to continue to the stadium.

"Not nice," I said quietly as we moved away.

"They're used to it, these people," the driver announced dismissively, as though Neapolitans were different from other Italians. "The area just to the north of here, which is called 'Il Triangolo della Morte', is where the Camorra reigns supreme." The driver repeated himself as though he had not heard me. "Everything thereabouts is the worst – unemployment, lack of housing, little fresh water, no hospitals, few police – " he suddenly blinked as though he'd been making a political statement. "And just think. Each season the football team has over 60,000 *abbonati*, season-ticket holders who choose to spend their money not caring for their families but instead on a pleasure that lasts under two hours. *Toh*!

"This contrast was especially noticeable when Napoli won their first *scudetto* at the close of the 1986–87 season. Fiorentina played here for the last home match in early May, the game which saw Napoli clinch its first *scudetto*." The driver shook his head. "Amazing. The carnivals in the streets were so overwhelming I thought the place would erupt in its frenzy. The celebrations lasted day after day. They brought in three hundred musicians, two hundred donkeys from Sardinia, a gigantic pizza which was created in the colours of Napoli and there was a firework display on Mount Vesuvius. The entire country almost ground to a halt. *Incredibile*."

The driver told me that he was a member of a family that originally came from Sicily – a well-to-do family that had included members of the gentry, medics, condottieri and even, he puffed out his chest, one who had become a bishop in the province of Naples. Eventually his branch of the family had made its way north to Piedmont in the nineteenth century although an uncle had been killed fighting for Garibaldi at the battle of Mentana in 1876, a fact of loyalty which he announced proudly.

"But you come from Piedmont?" I wondered as he drew up in front of the main stand.

He nodded but remained seated.

"Won't you be watching the game?" I poked my head in after I'd climbed out of the car.

"Certainly." He dug around in his pocket until finally he found his ticket. "A good seat, this, in the main stand. All thanks to Il Dottore. But I'll have to find a good place to park."

"I understand," I said. "Can you collect me here after the game?"

The chauffeur nodded and I started to walk away, but I'd taken only three or four steps when I swivelled round. "I'm sorry. We English. I learn much about your family, but I don't even know your name."

He smiled at me briefly. "Nucera," he said. "Antonio Nucera."

"Thank you. Forgive me again for being so rude. See you later." I shook his hand.

He nodded and gave a grin. "And have your ten thousand lire note ready."

I made my way to the press box. The only person I'd know there would be Sergio Triscardo but I couldn't be sure what kind of attitude he'd take towards me after the events of Monday evening. He hadn't yet arrived so I chose a seat towards the back of the box and took out those papers which would give me details on who was taking part on the field of play. Though, naturally, I was determined to spend the whole game examining the attitudes and play of Byron; see how he managed to perform when all the emotional weight of being involved in an unwanted pregnancy was off his shoulders.

Just after the two teams came out for their pre-match warm-up session I felt a tap on my left shoulder and a voice said, "Permesso?" It was Sergio Triscardo.

"Not at all," I said. "Shouldn't it rather be a case of do you mind after having to watch me stand by Byron on Monday evening. Please try and forgive me."

"No question of that." He smiled, gave a quick shrug and settled into the seat on my immediate right. "He's been carrying on like that during every occasion we've played recently. I thought it very worrying at first but then I came to see how I could use it for my own ends."

I looked a question.

"Someone who habitually cheats rarely plays through any game with the utmost concentration. One part of his mind is always employed making value judgments that are either rash or biased in some form or other. And I soon noticed the manner in which Gary was looking at that cigarette case to get a reflection of the cards being dealt."

"He must have had a fair amount of practice," I thought aloud.

"Considerable, I'd say. Considerable. His first target was Bordi, who's little more than a conceited loud mouth."

"I thought so too."

Triscardo nodded. "A real lightweight, for all his bluster and aggression. Gary used to make sure that he sat next to him. In proper poker you are accustomed to draw for seats but as we were playing together frequently that rule was dispensed with. The next victim was Richard Strickland and on the last two occasions young Byron has sat next to me."

"And you don't object?"

Triscardo shook his head. "A vast proportion of the money that changes hands is put in by Richard Strickland, a bit by Bordi and usually a bit by our guest player. But I've my own private method of making sure that I keep in step with what is going on. First," he held up his forefinger, "I have a good memory for cards. Second," a thumb this time, "I keep a notebook which I fill in when I reach home concerning the patterns shown by the other players in all games. When they play carefully or riskily, when they bet strangely, when they withdraw from the game – all these and many other factors I keep in my book. Never mind," he broke off suddenly and fixed a hard stare on the pitch. "Let's concentrate on what is happening out there."

He went on to confirm the suspicion concerning Alex Gooding, a fearsome Argentinian central defender who decidedly did not live up to the image given by his blond locks and surname. Throughout the world of Italian football he was known as "Il Pirata", due to his cavalier disregard for the welfare of his opponents. Although the world-famous stopper, whom Napoli signed in the June of 1988, had passed a last-minute fitness test on his right knee, he could be considered to be a risk. The previous Sunday, during the final minutes of Napoli's away game against Torino, Gooding had been fiercely tackled after he had played the ball by the central striker of the home side. Although the attacker had been sent off (a decision which brought forth from the crowd lengthy whistles of disapproval), it had also meant that the Argentinian star had been taken off on a stretcher, and hadn't trained during the first half of the week. His lack of fitness might lead to disorganisation among his team-mates since Napoli had consciously built up their defence around him. This was a further blow to morale since the added absence of Diego Maradona robbed the team of his superlative skills in attack.

"Could be an interesting game," I remarked.

So it turned out to be – but for entirely the wrong reasons. During the first half Fiorentina found themselves facing the sun and a gusty wind, but the conditions could hardly be used to explain the poverty of their play. I'd read that they were a side that travelled badly, one that always tended to play considerably better at the Stadio Comunale in Florence than elsewhere, but it took them at least quarter of an hour to come to any sort of grips with the opposing attack which was being led in masterly fashion by Bo Christophersson, the Swedish deep-lying centre-forward. He scored himself by courageously diving among feet to make a goal with a near-post header, laid on a quick interchange with a wing who ran on to score and was desperately unfortunate not to have a hand in another goal just before half-time when the ball hit a post. Their midfield star, Gregorio Stabile, was commanding their attacks with a display of glorious passes, gliding forward to join the attack on the right and proving a constant thorn in the visitors' defence.

Against this incisive play Fiorentina offered very little. Cianfanelli made some spirited runs at the heart of their defence but, finding himself given too little support, he gradually faded from the game. Byron did little of note apart from conceding a free-kick on the edge of the penalty area, which the Fiorentina goalkeeper spread himself at the very last moment to turn the ball around the post. In fact he put on a thoroughly abject display throughout the half, immediately getting rid of the ball whenever he received it, passing without any sign of intelligence and never once made a penetrative run into the attack. If another Fiorentina player hadn't been injured towards the end of the first half there must have been a good chance of his being substituted at half-time.

The break was greeted by the home supporters with an extravagant display of fireworks, flares and coloured rockets. I looked across at Triscardo but he was busy talking into a telephone, so I went off alone, took an espresso, and tried to think of excuses for Byron's atrocious form. Maybe the news would have taken some time to sink in. Maybe he had other worries of even greater import. Like blackmail. Maybe he had driven himself ill with worrying. It was very much a case of *forse, forse, forse*. By the time I reached my seat I was becoming tense with agitation. Triscardo was still on the phone.

Soon after, however, I was given a swift pick-me-up when the players came on to the field at the start of the second half.

Byron had changed his jersey, the one he'd worn in the first half having been dirtied, but that was not the only new feature about him. He moved on to the pitch with a real spring in his step, and when he'd taken up his position for the kick-off started to perform some loosening-up exercises. This was followed by his looking towards every other member of the team and giving each words of encouragement. It was Fiorentina's turn to kick-off, but when Cianfanelli passed the ball back to him, Byron jinked his way past an opponent and having slid a perfect pass to the right wing raced forward to meet the centre, which he struck hard into the corner of the goal with his right foot. In all the move couldn't have taken more than twelve seconds, and it was difficult to appreciate who had been the more thunderstruck: the Napoli players or their supporters, who started to discuss loudly what had gone wrong. This shell-shock when they had just become settled after the interval!

Napoli started to play as though they were suffering from nemesis, and found it extremely difficult to cope with this newly-motivated adversary. In addition to performing as though he possessed enormous stamina and acute skills, Byron acted as a catalyst on the other Fiorentina players who also started to play as if they were new men. The attack came up with several fruitful ideas and, after twenty minutes, a second goal was scored by Cianfanelli who ran into the Napoli penalty area and fearlessly dived down at the feet of Gooding to head a crossed ball into the goal. Two goals apiece then, and with the season in its last third both teams felt the special urge to gain a victory that might go a long way to securing a place in a European club competition in the following year.

The fifth, and final, goal of the match came in the eighty-fifth minute, after Gregorio Stabile had been carried off on a stretcher following a vicious tussle with Matteo Mandarini who was going into tackles with the zest of a Turk. Byron, receiving the ball on his right-hand side and just over the half-way line, ran forward three paces and then struck a stupendous thirty-metre pass across to the left touchline – a pass which had all the defenders moving in the wrong direction and completely off-balance – where lurked young Cianfanelli, who'd moved away from the centre of the attack. He sped inwards and, despite being half-tripped by Gooding when inside the penalty area, managed to retain enough balance to slide the ball home with his right foot. Three–two to Fiorentina, and for the last five minutes play was most disjointed as Napoli tried to force an equaliser. I found myself sitting on the edge of my seat, and leant back in relief when the final whistle went.

I turned to Triscardo but he was again on the phone, so made my way downstairs to offer Byron my congratulations. We found ourselves being allowed into the changing-room after the obligatory pause while the manager had his say but when I came through the door I bumped into Taccone who, shaking his head, exclaimed, "That is what we bought him for. And all three goals being scored by young players. *Incredibile. Incredibile. Incredibile.*" He slowly walked away as though he'd been sand-bagged.

When I reached Byron I found him surrounded by journalists, talking to them in Italian. He waited until the crowd had dispersed before taking several steps over to me, seized me by the arms and hugged me close. "You would never believe how delighted I am," he said. "So, so delighted."

I told him the fact about the game that puzzled me, the difference in the standard of his play during each half.

"*Cretino io!*" he exclaimed hitting his forehead with the palm of his hand. "You know they called me in when Franco Palmieri went down with a virus? I was in such a state before the match began that I needed to be entirely alone."

He gave a smile. "I spoke to no one while I was getting changed; even when Roberto kindly wished me good fortune for the game I turned away. But when I went in after the first half Taccone came over to inform me that I'd probably be substituted during the second half. I felt so depressed until I happened to notice the telegram from Giuliana, which I hadn't opened." He reached down to the bench beside him and from under his clothes produced it. ALL'S WELL AND I LOVE YOU SO MUCH G.

The next moment he snatched back the telegram and the smile went off his face. "But how in hell did you know about this?" he said in strained tones, thrusting it towards me.

I explained that Giuliana had telephoned me first, but had been unable to get in touch with him.

We parted company promising to contact each other the following day. But soon after my heart chilled when I saw coming into the dressing-room none other than someone I'd suspected I'd seen earlier during the match – Richard Stokes, the investigator whom Dal Bosco had mentioned to me just two days before. I continued towards the door as though I'd not seen him. There I turned round, however, and was delighted to see Gary refusing to answer any of his questions but instead preferring to get changed. Just before I left I spent a moment with Roberto Cianfanelli who'd just finishing giving an interview.

"Thank you," he said, and peeled some mud away from his boots. "The person I'm most pleased for, however, is the manager. He must be delighted with the manner in which we played during the second half. Delighted and vindicated. And Byron . . ." His silence said more than could have a thousand words.

When eventually I made my way outside and found Nucera waiting for me, he didn't say a word but merely held out a ten thousand lire note.

I shook my head. "Keep it," I said and gave a wry smile.

"But . . ."

"Let's just say that I received advance information which made it an unfair wager."

"Do you mean that?"

"I'm positive."

"Thank you," he said tucking the note away in his black plastic wallet. "But wouldn't it have been worth losing a hundred thousand to watch Byron in that second half? In the first half I thought my money was safe and would be doubled. But his performance after the interval really had to be seen to be believed! Mention the names of all the most famous players in the world and few of them could have played like that. Let's hope that from now on he plays like that every time. *Speriamo. Speriamo.*" Nucera stuttered slightly as his voice became more excited.

"*Speriamo,*" I murmured in agreement.

We eased ourselves into our seats and moved off in the direction of the airport in the falling light. Nucera asked sharply after perhaps ten minutes of silence, "Why?"

"Why what?" I replied.

"Two things puzzle me. Why should Byron suddenly find such glorious form after so many poor games? And second, why does he put on this display here against Napoli and not in the Stadio Comunale before his home-based supporters?" He began to shake his head, as though these questions had become rhetorical.

"Taccone must have given him a really vicious talking-to at half-time," I suggested.

He nodded in agreement, but my mind kept savouring the rich irony that it had been after the first game between Fiorentina and Napoli that this affair had started in earnest, and after the second game between the two sides that it had seen an eventual happy outcome.

16

Sunday, 25th February

I arrived back at the Lungarno Corsini at eight-fifteen and immediately rang through to the Stirata villa at Strada-in-Chianti where I asked to be put through to Giuliana.

"Can you slip away for a few minutes and give me a call?" I sounded urgent. "I've lots to tell you."

She rang five minutes later from a public telephone. "Tell me everything," she said breathlessly as though she had been running.

I told her in some detail about the noticeable difference between Byron's play in each half.

"But . . ." she began to say.

"I know, I know," I cut in, carrying on to explain. When I broke off I could imagine her sense of delight. "I can realise how the second forty-five minutes might have been the best form that he's ever shown for the club. In fact the difference between that and his sluggishness of the first half made some people wonder if he'd taken a stimulant."

"Had he?" She sounded anxious.

"No," I said firmly. "He was one of the Fiorentina players chosen for testing and no drug was discovered." I went on to relate the delight shown by Taccone.

"I can believe that." She gave an excited laugh. "When Papa arrived home two hours ago he was so thrilled. The highlights of the Napoli-Fiorentina game will be shown on television. Just the sort of lift he can use in his advertising. The whole of Italy will spend the next few days discussing the performance of Byron."

I hung up after we'd made our farewells and promised to make contact soon. However, whereas Giuliana might have reason to be happy, I'd been severely thrown off balance.

Until now the case had been comparatively straightforward. I'd been asked to come to Italy and try again to discover what sort of shape Gary Byrne was in and give Tom Kennart's club as accurate an assessment as possible of his potential. So far so good.

Or rather, so far so bad as far as my mission was concerned. Until the events of the afternoon I'd concluded that Gary Byrne would be the most risky of investments. He'd had many factors in his favour when he'd first arrived in Florence, but there could be little doubt that this unfortunate episode with Giuliana had altered his outlook on life: he'd begun to drift into a state of mind that removed him far from the realities in life, as illustrated by his cheating at poker and his senseless dabbling with drugs.

I considered my commitment to Kennart. He'd be advised as to the current form of the player soon enough, but I felt that since I'd become so involved with Gary's state of mind in recent days my commitment might have shifted in a subtle way. I had to pass on to someone in London a report about the events and emotions which I'd witnessed during the afternoon, but Dal Bosco seemed the more obvious person to ring, being the one who had the most interest in Gary Byrne. I'd continue to do everything possible for Tom Kennart, but a far more effective route of helping him might lie in my gaining absolute trust from the player and manager, and acting as a third man in the whole affair. Still outstanding was the agony of the blackmail, and until I could pin the person concerned this case would be very much still alive.

When my call to Eugenio Dal Bosco soon after ten went unanswered I assumed that he might have gone out for the evening, or, more likely, was eating his evening meal as usual at some restaurant in the Knightsbridge area, so I left a message on his answering-machine.

A shower, a drink and a toasted ham sandwich later confirmed that possibility.

"What's the news about our player?" he asked when he rang back.

"I presume you've heard about the Napoli-Fiorentina game?" I asked. Dal Bosco usually received summaries of each game from agency reports in Italy.

"I've merely heard the score but have been busy all day. So no time." He paused. "You sound very relaxed."

"Yes and no," I replied and went on to give Eugenio a summary of the events from Napoli. "And I can easily obtain for you a copy of the film of the entire match."

"At last," he exclaimed fulsomely, "at last *il ragazzo* has recovered and has played to his full potential. This is what I always hoped he would do."

"The first few weeks – " I began.

"*No, no, no.*" I could imagine him shaking his head and gesticulating energetically. "Although he was playing well in those first few weeks he must have been tense, was becoming used to foreign customs and pace of life, as well as polishing his Italian; all matters which might have affected his football." He paused, and couldn't keep the excitement out of his voice. "I must come to Italia at once, I must see this for myself, I must join in the postscript of this triumph – "

I cut him off before he had time to become too declamatory. "I was planning to leave tomorrow," I said. "Now I'm not so sure. There's still the question of the blackmail."

"Indeed there is, indeed there is. Wait in Firenze for me." Dal Bosco's voice sharpened but there remained the undercurrent of excitement. "I owe you, my friend, I owe you and should be with you very soon. I'll telephone in the morning with details of the time I arrive. *Arrivederci. Ci vediamo. Ciao, ciao, ciao,*" and the phone went dead.

He'd rung off before I'd had time to tell him about Taccone's delight, one which undoubtedly would have made him feel most proud. My mind went back to those first few weeks of Byron's in Florence when Dal Bosco had acted in the manner of a parent, telephoning three or four times a week to make sure that "his boy" was settling in well, making acquaintances and friends at the club, becoming used to the different attitudes in a foreign city.

Dal Bosco's eagerness to travel immediately out to Italy made me feel less troubled concerning my responsibilities. After he'd seen a videotape of the game between Napoli and Fiorentina he could help guide my next move as far as the immediate future of Byron was concerned.

Monday, 26th February
The telephone rang at five minutes past nine on the following morning.

"I'll be with you in just over three hours' time." Dal Bosco didn't waste any time with preliminaries of greeting. He still sounded ebullient, as though he'd made a considerable fortune on the Totocalcio.

172

"Wait a moment, Eugenio," I said. "You're flying to Pisa, right?"

"The first direct flight to Peretola leaves at midday, so I'm forced to fly to Pisa. That seems to be the quickest way of getting to Florence." There was humour in his voice.

"Very droll," I replied. "Tell me the time of your arrival. I'll come to meet you." To make sure I was with him for as long as possible.

"Five minutes after twelve," came the answer. "Your time," he added unnecessarily.

"I'll be there. *Arrivederci*," I replied and rang off before he could say anything else.

That gave me good time to go and meet him, and after a strenuous period of exercising, a shower and a light breakfast I set out on the autostrada which runs towards the west coast. Until I approached the link-road to Pistoia, half an hour's driving away, the journey was peaceful. That, however, was the point at which I became convinced of being followed, and changes of lane and of speed confirmed that suspicion.

When I reached Montecatini, fifteen kilometres further on, I slid off the autostrada, paid the toll and made my way into the exclusive resort. There it was still following me, a black Fiat 132 with tinted windows.

I pulled the gun out of the shoulder-holster and laid it across my thighs. This sort of complication I certainly didn't need. At the next turning I slid into a side-road, stamped on the brakes, scrambled out of the car, and was crouching low behind the Alfa holding the Beretta 9 when the black Fiat came past, slowing down, with the driver perplexed as to where his quarry had disappeared.

It took him two or three seconds to react to my presence as I sprinted to his car and opened the door.

"*Via fuori*," I snapped. "*Scendi, scendi!*"

He was a tall, well-built character with a nut-brown face. I'd not seen him before. He climbed out very sedately, but when he saw the Beretta he flung both hands up impulsively in the manner of one who'd never seen a gun, and began to shake his head, "*No. No. No.*"

"*Sì. Sì. Sì.* And put your hands on the roof."

I frisked him thoroughly before I moved away, but the gun stayed on the horizontal.

"Now explain why you were following me."

When he turned round I saw that he'd started to sweat. He gave a nervous shrug. "It's not for me." He shook his head. "I've another driver with me."

I waved the gun at the car. "Get him out. And move slowly."

He went and opened the passenger door and let out his companion, who looked understandably distraught. It was my chauffeur of the previous day, Antonio Nucera, who wore a similar uniform and walked towards me displaying his palms in front of him.

"Il Dottore Stirata wanted to follow your movements and make sure you were safe," he explained stiffly.

That seemed very possible. "And your companion?" I asked sharply.

"A new driver who's applying to start in a month's time. When Il Dottore asked me to keep a watch on you I thought it a good opportunity to see how expertly Franco drove."

"Franco who?"

"Franco Langella."

"And it's his car?"

"Yes."

I nodded at the newcomer before turning back to Nucera. "Most considerate of the kind Dottore," I remarked. "Most considerate and most generous." I put away the Beretta and looked at my watch. "I'm due to meet a friend of mine at a bar in Lucca in just under twenty-five minutes' time. If I don't get a move on I'll be late." I patted him on the shoulder in a friendly manner. "Now you can go back to the sympathetic Marcello Stirata, pass on my gratitude for his kindness and assure him that, in my humble opinion, I will be in no danger whatsoever. *D'accordo? D'accordo ed arrivederci.*"

I watched them until they'd climbed into the 132 and had driven off, but still had the sneaky feeling that I'd see them sooner rather than later. So it transpired. Just as I was about to enter Lucca the image of a Fiat 132 appeared in my rearview mirror with Nucera having taken over the controls. A dogged character, this Nucera, but driving around the picturesque city it wasn't too difficult to lose him again and soon I was on the minor road heading in the direction of Pisa without the attentions of my late keeper.

I assumed he'd been telling me the truth.

*

I arrived at Galileo Galilei Airport, three kilometres to the south of the historic city, in good time so was able to spend the following ten minutes purchasing and reading the three sporting papers on sale in addition to the sports reports in *La Nazione* and the *Corriere della Sera*. All five reports of the Napoli—Fiorentina game, naturally, stressed the thrilling difference between the first and second periods of the contest. *La Gazzetta dello Sport* awarded Byron a mark of 8 and was of the opinion that, during the second half, "*i magnifici quarantacinque minuti di Byrne*" had provided one of the most rewarding displays of the season. *Tuttosport* gave a mark of 7.5, while *Corriere dello Sport* registered one of 8 and wondered about the reason for such an astounding transformation. It went on to question if this had been primarily due to drugs – a motif that was taken up by the report which appeared in the *Corriere della Sera* and used the word "*drogato*" on three occasions in the space of five lines. The report in *La Nazione* finished up by wondering if that had not been the most magnificent performance shown by Byron since his move to Fiorentina in the summer. All eulogies gratefully accepted.

Eugenio should be well pleased, I thought, as I watched him descending from an Alitalia Douglas DC9. He was wearing a midnight-blue overcoat over a horribly expensive-looking light grey suit and carried only a briefcase.

"Where's the car?" he asked after we had greeted one another.

"In the forecourt," I replied. "Have you any luggage?"

He lifted his briefcase into the air. "Only this. I must return to London on the plane that leaves this afternoon." He gave a quick shake of the head and his brow quickly furrowed before coming smooth again. "I've a most important meeting tomorrow in Birmingham but when I heard your account of the match I simply had to come, didn't I?" He raised one finger in the air. "*Incredibile, incredibile*. After this recent spell of ill form, after all this torture, after all this recent disappointment, Byron triumphs over everyone else." He seemed as happy as a child who's just been given an unexpected present.

"There it is." I passed across the video-cassette, which I'd not wanted to let out of my sight.

"I can't wait to run it through."

The moment before we entered the Alfa I gave Eugenio the collection of papers which I'd bought at the airport kiosk. "If

175

reading in a car doesn't make you feel sick there are some match reports about the game you might like to look at while we are on our way."

"Very thoughtful of you," Dal Bosco exclaimed, squeezing my elbow.

"Superlative after hyperbole after panegyric," I remarked. "They'll soon have to invent a new word."

"Marvellous, marvellous, marvellous," Dal Bosco rhapsodised before he looked quickly at his watch. "We have slightly under three hours before my plane departs. It might be a risk but I desperately want to have a short talk with Taccone for a few minutes. He's agreed to meet me at the offices of Fiorentina at Via dei Mille. Let us see how quickly we can make it to Florence."

Dal Bosco spread out paper across his knees and started to read a report of the game between Fiorentina and Napoli from the day before. When he reached the passage describing how a Fiorentina player had been upended inside the Napoli area Dal Bosco became very agitated. *"Un arbitro venduto"* was the most savoury of the remarks he offered when he read that the referee had failed to award a penalty; then came a stream of invective against the luckless match official which advised him to perform various acts of buggery in addition to laying the most terrible blame on his mother for having brought such a miserable wretch on to the earth. Fortunately I was forced to suffer this explosion of bile on only the first occasion since subsequently Dal Bosco confined himself to merely murmuring his strictures during his perusal of the other reports, but by the time the Alfa reached the outskirts of Florence his blood-pressure must have risen several degrees.

We drove quickly along the north bank of the Arno, made a left turn and sped northwards until we reached the ground. In fact we caught the players at the last stages of a practice-session. Monday being a "rest day", these were in the main players from the reserve and the youth teams but as soon as we stopped the car Dal Bosco leapt out and rushed in the direction of Taccone.

"Eugenio", "Sergio", "Eugenio", "Sergio" – the cries were loud and very friendly before each man started to babble a stream of Italian without bothering to listen to what the other was saying. It was all beyond me. I went away in the direction of the training-field where various reserves who wanted to advertise their keenness were going through a variety of exercises that displayed their skill with the ball. I looked around for Byron and found him talking intently to a journalist from one of the major sporting papers. I overheard Gary say "*No*", "*No*", "*No*" several times and saw him vehemently shake his head, but that disagreement didn't prevent them shaking hands and finishing with smiles on their faces.

He wandered over to me when he had finished and held out his hand.

"What was all that about?" I asked as I took it.

"Oh, that," he replied. "Nothing really. Just an article he's writing for his paper. All this week will be a gradual build-up for the Switzerland match on Saturday, and he wants to do a feature about me tomorrow. The Swiss have a midfield player who can be gloriously creative." I noticed the "can be".

At this point someone blew a whistle. "I must go. You'll wait for me, won't you? I should be free in a moment or two."

I nodded. "I'll have a surprise for you when it's over."

It was a short and gentle training-session with emphasis being placed on skill rather than on stamina. The Byron we'd seen the day before was very much in evidence directing those around him with the authority of a conductor: "*Claudio, a destra*," "*Pinzo, avanti, avanti*," "*Domenico, a piedi*." Throughout he was treated with great respect – a factor which had been noticeably absent during the previous week whenever I'd attended training-sessions. He was, of course, only playing with reserves but even so there was something reverent in their attitude towards him.

When the training-session was finished and Byron came over I started to say "This is the surprise I . . .", but before I could finish my sentence Dal Bosco and he were embracing each other and talking twenty-four to the dozen.

"This rogue," Eugenio poked me in the chest, "told me about the Napoli game last night so I simply had to come and see for myself." He pointed together the fingers of his right hand and gestured in the air. "This is what we've been waiting for, this will cause people to stop bemoaning that injury to Pablo Cortes." He paused for a moment to look at his watch, then turned to me. "But come on, come on, or else I shall miss my plane."

"Thank you so much for taking the effort to come out," Gary said to Dal Bosco as we walked to the car. "You can't know how grateful I am. Thank you again."

Dal Bosco looked suitably grateful. "*Niente. Niente.* It was a pleasure, a most special pleasure."

Byron turned swiftly to me. "Before you set off, Ross, I was wondering whether you'd mind sitting in on another poker session?"

"When?"

"Tonight, I'm afraid. It's very short notice I know, but Sergio, who's been called out of town at the last minute, asked me to find someone who could take his place. Please say yes."

I'd simply become too interested in the young man's fortunes to be able to refuse. "Where?" I asked.

"Oh, great!" Byron exclaimed enthusiastically, and started to give me directions. He finally shook his head. "Can you collect me at half past seven and I'll take you there." He embraced Dal Bosco and, after giving me a nod and a smile, slipped off towards the changing-rooms between a small crowd of supporters who'd remained behind to applaud him and ask for his autograph.

"Thank you very much, my friend, thank you very much," said Dal Bosco effusively as we drove towards the west of the city.

"Don't mention it, Eugenio," I replied, "I'm very pleased that you came."

"You've probably wondered why last summer I allowed Byron to move to Italy on such comparatively poor terms?" I could sense him staring at me.

"You must have had a strong reason."

"I had, I had. I told you some days ago that I'd always had my eye on him, thought him a fraction too inexperienced, but that things fell neatly into place after that injury to Pablo Cortes. But I don't think I would have let him move if the person involved hadn't been as considerate as Sergio Taccone."

"Interesting," I remarked. "But what now?"

He shook his head and I could imagine his frowning. "How do you mean, 'what now?'"

"Concerning a possible transfer back to England."

There was a lengthy silence during which Dal Bosco looked out of the window.

"I'm sorry, Eugenio," I continued, "but you know that was why I was sent to Italy ten days ago. My instructions were clear, and I'd be failing in my duty if I returned home attempting to conceal the truth. I understand how you might have a feeling of fulfilment at the player showing such glorious form and playing up to the level which you'd promised. My primary concern, however, is involved not with the state of the player in absolute terms but rather with his potential value to an English side. Before I write my final report I must talk to Byron himself and try to see whether he's still interested in the move." I pointed in the direction of the briefcase resting on the seat between us. "I'm sorry, but I'm sure that that video recording will give you a more worthwhile impression than would a score of articles."

Dal Bosco gave a sigh of acceptance, and maintained an eloquent silence all the way to Pisa.

Moments before we had to leave each other, he turned to me and said nervously "You're right, of course, quite right. But thank you for such an enjoyable day. Don't worry, I'll make sure that Tom Kennart gets this," he patted his briefcase.

As he disappeared from my sight I could faintly hear him talking to himself.

During my return journey I began to wonder what precisely Dal Bosco and Taccone had discussed when they had had their tête-à-tête at the training-ground.

17

Monday, 26th February

This time I was allowed to cross north to Florence in less hectic fashion and didn't arrive at the apartment until soon after half past four. That gave enough time, however, in which to have a rest, a shower and a change of clothing before setting off the short distance to collect Byron. Just before I left the Lungarno Corsini I caught a glimpse of a black Fiat 132 turning the corner and wondered for how long the unfortunate Nucera had driven around Lucca before he realised that he'd pulled only the short straw.

Byron looked awkward and nervous when he pulled open the door. Glancing past his shoulder I noticed Giuliana Stirata standing close to the window with a drink in her hand. When she saw who it was she gave a sharp cry of pleasure, placed her drink on a small table and moved across quickly to give me an embrace.

"Thank you so much for telephoning yesterday evening," she exclaimed in a rush of words.

I smiled and gently shook my head. "You had to be the first to know."

She was wearing a midnight-blue coat over a knitted dress in cream, while around her neck and wrists were several thousands' lire worth of gold. She still looked almost anorexic, but standing close to, I noticed a sparkle in her eyes which hadn't been there before while on her lips was a smile that caused her to look years younger and exceedingly more striking.

"It was very considerate of you, in any case. Thank you again." She looked at her watch and gave a sigh. "I must leave now, I'm afraid. Will I see you tomorrow?" she asked, looking anxiously at Gary.

"Of course," he replied, coming over to take her elbow. "I think I'll be back too late tonight, but I promise to telephone you in the morning." He leant down and gave her a light kiss on the mouth.

She gave a smile of relief. "About what time?"

"Say ten?" he enquired.

"I'll look forward to it." She stepped towards him and brushed his mouth with hers.

"Wait a moment," said Byron looking at his watch. "We might as well leave now too."

He slipped on his dark green jacket, made sure that he had his keys, checked that the windows were closed, and then shepherded us into the hallway. He waited for the door to slam shut before he brushed past me and made sure that he was descending the stairs close to Giuliana. When we were in the street he waited until she had driven away before we set off on our short trip across the river.

Fulvio Bordi had an apartment on the top floor of a house sited just where the Via dei Seragli meets the Arno at the Ponte alla Carraia. Typical of the homes of many journalists it housed shelf after shelf of reference books plus hundreds of volumes of non-fiction, all of which journeyed up from the floor to the ceiling along three walls of his principal room. Copies of newspapers were scattered on the tables as well as on the desk: when we arrived Bordi himself was checking through an article he'd just finished.

"I thought you asked us for eight," Byron said matter-of-factly. His voice was not apologetic.

"I did, I did," the journalist replied. "I simply had to have this piece finished for tomorrow. A kidnapping concerned with a wealthy banker who has a second home close to Volterra." He paused. "He'll pay, I expect, but I was first on to an incident that should help to sell thousands of additional copies." He'd been talking at a fast pace and, although the evening was cool, he was perspiring at the temples.

"I'm sure I'll have as rewarding an evening as the last time I was invited to play," I responded, shaking him by the hand.

"As long as I win some money," Bordi grunted, moving away. "These last two or three occasions have seen me lose several hundred thousands."

Richard Strickland came in next followed approximately five minutes later by Bordi's guest. A tall and lean character in his early forties, Corrado Poccudu had the type of presence that instantly makes people slightly wary.

Byron had told me what he knew concerning Fulvio Bordi's guest while we'd been making our way to his apartment.

181

Poccudu was a Sardinian who had come to the mainland from his native village of Villacidro in the early seventies in order to find work in the leather industry – and where better than Florence? He'd been very uncommunicative about his past, but I gathered that, since he arrived in Florence, Poccudu had been engaged in a well-publicised affair with a Sardinian beauty who was starting to make her name in the entertainment world. She'd almost been killed in a road accident near Pavia at a time in her career when she was starting to attract attention from the critics and, more meaningfully for her finances, also from the studios. News of the accident had turned Poccudu into a heavy drinker who subsequently appeared to have alternated increasingly frequent periods spent in jail with liaisons with well-known Florentine women – most of which had been chronicled in the gossip column of *La Nazione*. Although people referred to him as being "*un uomo donnaiolo*", a man who cared about women, he was celebrated throughout the city as being something of a crude sex maniac.

A man of very few words, he sat down abruptly and composed himself for the game that was to come. He looked the type who would have to shave twice a day to remain smooth-faced. His nose had been broken and along the left angle of his jawbone was slashed a finger-length scar. It seemed to be only a few months old and he was extremely fortunate that the cut had been slightly above his jugular vein. I wondered what had happened to his opponent. The final verses in this catalogue of the unnatural were his eyes which were ingrained like bullet-holes. He reeked of evil.

My foremost attention, of course, was taken up with considering Byron's behaviour, but although I was particularly on the look-out for any glimpses of cheating, during the first few hands I was unable to spot any sign of it. The notorious cigarette case was not there and his behaviour was noticeably more relaxed than on the previous occasion. He didn't smoke, drank only sparingly and concentrated on the game in an entirely different manner: one during which he made none of his ham-fisted attempts to ingratiate himself with his fellow-players but rather, in the manner of the absent Sergio Triscardo, always followed the dealings of the cards with precision, attempting to discern from the expressions of the players what strength of hand they held.

Few enormous hands were seen in the first two hours of play.

Bordi gained a large amount from me only to lose most of it on the following hand to Poccudu. Another large win by the Sardinian rashly prompted Bordi to comment stupidly, "*Beh, le donne, Corrado, le donne*" only for his guest to look up and give him a piercing stare. Byron won a fair amount in a game during which Richard Strickland was his principal opponent – after which the charming American gave a chuckle and a resigned shake of the head. I lost a fraction more than I had won but I'd been concentrating more on my fellow-players than on the game in hand.

We were forced to take a break from the play while Bordi went to answer a call from a motorcycle messenger from *La Nazione*. That short period, however, proved very illuminating.

I took the opportunity to remark to Strickland while Byron visited the bathroom, "Please *never, never, never* give Byron any more hash."

The handsome American looked shocked. "He didn't much care for the stuff I provided?"

I shook my head, and took out my wallet. "No. How much do I owe you?"

Strickland flushed. "Put it away. I didn't think. We don't want him to be ruined, do we?" He was clearly getting rather upset.

"No. We don't."

We sat in silence for a couple of minutes until Byron returned.

"Hey, Byron," said the American, "I was thinking of visiting Milano soon. I could make it this weekend. If you'll be there maybe we could meet up some place?"

Byron gave a warm smile. "Nothing could be easier. We've got a few days off this week and I was planning to spend them in Milan. Why not stay at my apartment? It's not too far from the city centre."

"You're sure?"

"Of course. And maybe we can go to a football match together and I can explain some of the rules."

"I'd like that." Strickland laughed.

Gary jotted down an address and phone number and slipped it across the table.

Via Carlo Crivelli 20
Milano 20122
58 26 88

"That's an apartment owned by my aunt. She's due to arrive some time tomorrow, but I don't think she's planning to stay long and should have left by Saturday at the latest."

"And she won't mind?" Strickland sounded genuinely concerned.

Byron shook his head. "If I'm not in you can get the key from the caretaker. I'll tell him to expect you. The apartment you want is in the name of Domenico Mozzolino."

"That's most kind of you," Strickland remarked, tucking away the slip of paper in his wallet.

"I plan to leave Italy tomorrow," I said, turning towards Byron, "but I have to call in at our office in Milan to collect documents concerning another case. Perhaps I could give you a lift." It might be interesting to have some extra time spent talking to Byron.

"I'm not sure exactly when I'll be leaving," came the reply. "Can I let you know?"

"Do," I replied, "but the offer's there."

"Thanks."

As though he was a character in a script Bordi chose this moment to enter the room, complaining noisily about the messenger who'd dared to countermand his orders. Perhaps it was that, perhaps an increase of communal tension in the room, but the tranquillity evident before the hiatus had plainly vanished. When Poccudu found his Flush in Diamonds being beaten by Richard Strickland, who held a Full House of Kings over Sevens, he became increasingly short-tempered and edgy. He appeared to be most distressed since Strickland had used a wild card whereas his own hand consisted of five Diamonds. Rules are rules, as regulations are regulations, and since he'd been clearly informed of these before the session had started, Poccudu could have no real cause for complaint.

Very soon afterwards a similar incident nearly brought the gaming of the evening to an abrupt close, and again Corrado Poccudu was one of those involved. The other person, sadly, was Byron who up till then had been the soul of charm and good humour. The crucial hand was rare in poker, a hand in which each of the players holds strong cards and bids for a lengthy period of time. I was the earliest to duck out holding two pairs, Jacks over Eights, and from the expressions of both Bordi and Strickland I could deduce that although their particular hands had been powerful they lacked courage to proceed with the bidding.

Poccudu and Byron, however, were long past the point of playing with reason. Both wore in their eyes that gleam of excitement known to the hardened gambler, so both played carefully as though to prolong the personal pleasure as well as to heighten the tension. It finished with the Sardinian being called and placing down his hand to reveal three Nines and a Two. As he leant forward to collect his winnings, however, Byron uttered a soft "*No*" and very carefully placed down his own cards, three Queens together with a Two.

His eyes flashing, Poccudu heatedly pointed his right forefinger at the footballer. "I shall remember you," he said in a voice as friendly as a length of barbed wire. He slowly gathered his winnings, stood up and left the room without having the grace to thank a flustered Bordi. No one else appeared eager to make a move.

Byron gave a look not of fear but one instead of astonishment. No one had ever talked to him like that.

We didn't continue playing for long after that abrupt departure by Poccudu, but just before we left a flustered Bordi put his hand on Byron's shoulder and apologised on behalf of his friend. "Please excuse that," he said. "Corrado has always been cold and reserved. He is due to come before the magistrates next week on yet another charge. These present troubles have not made him any more companionable," he finished lamely as though offering an explanation.

Trust Bordi to make a friendship like that, I thought, but Byron was far more polite. "Never mind, Fulvio. I'm going north for a few days soon and expect to have more exacting matters to worry about than that." He gestured in the direction of the door and gave a brief smile.

After we exchanged farewells with Bordi – Byron being guarded about exactly when he planned to return to Florence – I drove back to his apartment quickly along streets almost deserted of traffic. The dark wedges of cloud which had been threatening during the late afternoon had made up their minds and the rain which came down now appeared to be set for the next few hours.

"I know it's late," Gary remarked when we arrived outside his front door, "but you'd be very welcome to come up for a nightcap." His invitation could not have sounded less enthusiastic.

A glance at my watch told me that it was after one o'clock. "I would like that," I replied, "but can I take a rain-check? Why don't we have breakfast together in that bar in the Piazza di Ognisanti?" I tried to give him no possible notion of the many questions that remained unanswered.

He bit his lower lip as though thinking of something entirely different before looking back at me. "I'll see you there." We both got out of the car, and he shook my hand. "Shall we say at nine o'clock." It was a statement rather than a question.

"Thanks, Gary." I watched him walk across to his own apartment building before I set out on the short journey to the Lungarno Corsini.

I couldn't, for the life of me, explain it but Byron seemed to have been kissed by the gods. Almost everyone I'd met while I had been involved in this case had gone out of their way to help him. Even the most blessed angels, however, carried some scars and I hoped that Byron would not hear again from the viperish Corrado Poccudu. More urgently, I was still worried at not being any nearer finding a solution to the problem of whether Byron was being blackmailed, and if so by whom.

18

Tuesday, 27th February

I telephoned Dal Bosco later that morning and reminded him to drop the video round to the office of Tom Kennart as the British manager who'd first shown interest in purchasing Gary Byrne.

"He should get it by this afternoon," came the reply. "The club has to play a game at home this evening, a match postponed from January, but I'll contact Kennart this morning and see if he can spare a moment to see me when he's not too rushed."

"Good," I replied wanting to maintain the pressure on Dal Bosco to perform the best for Byron as the player himself saw it, and sensing anyway that the agent was beginning to perk up at the prospect of ten per cent of another lucrative deal. "Eugenio, please remember what we discussed on the way back to Pisa yesterday afternoon. I'll be driving to Milan later this morning and flying into Heathrow this evening. I'll telephone again after I've reached home."

"What about Byron?" Dal Bosco asked anxiously.

"I'll tell you more tonight when I've discovered precisely what he intends to do in the near future. I'm due to have breakfast with him and mean to get answers to some questions that have been worrying us both."

There was a lengthy silence at the other end, spoilt only by the sound of Dal Bosco's strenuous breathing.

"Good luck, my friend," he said at last. "I hope it turns out to be a straightforward matter, and that soon he can give his whole attention to playing football. When I saw that video myself I could have wept for joy."

"It was astonishing," I agreed. "But he talked about expecting to have other matters to worry about in Milan. I wonder what they could be."

"We can only hope for the best," Dal Bosco remarked. He was becoming increasingly measured in his use of words, almost pompous. "He might have a friend in Milan to whom he is indebted, he might owe money to a Milanese bank, he might be keeping an appointment concerned with his career as a model – something minor such as those." He splayed his hands in the air and gave a knowing shrug.

"Possible," I replied, "but he did use the word 'serious' when speaking to me the other day. We'll see what he comes up with in a few minutes' time."

"You'll let me know the moment you discover anything?" Dal Bosco broke in anxiously.

"No, Eugenio," I informed him. "But I promise to ring tonight when I reach my flat." I did not make promises readily. "Please make sure that the video reaches Tom Kennart as soon as possible. That's most crucial at this moment." A crackle over our conversation reminded me of the impending meeting with Byron. We exchanged farewells and I hung up, but soon afterwards, as I was having a shave, the phone sounded again.

It was Stirata himself at the other end and he couldn't have sounded more unfriendly, entirely the opposite from the last time we'd spoken.

"Mr Armstrong?" His voice had an unhappy ring to it.

"Good morning, Dottore," I replied politely. "I was just about to contact you to thank you for your various kindnesses during my stay. I'm on the point of leaving Florence."

"How could you repay my friendship in this manner?" He spoke as though he was talking through broken glass.

I paused for a long time before replying that I'd not the faintest idea what he was talking about. For a moment fear ran through me that Marcello Stirata might have discovered the panic which had surrounded his daughter during the previous few weeks.

"Antonio Nucera has been known to me for over four years," said Stirata stiffly, his voice becoming more pointed. "During that entire period he's given me no reason whatsoever to feel dissatisfied with his services. He told me yesterday morning that he was following you to Lucca."

I could imagine him becoming embarrassed. "I was on my way to meet a friend at Pisa airport," I said quickly. "Nucera informed me that he had been sent to watch over my movements by none other than your good self." I kept my voice calm.

"He telephoned fifteen minutes ago to tell me that after

encountering you he'd been forced to go for treatment at the Ospedale Generale in Pisa."

That came as a surprise. The last occasion on which I'd seen Nucera he appeared to be completely in control of all his faculties. I informed Stirata of this. "What on earth for?"

Stirata gave a tight reply. "You name them, Nucera had them. An arm that had been broken, cuts on his face, bruises all about his body." He paused again. "Maybe now it is your turn to speak."

I was starting to feel irritated. "And in your opinion it's I who am responsible for the attack?" I asked incredulously.

A snarl of laughter came over the line, one that savagely lacked humour. "Let us merely say, Mr Armstrong, that your name appears very high on a short-list of one."

"Why should you think I was responsible, Dottore?" I asked calmly. "I try to make sure that people get on well together. I don't spend my time committing random acts of violence."

There followed a long pause after which Stirata sounded rational and much more calm. "You're stating that you have no idea whatsoever concerning this attack."

"None at all. I can only repeat that the last occasion I saw Nucera was in Lucca." I'd had a suspicion that his fellow-driver, Franco Langella, might have been involved, but the thought passed away quickly. Although Langella had more muscular features that Nucera, he'd struck me as being essentially pacific. I hoped that Stirata would believe me. I wanted to be on time for my next appointment. "Can you be positive that these injuries were not caused by an accident?"

"From what Nucera himself had just told me, they can't have been."

"Have you seen him?" I was becoming confused.

"No. Every day Nucera presents himself outside the front of the villa at eight o'clock ready to drive me into Florence – either to the football club or to my office. This morning he failed to show up. On searching his room, one of the other servants discovered that Nucera hadn't slept in his bed last night. Roughly ten minutes ago he telephoned himself, informed me of the facts to do with the attack, explained that he had been kept in Pisa Generale hospital overnight for observation and asked to be collected." There was a sudden silence.

At no time had I been concerned with any part of this fantastic story and went on to inform Stirata of my actual movements during the period in question. "I drove Eugenio Dal Bosco to the airport at Pisa for him to catch the afternoon plane for London. I give you my word that I drove straight back to the apartment and didn't see Antonio Nucera again."

"And how was Eugenio?" Stirata asked. His voice had become considerably less hostile.

"On fine form."

"Good." Another break. "Mr Armstrong, I'll accept your word that you weren't involved in any way with what happened to Nucera yesterday. But you should have been more truthful with me from the start of your time in Florence."

It was my turn to make the apologies. "There are lies and lies, Dottore, and I felt mine were of the more unimportant type. But please forgive me."

"I was told last night by Taccone that he suspected that Byrne was eager to return to England, and that you were being employed by someone in England to give them a briefing," Stirata continued as though he'd barely heard me. "Last night, I agreed terms with Sergio Taccone for a new contract for next season, which should make sure that the amount of discord inside the club is minimised.

"When you have in charge a psychologist as subtle as Taccone you can be confident that the club will be administered on the correct sort of lines." He stopped his assessment. "Mr Armstrong, I realise that you're a busy man, but I'd be exceedingly grateful if you could collect Nucera from where he is at the moment and bring him back. My other driver has had to remain overnight in Rome."

"Of course I will," I said. Stirata had gone out of his way to be helpful, and I felt in his debt.

As soon as I'd made my reply Stirata cemented his request. "I am exceedingly grateful to you for this kindness, Mr Armstrong. You can be sure that you will be handsomely reimbursed. Name your fee on your return."

He rang off before I could reply, but I wasn't looking forward to that meeting. No one likes having to apologise.

I telephoned Byron and informed him that our working breakfast would have to be cancelled.

He sounded bitterly disappointed. "Can't we meet later in the day?" He appeared so desperate to have a conference I felt again that I'd metamorphosed into a Monsignor Armstrong.

I promised to get in touch with him "as soon as possible", but I couldn't be sure how long this new mission might take. It might, however, be in his long-term interests that I perform this seemingly essential mission for Stirata. Were Tom Kennart to make an offer for the player, any eventual transfer might still depend on the ability of the two parties to talk the same language and, in such circumstances, it could be significant that I put the president of Fiorentina in my debt by volunteering to act as a private ambulance driver.

I set out on this dubious errand with a measure of interest overcoming my feelings of natural doubt. Franco Langella hadn't worn the smell of evil about him, so what had Nucera been involved in after I'd seen him on the fringes of Lucca? And to what, if any, degree were his activities involved in the particular case of Byron?

The Ospedale Generale lay within the boundaries of the Piazza dei Miracoli on the southern side of the Piazza Duomo. Comprising some thirty or forty buildings in stone that was the colour of terracotta, there were many notices that proclaimed for the hospital a world-famous reputation in diseases of the kidney, lung and heart and in addition lauded its prowess in general surgery. Not wanting to waste precious time I approached a sallow man wearing an ebony uniform sitting inside a box near the entrance who directed me straight away to the casualty department.

The administrator in charge of the unit was a tall woman in her early forties, who wore her black hair pulled back into a bun and a clip on the left lapel of her white coat that announced her as being Dottoressa Francesca Dell'Orto. When I entered her room she was standing awkwardly in a corner searching through some folders. "Can I help?" she enquired in a low voice, without troubling to look across in my direction.

I explained that I had come to collect Antonio Nucera who had been brought in the previous evening.

"Nucera Antonio," she said steadily, and then shook her head. "No. There has been no one of that name in casualty recently."

"Are you positive?"

"*Ma*!" She arched her eyebrows. "I've been on duty all night and that particular name is new to me." She was looking at a pale green card which she held in her hand.

"When did you start your spell of duty?" I enquired and was

given a cold stare by grey eyes which hardened. "Forgive this inquisition, Doctor, but I've the curious feeling that I might have been sent on a wild goose chase."

She gave a flicker of a smile. "I was on the point of ordering you to leave. A man, who's clearly not injured, barges into my office as though he owns the entire hospital, asks questions concerning a patient who doesn't exist and prevents me from doing the work I am paid to do."

"I'm sorry for having caused you this trouble." My voice sounded pleading. "But – "

"But," she continued, "you'd be most grateful if I could confirm that he wasn't admitted yesterday?"

I gave a quick nod. "Please."

She walked away from me, looked briefly at some green folders and then shook her head. "I'll just make double-sure." She pressed a bell on her desk-top and spoke very fast. I guessed that she didn't come from anywhere nearby – a region in which people tend to speak with a flat tongue – but maybe from further north. "*Un momentino*," she said when she'd finished and, pointing to a chair on which I could sit, resumed writing her notes.

Two minutes later there was a knock at the door and a stout bespectacled girl with short black curls came in, shaking her head. The two of them held a brief conversation after which the girl left.

"As I thought." The administrator turned towards me after watching her assistant leave. A spark of laughter lay in her eyes. "The answer is in the negative. The most approximate names we have to Nucera are Noci and Nuterino." She flashed a smile. "I'm very sorry."

"Could you define the period you were referring to when you said 'recently' a moment ago?" I enquired after a time.

The smile broadened. "Of course. Just over three years ago we saw in casualty an Antonio Nucera who'd been injured when involved in an accident. Cuts and bruises all across his face and we had to strap up a shoulder that was dislocated."

"Just over three years ago?"

She nodded.

"But nothing more recent?"

She shook her head. "There's no record in his file."

I walked over to her and shook her hand. "Please forgive me for having wasted your time."

She raised her head slightly. "There are several more hospitals within the city if you wish to pursue your enquiries any further. You have the addresses?" It was a polite question, yet one asked in a tone that suggested I leave.

I shook my head. "I suspect that each will provide an answer similar to yours." I made for the door. "Thank you again."

"*Prego*," came the reply. She was already at her desk making notes concerning another case.

Three hours are three hours are three hours, precious moments of time which had been spent in a futile journey west of Florence instead of driving north to Milan. The last plane for London was scheduled to depart at five minutes before seven but given the several matters which I had to see to in Florence, I was unlikely to be among its passengers. It was well after one o'clock when I reached the Stirata villa and my mood with the various bodyguards was surly.

Stirata was taking an aperitif before his lunch when I made my way into his dining-room. Always someone whose manners were impeccable, he stood up at once and held out his hand.

"Mr Armstrong! Back so quickly?" he said in tones of surprise. "I really didn't expect to see you again before this afternoon." He glanced past my right shoulder. "But where's Nucera. Has he gone straight to his room?"

"His last visit at the Ospedale Generale was during November 1986. That's over three years ago and although I didn't search any other hospital; I suspect you'll find that he has simply disappeared."

Stirata went paler and appeared at first to be incapable of speech. "Disappeared?" he said eventually in a faint voice. The possibility had obviously never occurred to him.

"Or has been *made* to disappear," I continued. "At what time exactly did he ring you this morning?"

He looked down at the table, his eyebrows drawn towards each other in a frown of concentration. "The telephone sounded just before eight o'clock as I was having my coffee and roll. I rang through to you as soon as I discovered that my other driver was away." He was clearly disgusted at having been lied to by an employee.

"You're absolutely certain it was Nucera?"

Stirata made an expressive gesture. "Of course I'm certain. The man has worked for me for a long period of time and I would know his voice anywhere. As you might have noticed yesterday when Nucera says certain words or becomes excited he stutters slightly."

I nodded. "I did, Dottore, I did. But the best thing to do now is to call in the police."

Stirata thought for a moment. "Them I can do without." His voice rose slightly. "Not for myself, you understand, but for poor Nucera. About a year after he started in service with me, he had the misfortune to be wrongly implicated when a major theft of jewellery took place from a shop in Fiesole. I was able to prove that at the time of the incident, Nucera was over eighty kilometres distant from Fiesole. However, the authorities still have his name on their files."

Eighty kilometres distant from Fiesole, he'd said. I took a chance. "It wouldn't have been in or near Pisa that Nucera had been?" I stayed matter-of-fact.

Stirata's eyes narrowed. "How in heaven's name do you know that?" He sounded startled.

I told him everything I'd learnt at the Ospedale Generale. "I think you'd better tell me what exactly happened."

Stirata laboriously circled the small table before resuming his original position. "Nucera became involved in a fight on his day off."

"Who with?"

"He wouldn't say. You see, as one of the perks with the job I gave permission to my drivers to make use of my cars while off duty. Normally this involved trips to Florence and back. On this occasion, however, Nucera had driven further afield and although irritated by this, my sentiments were soon overhauled by the action which the police attempted to bring against him, clearly the innocent party." He looked at me intensely. "You've met Nucera. Have you come across anyone more mild?"

"No."

"Precisely. That business, however, was over three years ago." He paused. "But regarding this present affair, I hoped that you might be able to suggest something." He couldn't have been more imploring without actually using the precise words.

I told him that unfortunately I was already employed on an assignment, one I was especially keen to finish. "I'm anxious to return to England as soon as possible."

"I could reimburse you well."

I shook my head. "I'm sure you can, Dottore, I'm sure you can. However, I gave my word to the man who employed me that I would spend all my time occupied with work for him . . ."

"So be it," sighed Stirata and followed me as I made my way to the door.

The hallway housed various memorabilia concerned with Fiorentina, which I'd not seen on my earlier visit. Photographs of the teams which had won the *scudetto* in 1955–54 and 1968–69 were given pride of place and also on view were caricatures of several players who had brought distinction to the Club by gaining selection for the national team. There was a row of signed portraits of past stars, among whom I noted a sepia photograph of Guiseppe Chiappella, but my eye was instantly caught by coloured portraits of heroes from the recent past: Giancarlo De Sisti, and the golden boy of the seventies and eighties, Giancarlo Antognoni.

I shook Stirata by the hand. "I trust the mystery concerning the disappearance of Nucera clears up soon."

"It will turn out to be very simple, I'm sure," Stirata murmured in an offhand manner. He didn't sound too confident, though, and gave me another pleading look.

"Please remember me to Giuliana," I said as a servant opened the door of the Alfa 90 but Stirata was already striding back in the direction of the dining-room.

All of which left me wondering not only why Ross Armstrong had suddenly become flavour of the month, but also what kind of mischiefs Antonio Nucera had been involved in before he took up employment with Stirata. More important, though, was discovering what kind of mischief he was involved in at the present. If he was. He'd struck me as being very calm and reasonable when we'd met two days earlier.

Added to which remained the running sore of the blackmail.

19

Tuesday, 27th February

Although I returned to Florence as quickly as possible it was already well past three o'clock when I let myself into Francesco Barberini's apartment. That left roughly three and a half hours to travel to Linate Airport, a few kilometres to the east of Milan, which was perfectly feasible, given the car I'd hired.

However the fruitless odyssey I'd carried out during the morning had taken toll of my patience and I gladly recalled the information I'd been given by Eugenio Dal Bosco; that Tom Kennart would be out of reach for the coming twenty-four hours – news that made me revise my timetable. I now planned on driving to Milan at less than breakneck speed, writing up the report during the evening and catching a plane the following morning.

My new resolution was given further substance when I switched on the answering device attached to the telephone. Byron had attempted to make contact on three occasions.

"Thanks for calling back," he said, having picked up the phone after only the second ring. "I was starting to become worried you might have already left." He sounded tense.

"I wouldn't have done that without getting in touch," I said firmly. "How can I help?"

"I wondered whether your offer of a lift up to Milan was still free." He sounded painfully awkward.

"Of course," I replied. "I was planning to leave in an hour or so."

"Great!" he exclaimed. "Shall I come to your place in half an hour's time?"

"Fine. See you later." Reminding him of the address of the apartment I was using, I put down the receiver before he could reply.

The bell sounded forty minutes later and I could appreciate instantly why Stirata had chosen Byron to model clothes. He wore a three-piece suit in dove-grey over a shirt in pale lilac and a maroon tie. In his right hand was a grip which must have weighed about twenty kilograms but which he carried as though it was almost weightless.

"Third floor," I said, and followed him up.

I'd purchased for Barberini an ornate casket as a present of thanks and I quickly scribbled a note expressing gratitude for the use of his apartment, which had certainly reduced my expenses. I left a gratuity for the woman who came twice a week to ensure the apartment was kept clean and soon after we were able to depart.

I could guess how eager Byron was to start talking, but I managed to keep him quiet until we were travelling northwards on the Autostrada del Sole. Although I could feel that he was bursting to scream out a catalogue of incidents that were both bizarre and sensational, I made it clear that, since we'd several hours ahead of us, nothing would be gained from rushing through his tale. A tale, I hoped, that would tie many ends together.

"Right," I said when I was ready. "Tell me precisely what Sian is using to blackmail you."

I could feel Byron throw a startled look towards me before he uttered a low moan and became deathly silent.

"I was bound to find out, wasn't I, and it had to be her, hadn't it?" I'd reduced the possible suspects to his poker-playing colleagues, but the only one of those who seemed likely was Fulvio Bordi, and he clearly hadn't the personality of a blackmailer. So it had to be someone from his past. The only good thing to come from my drive to Pisa was that I had narrowed it down to Sian.

I thought at first Gary had stopped breathing, he was so frozen. He finally started speaking just as we were about to approach one of the many tunnels on the stretch of autostrada between Florence and Bologna. Though on occasions his voice fell to a murmur so that it became difficult to hear over the normal sounds of the motorway, and although I knew some of this tragedy already, I was careful not to interrupt. It seemed absolutely essential that I didn't insult the confidence which Gary had placed in me.

He told me about the troubles he'd become involved in when he was thirteen and fourteen, and about the mugging of the old lady which ended in her being badly beaten up and robbed.

197

Matters had looked very bleak for him until the appearance of a saviour.

When she'd been apprised of the facts along had come Sian Wright, his mother's younger sister, who straight away agreed to have the boy to live with her, given that he was placed under a regular Supervision Order.

"I must have been bloody impossible at times, bloody impossible," Gary confided, reiterating much of what Sian had told me the previous week. I was sure that he had.

"For eighteen months," he continued pitifully, "I drove them close to distraction. Then it happened. Coming home from school one day – it must have been inside the space of just half-an-hour – I realised precisely the enormous sacrifices which they must have made for me, especially my aunt." He turned to look across at me. "I presumed it was because she couldn't have children."

"She told me."

"She was intensely jealous of my mother, her elder sister, having given birth to four children. Intensely, almost insanely jealous though heaven knows what else there was to be jealous about. Mam got wed soon after leaving school, but looking back I can see the man she married was an authentic no-hoper." A disloyal way to refer to his father, I thought, unless his thoughts had been influenced by his aunt.

"I can see that now. Sian had a far better brain, far better looks, far more presence and I gathered that as the two sisters grew up there started to be a divide between them that only became more and more rancid."

Although I'd been right in my suspicion that the information he had to impart was little more than a rerun of that I'd heard some days earlier from Sian, what impressed me deeply was the clinical manner in which he'd absorbed these facts and was now recounting them with an accuracy that suggested that he'd played and replayed them through his mind on numerous occasions – many of them ridden with guilt.

"I settled down in time," Gary's voice became less severe. "Each night, when I got home, I'd combine homework with playing football out in the garden. I forced my way into the school Under-16s team, and when I was a year older I was chosen for a Yorkshire Schools side. Everything in my life had changed for the better – and I could sense the admiration and pride felt by my aunt."

Their relationship became very close – most obviously because she was the sister of his mother, but also due to the fact that on weekdays his uncle seldom returned home from wherever his case happened to be much before ten at night. Frequently he came home to find Sian and her nephew either watching a television documentary, listening to a record or discussing various topics – for all the world as though they were mother and son.

"Another important factor that brought us closer together was religion. I was brought up in a house that was firmly agnostic: none of us kids even used to attend Sunday school. During those years in Yorkshire came the time when I started to accompany my aunt to church." I could sense him looking fixedly out of the window as he explained. "She frequently asked if I'd like to go with her, and when I finally made up my mind I found that religion gave me a world ordered by peace and goodness, a still and calm world where you could be your own person. Soon after I became a Catholic convert myself."

"You must have been either sixteen or seventeen?"

"Although I was seventeen and a bit when I was first received into the Church, I began to attend when I was sixteen." He broke off and stared into his window as though it was a mirror. "My having become a Catholic seemed to be very important to the president, when he found out about it. Apparently after the death of Giuliana's mother he turned increasingly to religion to bring him comfort."

I couldn't remember Dal Bosco having mentioned it but all of a sudden many aspects of the case fell into place, such as Gary's heartfelt anguish a week before when I'd suggested he and Giuliana consider having their then expected child aborted.

Apparently soon after she came to live in Milan Sian had herself become a convert. She started to take instruction soon after her first husband proposed to her, and hoped that she'd find it easier to integrate into the country more completely by adopting its religion.

"In fact, during those years when I lived with her in the house in Silkstone she used to be full of praise for almost everything that came out of Italy. Clothes, books, music, cinema – you name it, she loved it. Whenever she spoke about Italy her voice would tend to become softer and filled with nostalgia. She'd reminisce endlessly about the times she'd spent in Milan, where she'd been praised so much as a beauty.

"'La Strega Gallese'," Byron murmured bitterly. "The Welsh Witch." Even in English the phrase was sinister, but in Italian it came across as considerably more cold and eerie.

In the evenings when his uncle was away Byron would sometimes find himself being indoctrinated by his aunt into the intricacies of gambling, which had taken place in private homes, in bars and clubs as well as in the few casinos in Italy in which gambling was legal. She described in detail those games in which she had been involved – poker, canasta, vingt-et-un, bestia, chemin-de-fer – as well as discussing in animated terms all those cases in which a participant had been discovered to be cheating. She had a peculiar obsession with this side of the game.

"She admired the elegance, the glittering jewellery, the formal dress, alcohol at three times the normal cost, players taking drugs – all existing because billions of lire could change hands merely on the turn of one card. She followed it with the fixation of a child, and it definitely brought out an animal passion in her. You could smell the excitement as it flooded out of her."

At that point Byron sank into silence. I could sense he was about to reach a crucial point in his narrative, and the atmosphere crackled with tension.

"For months I'd been able to tell that the marriage was becoming increasingly unpleasant. They'd always slept in single beds, but I could often hear them having fierce arguments about the most inconsequential matters. Sian's husband often behaved like a bully. He was someone who always liked the sound of his own voice and who regularly preferred to talk in a very theatrical manner, gesticulating wildly as though he was in court."

We motored on quietly for several further kilometres but it was only as we drove away to the north-east of Bologna that I turned to think about another personality in the puzzle.

"Exactly were does Andrea Cornelius figure in the narrative?" I asked soon after.

It turned out to be an accurate guess. Byron instantly swivelled his head and uttered a low groan. "How did you know about her?"

"Mike Townson told me about her."

They'd met soon after the events he'd just described, when Gary had left school and chosen to follow his career as a footballer. He moved into a house owned by the club, which used to give accommodation to some of the younger players attached to their sides. He found it easy to settle down because every lodger was encouraged to adapt to the homely atmosphere of the place and all were advised by the landlady not to indulge in petty jealousies of each other. The unmarried sister of one of the directors of the club, Laete Cornelius threw all her energies into the upkeep of a well-ordered house and taught those lucky enough to be sent to her as lodgers how important it was to hold fast to strong principles. Visitors of either sex were encouraged to be away from the premises by half past ten at night, she made it plain that she disapproved of smoking, came down heavily on those who were ever caught coming in drunk of an evening and encouraged her "lads" to write every week or ten days to their parents, or in the case of Gary, to his aunt as well. The atmosphere of the place might sound akin to that of a boarding-home but everyone who'd ever been involved with it often spoke about their time spent there with warmth and fondness and thought of Laete Cornelius as being a close substitute for a mother.

"And Andrea is her niece?" I enquired.

"Was," murmured Byron dramatically, and looked across at me. "Past tense, not the present."

"I know, Gary," I broke in gently. "Mike Townson told me about her driving over from Sheffield weekends to visit you. He also told me about her death."

"Oh Christ!" Glancing across I noticed the resigned look of someone who knew that all their secrets had been discovered.

Gary had come into the senior side three months after the start of the season and had grown accustomed to seeing in the daily papers on most mornings articles about himself, whether of five lines or fifty. Laete Cornelius had been instrumental in making him realise how transient all this adulation could be. "They'll not be slow to hurt you when you're down, Gary," she had pointed out in her soft Yorkshire accent. "Tek very little notice, if tha' wants my opinion."

After Gary performed outstandingly in one home match he received a visit from someone he claimed had changed his life: Andrea Cornelius, the daughter of a director of the club, and niece of his landlady. He'd been overawed at first, but in time the two of them had taken a great liking to each other and used to meet in secret. She chose to be very guarded in case the news reached the ears of her father, which delighted Gary since he'd become used to a life in which he had kept his own thoughts to himself.

"Tell me more about Sian," I said, in an attempt to turn his thoughts away from the tragedy of Andrea.

"She never went out to work." Byron stared out of his window. Dusk had started to melt into the darkness of night and spots of rain began to patter lazily on to the windscreen.

"She spent all her time translating?"

"No. She used to specialise at casting precious metals, and often spent days meticulously cleaning all the silver in the house."

"Was there much?"

"All the cutlery was handmade, as were most of the ornaments which hung on the walls. Sian used to have fads. When I came to live with her, her current craze was being a silversmith. In the attic was a furnace, files of varying coarseness, emery paper, polishing mops in addition to the basic necessities such as tools and hammers which could help to create the desired shape. Most days, while I was at school, Sian would isolate herself in front of her work-bench and sometimes, when she had to meet me from school, on her hands was the evidence that she'd been forced to leave before she had finished a particular task."

I didn't understand.

"Silversmiths always wear an apron of some type," he explained in a voice that had started to take on the timbre of a tape-recording, "but they can't wear gloves for the obvious reason that they require one hundred per cent feeling in their fingers when it comes to giving objects shape and form. On occasion it can be filthy, physical work – which explains why many women smiths prefer to be totally involved with jewellery. Perhaps the nastiest thing they work with is acid."

This hobby as a silversmith had started in Milan. When Sian was first married to Domenico Mozzolino, she learned that one of his forebears had been the Dominican Inquisitor of Lombardy, Sylvester Mozzolino. Sian had taken up an interest in the history of witchcraft during the sixteenth and seventeenth centuries which became intense after her first miscarriage. Having taught herself the skills of the silversmith she would pass hour after hour in a state of extreme depression about her inability to bear children, and would compensate by creating, as well as engraving, the artefacts held precious by every witch: silver caskets which could hold pieces of bone, silver vases that could take drops of blood, silver sticks that could be used to summon up Satan together with his disciples. That was the start of her being referred to as "La Strega Gallese", the Welsh Witch, and the name had stuck.

"You must have found this pretty weird?"

I glanced to my right and saw him nodding vehemently. Then as an answer to my unvoiced question he said "but" – and became increasingly voluble. When he'd compared his life as a sixteen-year-old with that which had gone before he realised how much he owed to his aunt for having agreed to look after him. Clearly, he felt, it was due to her inability to have children. Once, when they were by themselves, she confided that she'd miscarried on two occasions while married to her first husband. She'd then given a dazzling smile and had come across to kiss him on each cheek.

During the succeeding twenty months, especially after Gary stopped having to report to the authorities, aunt and nephew became closely drawn to each other. Her hold over him intensified. Sian continued to spend money lavishly at every possible opportunity and any occasion on which a celebration was called for – her birthday, his birthday, anniversaries of both her weddings, every time Gary was selected for another football team of importance – the pair of them would dine at Brooklands, a warm-hearted and handsomely-organised restaurant in the nearby village of Dodworth which was owned and run by a family of Italians. Each visit they made saw Sian paying the bill as though she could lay claim to millions and behaving as though she had not a responsibility in the world.

She frequently took him for a trip round the northern part of Wales, and they made two crossings to France. On the first occasion they visited some old friends of hers who inhabited an elegantly-furnished apartment in the centre of Paris, and twelve months later she accompanied Gary on a trip to Mont St Michel. Although Sian chose to help Gary herself by talking to him constantly in Italian as well as coming to his aid on the few occasions on which he needed advice about his homework, these short visits were intended to help her nephew prepare for A-level French by providing the "feel" of France and the French.

"Extremely thoughtful and generous," I remarked after a pause, "but what I've so far failed to note," I threw a swift glance in the direction of Byron who was again gazing out of his window, "is this. You experience difficult times when you are young, many thanks to your own stupidity. You grow away from those, thanks to the generosity of your aunt. Then comes the death of Andrea Cornelius, two years after you started to make your mark as a professional player. But so far I have heard absolutely nothing which implicates you with blackmail."

He proceeded to give me a portent of what was to follow. On that trip to France during the half-term break in the summer of 1985, the two of them had visited the glories of Mont St Michel in Normandy. Sian, who climbed with all the zeal of the former hockey star she'd been, had led the way and had been the first to reach a level above most of the crowds climbing up a steep flight of stairs, the summit of which reveals the most spectacular views to the front and to the right. These steps are wide and shallow, with cuttings of greenery visible at the top, over the wall to the front where the gardens can be glimpsed. At the top these lead to a wall with a superb view of the vast expanses – not so much sand as the exposed carpet of the sea leading to the edifice of Mont St Michel.

On her way up these steps Sian, who'd taken Gary's right arm, stumbled and almost fell, and took an inordinately lengthy time to regain her sense of balance. Gary assumed that she was rushing to the top to catch first sight of the edifice, to be among the first to emerge from the nook-and-cranny views that had only promised better things to come.

"I only later realised that her haste had been merely a ploy," Gary murmured, and went on to relate that Sian had followed this incident by frequently walking around the house scantily dressed and taking a vast amount of time getting ready when she had to go out. "It acted like a green light. I should have seen it coming, of course," he continued, "but it's so easy to be wise after the event."

And it had come.

On the morning of 14th August, 1986, Gary had woken very early since this was the week when the examiners sent results of A-level exams to the pupils. He'd been rising first for the previous three days and had come downstairs in his pyjamas to see if the post had arrived. That morning it had – although after he had opened his envelope and seen his good marks, Gary had forced himself to keep quiet since he knew that he'd have to wait for his aunt to appear before being able to celebrate completely.

She'd appeared fifteen minutes later wearing a towelling dressing-gown in sky-blue, and had been delighted when she heard his good news. He spent the rest of the morning walking on air, and rang some of his chums from school to find out how they'd fared, and where they would be going next. After Sian returned from her morning shopping expedition he had persuaded her to lend him her car in the afternoon so that he could go into Sheffield and have some words with the chief coach of Sheffield Wednesday, Graham Knight.

"Graham was very chuffed when I went in to see him, very chuffed indeed. He knows better than most how thin the line is in football between success and failure, and we opened a bottle of bubbly before I drove back to Silkstone for a celebratory dinner with my aunt and uncle.

"But when I got there it was to be told that my uncle had rung up to say that he wouldn't be coming back that night."

Sian had cooked some veal rolls stuffed with lamb, which she knew Gary was very fond of, and followed this with an apple trifle with almonds and raisins. There being only two of them, each had eaten copiously, and they had also drunk their way through two bottles of wine, and followed this with a double measure of strega.

"You know how it is," appealed Gary. "You know you've drunk too much, but are so enjoying yourself that you lose all sense of when to stop."

She'd unloosened the belt of her antique white dress, under which she was wearing nothing, and had slowly pulled the confused boy down until the two of them were kneeling on a large black rug which lay in the middle of the beige carpet. She needed little time to make him come fully erect.

Although Gary had seen many photographs and paintings of nude women, what had mesmerised him most was not the firmness of her small breasts nor the pale slenderness of her waist but instead the thick dark luxury of her sex.

"I should have seen it coming, of course, I should have seen it coming," Gary said in strained tones.

"And the blackmail followed that?"

It had.

After he'd been seduced a second time Gary was allowed to leave. He stumbled up to his room and locked the door; the thrill he had felt on receiving his exam results having been completely overwhelmed by feelings of disgust at how his aunt had treated him. He spent the whole night in chilling numbness, feeling totally degraded and humiliated, in a state of crushing disbelief that he had allowed himself to be over-powered and humiliated in such an easy way. The following morning his aunt made no attempt to enter his room.

Ever since he had come to live in Silkstone Gary had received a diary among his Christmas presents, a generously-spaced journal which gave a page for each day's entry. It also had a small lock, and he was always encouraged to consider it his private property. The first he received had been used to a pitifully small extent, but that for the following year had been filled in generously, and after Gary had become a convert to Catholicism he started to treat the book as a type of daily confessional, and locked it after each time he had used it.

After he had been humiliated so painfully by his aunt Gary used the diary to express his sense of shame. Page after page after page the confession went on, written in a scrawly hand in ball-point pen, until he found that he could say nothing else. He didn't read through what he had written and stayed in his room until called down for the evening meal.

During the following two days Gary had remained resolutely isolated in his room, coming downstairs only when he knew his uncle would be present. He rarely looked at his aunt. Not once did she offer any signs of remorse for the amorality of what she had done, nor any sense of guilt or shame. The two of them grew further apart in the following few days but it still came as a shock to Sian when Gary told her that he intended to follow a career as a footballer, even though he had been offered a place at Bedford College, London, to read Italian. He'd been in touch with the manager's office at Sheffield Wednesday, and had been told to report there as soon as possible.

"Was that when the blackmail started?" I said, glancing across at Byron's grey face.

It had come almost two years later, following his transfer to Stoke City. He'd been upset at leaving the warmth and friendliness of the home of Laete Cornelius, and although he made a pledge to remain in touch with Andrea, his departure for Stoke was hurried and he forgot to take with him two or three items, including some of his old diaries. These were discovered by Laete and forwarded to the only address she knew: Hilldrop House in Silkstone.

That was when Sian played her hand very adroitly. Long

after Gary had done his best to push the memory out of his mind, she'd written to him in Stoke and had threatened to sell his diary to one of the tabloids unless he paid her two hundred pounds a week. For a brief moment he was overcome with fury at being reminded of his mindless surrender on that tumultuous August evening two years previously, and was on the verge of contacting his aunt with the message to publish and be damned – and hang the consequences.

Gradually, however, he'd come to see how a viper like Sian might make use of only part of his confession to make it appear like an act of rape, opted to pay, and thereby set himself on the road to self-destruction.

The crippling blackmail started twelve months later when Sian had learned of the intense Catholic fervour of the president of the new club that had bought Gary, AC Fiorentina. She assumed that were Marcello Stirata to discover the story, Gary's footballing career would be over. In Italy, at least. On finding out what comparative riches Gary was now being paid she had struck, demanding that on the first Monday of each month he should make his way to her flat in the Via Carlo Crivelli and pay her his "blood money". A monthly sum of ten million lire.

"She's doing this purely from spite. She's always been able to lay her hands on as much money as she required." Gary sounded particularly bitter. "But now I've had enough, Christ knows, of being always under her control, always having her at the back of my mind." His voice became sharp. "And since I want to finally rid myself of this torture, I'm going to refuse to be blackmailed any longer." Which implied that I'd been asked along in the role of prime witness.

"But today is Tuesday?"

"She couldn't come yesterday."

"She didn't give an explanation?"

Gary shook his head. "She never did. She never does. The bitch."

Another prolonged interval, before I mentioned a different topic, one that had greatly puzzled me. "It's to go back several paragraphs, Gary, but I've never heard you mention church. Catholic or otherwise."

"No." The word sliced into my brain like a knife. Catholic converts frequently have higher expectations than do cradle Catholics, and becoming a Catholic must have meant a great deal to Gary. However, I was right in my assumption that as well as helping to influence his life in other ways, Sian's behaviour that morning had helped to form a religious watershed. "I ceased to believe on 14th August, 1986." When Gary had been less than eighteen and a half.

When I glanced across two minutes later I saw that tears of anguish had started to trickle down his cheeks.

Part Four

When the crash occurred he'd just started to serve a three-year sentence at the prison at the Via Ghibellina for maliciously attacking the manager of a shop who'd refused to purchase any of his shoes – an attack that nearly cost the victim his life. A conscientious salesman he was not – but considerations about his career were entirely forgotten after he learned that his ex-fiancée had been dramatically injured in a traffic accident.

Although he'd been employed in Florence for several years, he had made only a handful of friends, none of whom visited him in prison. In the first few days of his sentence he'd been an archetypal loner. He'd talked with nobody, and nobody had talked to him.

He'd only learned about the accident when he'd seen her name in a headline in La Nazione. GRAVE INCIDENTE ALLA STELLA DONATELLA SPEZIA. Beneath had been a grainy photograph of the damaged Maserati in addition to a report which gave the names of the other passengers.

In a state of trauma the near-illiterate Poccudu had made his cell-mate read the story to him and was told that the girl he'd felt responsible for almost since her childhood, the girl he'd been deeply in love with, the girl he'd followed to Milan, had not only been horribly disfigured but had also lost her mind. She was being cared for in a home to the north of Milan – still alive but now effectively turned into a person who could best be described as a "living vegetable".

For the first time in his life Corrado Poccudu had allowed himself to sit down and weep.

After some time, however, grief had turned to wrath and he'd vowed vengeance. Vengeance against the one person to have survived unscathed an accident that destroyed the only person he'd ever truly loved.

20

Tuesday, 27th February

I reduced speed during the last third of the journey. Byron had pleaded with me to stay and meet his aunt, and all thoughts of catching a plane back to London had paled into insignificance when set alongside the agony of the story he'd told me.

He'd fallen asleep, clearly exhausted by having had to dredge up harrowing memories from the past, and soon after we'd passed the slip-roads leading to Piacenza, patches of fog started to appear, making the final sixty kilometres of our trip something of a visual steeplechase.

I would be eternally grateful to Keith Nightingale for ordering me to continue my investigation of this case. And what a case it was turning out to be! During the rest of the journey I tried to examine the reasoning behind the blackmailing of Gary, for whom I felt intense sympathy.

That Sian was born after their previous baby had been stillborn only heightened the interest in her shown by her parents. From the start she had been outstanding, in beauty as well as in cleverness, and where her sister Gwyneth had shown herself to be relatively ordinary and unremarkable at school, Sian had been blessed with commanding intelligence and poise. While Gwyneth had left school when she was sixteen, Sian had gone to university, had taken a good degree and was celebrated for being the perennial centre of attraction, wherever she went. Where her sister had married a drunken dullard, she had married an elegant and respected barrister, and his being a foreigner gave him an automatically appealing aura. Instead of five, she looked at least ten years younger than her elder sister. She seemed truly to be one of those people for whom life presented no challenge.

The only thing she couldn't do which her sister had done was to bear children – a failure which made her feel an intense sense of shame. Having her first miscarriage when Gwyneth had her third child brought the problem cruelly into focus. There still had remained hope that her wish to become a mother would be granted, but the second miscarriage had been crucial.

When Gary had got into trouble, she had leapt in with an offer to help which Gwyneth found it hard to refuse, whatever misgivings she may have had about "losing" her child. Why, hadn't Sian always been a constant caller before she had become married for the second time, and a not infrequent visitor after she had moved to Yorkshire?

As the eldest child and only boy in the family Gary felt himself being deprived of maternal attention and was therefore vulnerable to becoming intensely attached to someone like Sian who was caring and attentive to him. As an adolescent boy it was easy for his feelings to become eroticised and for him to feel that he was partly in love with his aunt. This was especially noticeable after the incident at Mont St Michel when Sian often became subtly tempting. Increasingly elated by Gary's company she started to demonstrate provocative behaviour. By taking breakfast in her negligee or leaving the bathroom door open when she was taking a shower or often making a point of kissing him goodnight, Sian enjoyed (perhaps subsconsciously) a situation of power over Gary – and by extension, her sister.

At that dinner on 14th August, 1986 when Gary arrived already having drunk some champagne, this relationship was horrifyingly consummated. Sian had plied him with drink, and as the emotional temperature of the evening heightened she'd begun to make overt advances to Gary who was still excited, drunk and confused, eventually seducing him selfishly and cruelly. The equivalent of a sexual crucifixion in which Sian, by proxy, felt as though she was gaining revenge on her sister.

Overcome by a feeling of shame and humiliation which he didn't fully understand Gary responded by escaping; walking out of his present life with Sian and Richard, as well as on those academic achievements and ambitions which were very much a part of that life. I realised that his feelings of humiliation in a sense matched those of Sian in not being able to bear a child.

The closer we came to Milan the more I thought about the character of Andrea and the more sympathy I felt for her. How had Mike Townson described the girl when I visited him at Stoke? "Quietly spoken" and "thoroughly likeable". I'd not seen her photograph, but I wondered fleetingly how similar to Giuliana she'd looked.

Sian's life seemed to be made up of many paradoxes. She'd

married someone who was involved in the same profession as her first husband, but a man who was more than ten years her elder. I'd only caught a glimpse of his features in a photograph on top of a table in their house in Yorkshire; a handsome face with the weather-worn look of someone who spends weekends outside, with dark hair that was starting to grey at the temples. Her marriage might be sexless. The inexpert way she'd tried to seduce me suggested that she had stopped living a life in which sex played any significant part. Since her husband was forced to spend much of the week away, if Sian needed to she could have affairs with other men and nobody need be any the wiser. But she had chosen not to.

The street proved simple to find and lay very close to the Piazza Medaglie D'Oro, the junction at which the Corso Lodi interconnected with the thoroughfare which cut into the city centre from the south-east, Corso Porta Romana.

Via Carlo Crivelli 20 was an elegant block of flats set near the corner of the street. Since Byron possessed a key to the building (a gift from his aunt when she was told about his move to Fiorentina, and started to blackmail him more heavily) we were soon able to transfer our luggage and two minutes later I was examining the apartment, which was on the first floor. Living-room, a large kitchen which had a dining-area, two bedrooms and a bathroom.

The walls of the living-room had been dressed in off-white and decorated with many prints which appeared to be over two hundred years old and were, I presumed, highly valuable. Although the pair of sofas, in addition to the sectional seating, were in black the cushions lying on them were in a sapphire-blue as were those which rested on the cream coverlets on the beds. The colour had faded in the sunlight and miserably failed to suggest that hint of mystery hidden behind Sian's eyes. Nothing could, of course, but they struck me as having been chosen years before and having been retained for a purpose other than that of decoration. The décor of the room didn't seem to have an identity of its own, most noticeable in that it still housed several shelves filled with legal tomes.

The chairs and table in the kitchen-diner were glossy white, while three of the walls were covered by wall units that were made from wood which had then been stained charcoal grey. Two prints by Kandinsky looked out on to each other and the "open" portions of the wall furniture were used to store glasses, decorations and cookery books. None of these was in a recent edition, which made me think that Sian didn't make much use of the place.

"You take the room next to Sian's," said Byron as I peeked into one of the bedrooms.

I shook my head and eventually persuaded him that I'd be fine on a bed in the living-room. "What time do you expect her to be here?"

Byron looked doubtful. "Can't say exactly. Her plane is due at Linate at twenty-five past seven but the fog might have delayed things. I'll telephone soon to find out. First, let's get you settled." The perfect host, who made my bed, produced clean towels and made sure that I was well cared for before he went to telephone enquiries at the airport.

When he returned there was a look of frustration stamped on his features. "As I thought, due to this bloody fog her plane has been re-routed to Turin." He glanced down at the slip of paper he'd written on. "Say that it arrives in Turin at about seven thirty and, given she gets through customs without being stopped, it'll be at least ten thirty before she arrives here."

He was still in control of himself but only just. I realised suddenly what was perturbing him – Sian would be tired after her arduous journey. He perhaps felt, in all honesty, that he could not put the record straight while she was so exhausted. He wanted her as she'd been at her prime when the blackmailing started. He wanted to render her speechless with indignation at his words. He desperately wanted to enjoy that moment he thought would rid him of his load, and he wanted me along to give moral support.

Suddenly, he reached for his set of keys and slid past me. "I'll nip out and buy some groceries." He sounded anxious and strained.

"Shall I come?"

Byron shook his head. "No need. It's only about fifty metres away, the *panetteria*, just around the corner. I'll look after myself. Don't worry." He pointed down the street.

"You're sure?"

"Of course. At last I'm starting to wake up." He gave a boyish grin before letting himself out of the room. He didn't put the door on the latch.

This seemed a good moment to make contact with Dal

Bosco. The number seemed simple enough but I was only able to make a connection at my fourth attempt at dialling.

Eugenio had just returned to his suite of rooms. "How was Byron?" he asked amidst huge gasps while he took fresh air into his lungs.

"Tom Kennart?" I prompted. "Have you been able to see him?"

"Let me get my breath back." Eugenio's voice started to become more audible. "Indeed. I've only this minute returned from his office. Another manager, Mark Snelling, saw a clip yesterday morning on BBC Television and has started to nose around. Kennart didn't anticipate any competition so soon and has spent much of the last thirty-six hours in a state of alarm, waiting to hear from you."

I explained the reasons for my delay but promised to be back in England by the morning.

"His display against Napoli can only help increase the price Fiorentina might ask," Dal Bosco pointed out.

Why state the obvious, I wondered?

"They might ask for a larger fee than Kennart is prepared to offer," Dal Bosco continued, in a tone that suggested he was talking to himself, and enjoying the conversation.

So that was his game. "Now, Eugenio, we agreed on the journey to Pisa." I sounded commanding. "At this moment the affair is between Kennart's club in London and Fiorentina in Florence. I've done my part and will have my report on Kennart's desk tomorrow afternoon. You do your part and stop stirring. Okay?"

Dal Bosco gave a throaty chuckle, made the promise and we exchanged farewells.

Kennart was out when I tried his number but soon after I'd replaced the receiver, Byron returned carrying a shopping-bag which contained rolls, eggs, butter and a litre of milk. "Enough to see us through until breakfast," he announced in a detached voice. He glanced at his watch. "I thought that we might go to a restaurant around the corner for our supper."

"What about Sian?" I enquired.

"We'll leave a note." Byron wrote an address on a slip of paper. "Gone to the Viale Beatrice D'Este." "It's the wide road just a hundred metres to the south and parallel with this street. She always used to go a particular trattoria with her first husband. We'll go there. They know me pretty well by now."

He shrugged his shoulders and said in mulish tones. "In any case, she might be later than we suppose."

Without waiting for an answer he turned on his heel and went into a bedroom to run a comb through his hair. The spark of life had re-entered his eyes.

"Come on," he ordered when he returned to the living-room and pulled his shoulders back as though he was reporting for guard duty. The trip out appeared to have imbued in him an attitude that was icily authoritarian, and I feared the antics he could display when later faced with Sian.

As we walked down the Via Porta Vigentina Byron explained what was in his holdall. "At this period of the season, clubs are more concerned about their players receiving injuries than anything else. But I did bring along a tracksuit and trainers so that I could run around and keep fit."

Thankfully we were given a table near the rear of the restaurant. Byron deliberately sat with his back to the door letting only the waiters have a close look at him. Andrea Trapani, the proprietor, had been an ardent supporter of AC Milan since the early fifties and the wall facing me was decorated with coloured photographs and memorabilia from previous teams. As if to underline the point a bottle of Grignolino '83 was placed on our table, a fresh red wine which came from grapes grown on vineyards owned by Nils Liedholm, a famous figure in Italian football during the previous forty years.

At that moment the proprietor returned to our table and sat down on a spare chair. Byron introduced us but before he was allowed to continue, Andrea Trapani remarked how much he had been enthralled by the televised football on Sunday evening. He repeated only comments which we had heard several times before, naturally, but the manner in which he embraced the player was the most eloquent statement of all.

I learned that his love affair with AC Milan had been with him since birth, and that he could say the word "Milan" before he could utter the word "Mama". But it had truly been sparked by his enthusiasm for that trio of Swedish imports who had graced the roster of the team in the early fifties and who came to be known by the collective of Gre-no-li: Gunnar Gren, known as "The Professor", Gunnar Nordahl, the massive centre forward and Nils Liedholm. In fact, Andrea cherished a photograph taken of all three of them showing Nordahl standing between Gren and Liedholm.

"Then along came my son," Trapani gave a shrug, "who supports Internazionale because when he was young Inter was all the rage in the city, and claims that the thought of AC Milan brings him out in a hot rash. *Ma che buffone!*" He indicated the wall close to him which was decorated with photographs of those Internazionale teams which had won the *scudetto*. I gathered that during the week prior to any local "derby" between the sides, father and son remained incommunicado and addressed each other only through inter-mediaries.

"The picture I cherish most," Trapani continued, "is that." He pointed to a signed photograph of Gianni Rivera. "The side that won the title for the tenth time in 1978–79 may have not been the most gifted the *tifosi* have seen, but after experiencing the moment of triumph, I could have happily died on the spot. Even though the deciding match was a goal-less draw and even though our opponents that day, Bologna, were at the foot of the Serie A."

He paused and then, as I feared he would, went on. "My next moment of real joy came last Sunday when I watched Napoli-Fiorentina on the television." He gave Byron's elbow a squeeze of affection before thankfully standing up and moving to welcome a quartet of new customers.

"A firm friend," commented Byron after Trapani had moved out of earshot. "After we first met in October, there were many occasions on which 'Toto' (Byron used a diminutive despite the fact that Trapani was tall and as thin as a stalk) used to ring me up from Milan to offer words of advice. After I returned to playing cards, he would recall the times he had passed gambling himself."

Some time later Trapani returned with a bright light in his eyes. "I have a surprise for you. As my guest, I insist that we go and do some gambling."

He would take no protests, listen to no arguments. "It's such a real pleasure to see you again," he said to Byron "and your friend, I'm certain, would not be annoyed by a little diversion. I know the password to Il Gatto con gli Stivali club and," he raised his left wrist imperiously, "I shall be free to leave in ten minutes."

Byron was caught in two minds. The idea obviously appealed to him greatly but he also had obligations to fulfil, one of which was the forthcoming meeting with Sian at which he planned to break free entirely from any financial restrictions which she could continue to place on him.

"I'd like that very much," he said softly and looked across towards me. "However we have a duty to meet my aunt who by now should hopefully have arrived from England."

"Duty! Duty! Duty!" Trapani gave a laugh. "You English never cease to amaze me. Why not use the phone to discover whether she's arrived yet. If the answer is yes, please remember me to her and explain that you will be delayed. If the answer is no, then the answer is no." He gave a shrug as he delivered this vein of logic.

"That's kind of you," Byron remarked politely, but I could see that flickers of doubt had come into his eyes.

I slid myself out of my chair.

"Maybe Sian might like to accompany us?" asked Trapani expectantly. I doubted that. After having had to spend hours of tedium on planes and coaches, the least attractive proposal would be to have to sally out again straight away. Any normal person would want to take life very easy.

Byron muttered to me in English, "Let's hope that she's already arrived and wants to remain at home."

Trapani showed me the way to the rear of the trattoria and then to his phone which had been appointed in the colours of AC Milan, red and black. I was amused at seeing another example of his fanaticism but the next moment my heart became icy.

The call was answered after the second tone. A woman merely had time to scream, "*Aiuto! Aiuto! Aiu –* " before the receiver was snatched away and thrown back in its cradle.

21

Tuesday, 27th February

I sprinted along the Viale Beatrice D'Este in the direction of Sian's apartment. The fog had become more dense during the previous two hours, making the traffic crawl at a snail's pace as well as affecting my confidence. I slid out the Beretta 92F as I turned off the main thoroughfare and moved north a hundred metres along the Via Luigi Anelli.

While still at the trattoria, I'd first dashed across to Byron to collect the keys for the apartment. That precaution might have been a crucial mistake because the moment I turned into Via Carlo Crivelli I heard a car being started at the eastern corner of the street, soon followed by an angry squeal of tyres as it negotiated the corner and sped southwards along the Via Porta Vigentina, the street down which we'd walked on our way to the trattoria.

I leapt up the short flight of stairs outside the building and feverishly let myself in, hoping against hope that the female who'd answered my call (I presumed it to have been Sian) had been left behind. A quick survey of the rooms confirmed that she'd been seized.

In her bedroom I found a smart suitcase in deerskin which held labels from Alitalia Airways as well as a handbag in light grey suede. Both were unopened, suggesting that the intruders had been anticipating her arrival.

I moved back into the living-room and was replacing the Beretta when Byron burst into the room and double-checked my search. "We'd better contact the Nucleo Investigativo." He sounded brittle and his eyes looked startled, making me feel guilty for having been seduced for a moment by the suspicion that he himself might have been involved in this dramatic seizure. Calmer logic made me realise that Byron must have spent the previous few hours building himself up for the confrontation and would hardly have arranged for his potential victim to be kidnapped before he was given the opportunity of speaking his mind.

I seized him before he reached the phone.

"It's our duty!" he exclaimed as he started to struggle. His voice sounded distraught as he repeated the phrase. "Can't you see! We must contact someone in authority."

"Of course we must," I replied, before steering him away by the elbow, "of course we must. But is there another extension in the apartment? There might be some useful prints on this receiver." I pointed towards the telephone.

Byron took a quick step back as though the telephone possessed powers of refraction, but his eyes soon mellowed as he realised the importance of my remark and gave a brief nod. "In Sian's bedroom." He gave a gesture. "Would *you* like to make the call?"

I shook my head. "I'll pretend I can't speak Italian well enough."

Byron looked perplexed. "You're almost fluent!"

"I am. But that's for later."

"I don't understand."

"It could be very useful to pretend not to understand a question. Gives you more time to think of a reply. At this time of the night I doubt whether there'll be anyone on duty who can speak good English. I'll leave the call to you." Before he could express further doubts I said, "636.886."

"Thanks." Byron slid into the bedroom. Soon afterwards I heard him talking Italian, his voice pitched high as though he was in a state of hysteria.

That gave me a chance to glance round the room. The fragrance of Sian's perfume still lingered in the air, recalling memories of my visit to her house a week earlier. A small table had been turned on to its side, a cushion was thrown on to the floor and along the matching cushion still on the sofa had dried a streak of blood. The sofa itself bore a couple of small blood-stains. Those aside, I could see no other signs of a fight having taken place.

When Byron had finished his conversation and returned to the room, I stressed the importance of causing no further disturbance and made it clear that we shouldn't move about the apartment unnecessarily. "It's amazing the amount of detail the police can acquire from only the slimmest amount of information. Why don't we move next door?"

I took his arm and we found seats in the kitchen-diner before I said, "Tell me about the call."

He had finally been put in touch with a captain in the plain-clothes branch of the Milan carabinieri called Enrico Morbelli. "I explained what had happened and he said that some of his people would be around as soon as possible. But with this fog," he gestured out of the window, "it could be twenty minutes before they arrive."

It turned out to be a shrewd estimation, and eventually we heard the noise of a car drawing up in the street outside. Byron descended to let the new arrivals into the apartment. There were three of them, Morbelli himself, together with another prune-faced detective called Giancarlo Oneste. The third man, who carried a suitcase full of implements, was introduced merely as Sasso, and immediately set to work in the drawing-room after the three of them had visited all the rooms in the apartment.

Morbelli and Oneste led us back to the kitchen and eagerly accepted Byron's offer to make some coffee. They were a neatly contrasting pair.

"At least that will prevent me chewing some of this revolting stuff," remarked Morbelli with a smile. He showed us a packet of nicotine-flavoured chewing-gum at which Byron pulled a face.

He looked to be in his late forties, but his hair was already streaked with grey and white and his eyebrows resembled puffs of white cloud. Of only average height, he'd obviously taken care to look after himself and, although thick-set, had only one chin and a firm stomach. He seemed to be the kind of man that one could talk to, and I trusted his mournful brown eyes.

Oneste, on the other hand, looked to be the direct antithesis of his name. Taller than his superior by four or five centimetres, his body possessed the type of sleekness known to those who spend long hours working-out in gymnasiums. He had a full head of raven-black hair, an aquiline nose, a firmly-set mouth and hard brown eyes that flicked everywhere like those of a falcon. Whereas Morbelli was dressed in a suit of comforting light ivory, that of Oneste was in an aggressive dark blue which glinted as though made of metal. He seemed to be a man whom one could take an uncomfortably long time to like. When it came to being interviewed separately, the preference for my initial interrogator would be simple. A session with Oneste could be too much for Byron to handle in his present mood.

After coffee had been served Morbelli took charge of the

proceedings. "While we're waiting to take you to the *Questura*," he began, taking a sip at his *espresso*, "let's go through the movements of both of you during the last few hours." He was staring at the central portion of the ceiling as though he expected it to provide information that would be useful. While Oneste busied himself taking out of his coat-pocket a notebook and pen, Morbelli's sad eyes finally dropped down to look at us. "Who will volunteer to tell me the information I wish to know?"

I pointed at Byron and said authoritatively, "He will."

I wished I hadn't.

There was little doubt but that the incidents of the previous half-hour had knocked my companion seriously off balance. He had steeled himself to confront his aunt with the news that he was no longer prepared to continue with her sordid game of blackmail. In his mind he had rehearsed his speech so that he knew it syllable by syllable.

His aunt's abduction, however, must have come as a great shock since he reminisced in halting tones until he reached the moment concerning the telephone conversation when he became inexplicably mute.

Morbelli, who'd resumed his inspection of the ceiling, lowered his eyes for a second time and glanced at me. "You'd better continue." His voice had become uncharacteristically harsh.

When I'd finished he said "But you didn't see their car?"

I shook my head.

"Perhaps we'll find some evidence in this apartment." He turned to Oneste and asked, "Why do you think that the Signora was given time to answer the phone?"

Oneste was far less sharp than he looked. After a lengthy pause, he replied sullenly, "I've no idea, Captain." At which Morbelli gave a grunt of irritation.

"Who can corroborate your story?" Morbelli turned to me. His voice was more gentle than it had been a moment earlier.

I gave the name of the trattoria, and that of the restaurateur, information which Oneste put down laboriously in his notebook.

At that moment I heard the noise of sirens approaching. "That will be Giorgio and Massimo," Oneste blurted out. "I ordered them to drive here in case we could make use of them."

Morbelli nodded his approval.

Both the new arrivals, however, were more interested in the

present cast of characters than they were in listening to Oneste. They'd watched television clips of the game against Napoli two days earlier which displayed the ethereal football played by Byron, and stood tongue-tied in the presence of the footballer after blurting out expressions of admiration. I half-expected them both to drop down on their knees to signify their respect.

"Yes. Yes. And yes." Morbelli broke the silence and turned to the recent arrivals. "Please remember that at present we are not holding a seminar on football but investigating a crime. We shall return to the *Questura* where we can take statements from both of you regarding recent events which might have affected this abduction. You," he indicated Oneste, "will drive Signor Armstrong while I," he tapped his black pullover, "will travel back to the Via Fatebenefratelli with Massimo and our celebrated guest." He took a pale-faced Byron by the elbow in an avuncular manner, and obviously intending to make him feel at ease he admitted, "I also much admired your performance before I came on duty on Sunday evening."

Byron gave a weak smile, one that showed relief.

We made our way northwards in silence, remaining close behind Morbelli. Massimo had his siren sounding – a racket that was imperative since, although the fog had cleared slightly, cars were being driven in the city centre at breakneck speeds. In addition Oneste was also making full use of his, causing the brace of cars to make an appalling racket.

At the *Questura* Morbelli shepherded Byron into his room, and, after taking Oneste to one side for a brief discussion, asked me to follow the junior detective into his office. I couldn't have expected to be inside a room that was more depressing. Offices are offices are offices the world over but even the most cheerless gives some hint about the character of its owner. That of Oneste had none, and could not have been more gloomy and clinical. Its walls were decorated solely with graphs – zig-zagging lines in blue or red or green. The top of the desk was bare apart from the regulation phones and battery of pencils. There were two hard-back chairs in front of it on which "visitors" could sit while two of the corners held filing cabinets in an unsavoury grey. It was a room which I couldn't wait to leave, and I made no attempt to disguise my feelings.

Oneste motioned for me to sit down and proceeded to ensure that I would be of very little help by ringing for another detective to come into the room.

"I feel that it's for the best if Marco here," he indicated the newcomer, a pickled character in his thirties who had little hair and wore a dun-coloured suit on top of a shirt striped in white and blue, "sits in on our discussion." The use of that particular word annoyed me even further, and my irritation was increased when Marco started to play around with a pair of black leather gloves. He'd obviously been watching too many "B" pictures.

I played it straight and answered most of Oneste's questions in a helpful way.

After half an hour Oneste disappeared, presumably to make his report and to note how his superior had been progressing. He was only out of the room for a couple of minutes, but when he came back his temper hadn't improved. "Up," he commanded. "The Captain wants to see you."

He accompanied me down the corridor to the door of Morbelli's office where he left me without a further word.

"Come in, come in." Morbelli's manner instantly made me feel more relaxed. This room was altogether a more urbane place than that I'd just left.

Of Byron, however, there was no sign.

"Your friend is taking a rest," Morbelli explained weightily.

"What have you done to him?" I snapped, moving towards his desk.

Morbelli held up both hands, shook his head and frowned. "Please, Signore, please. I'm not that type of man. No. He suddenly felt exhausted just before my colleague came along and I thought that he'd benefit from being able to lie down." He indicated a doorway at the rear of the room.

"Kind of you," I said after a long pause.

"You sound as though you don't believe me." Morbelli's voice rose sharply.

I passed a hand across my face and wiped away some of the fatigue. "Forgive me, but it's already been a very long day. Of course I do." I smiled. Morbelli had nothing to gain from not telling the truth. "In any case, the boy must also be tired almost mindless with all that he has experienced today."

Morbelli nodded sagely. "You must be exhausted. Signor Byrne has told me some details about your role in these recent events, but I'd be extremely grateful if you could tell me about your own involvement yourself." He gestured towards the door. "I gather from my colleague that your command of Italian is not perfect."

226

"It's adequate."

"I could summon a translator." Morbelli seemed very anxious to please. "There may still be one in the building."

"At this hour?" I exclaimed. "No. I'll be all right."

He gave a shrug. "In that case, take your own time." That was the reason for Morbelli having spoken so distinctly!

"So Oneste told you I couldn't speak Italian very well? Take no notice of that. It's sometimes a useful exercise to undermine the confidence of any interrogator whom one doesn't like. Him I didn't, but," I smiled, "my Italian is good enough."

"Thank you," Morbelli replied before repeating his request. He indicated a recording device attached to his desk.

"I'll sketch in the outlines of my movements during the previous fortnight," I replied. "Many of the members of the cast you'll never meet nor hear about again."

Morbelli spread his hands apart. "I realise that. But we've no time-limit. Kidnappers often don't make contact for several days, or even weeks, and often prefer to keep the hostages hidden. They usually like to cause as much anguish as possible before they reveal their whereabouts." He leant across and switched the tape-recorder on.

I must have spoken for over three hours, and my throat started to become dry despite the fact that Morbelli offered me several cups of coffee. Although both of us discarded our jackets and loosened our ties, my palms began to feel clammy.

"The aspect of the story I thought interesting was the poker, and the way in which Byron came to make use of it to bolster his earnings. Gambling can swallow up large amounts of money, as you well know, and often reason plays a very poor second to emotion. Agreed?" Morbelli again went into his imitation of a wise old owl. "And we may be looking for something that might have been an event which occurred during the last few days."

"Carry on."

"Look at the problem this way." He stood up from his chair and stretched his arms above his head before resuming his seat. "Just under eight years ago, on 2nd March, 1982, the Spanish centre-forward Quini was kidnapped from outside his apartment in Barcelona. He was held captive in a cellar in Zaragoza for just over three weeks before finally being freed by the police. And who were his captors? Not men after an enormous amount of wealth, though Quini wasn't poor and he played for a very prosperous club. No. His kidnap was organised and bungled by three unemployed electricians."

"You think it might have been this type of person who kidnapped Byron's aunt?"

"Exactly. And the reason may be something connected with the past as well as the present." Morbelli paused, and started to tap the top of his desk with a pencil. "How long has Sian Mozzolino been resident at that apartment?"

"About fifteen years," I replied. "Give or take a few months."

"Correct. So she inhabited the city during the era when kidnappings in Milan were frequent."

I nodded.

"So why wasn't she seized during that particular period? Why the delay until the present time?" He shook his head. "No. The truth is closer to us than we probably realise."

It might have been that statement that turned back my mental clock by thirty hours. I suddenly caught a glimpse of those demented eyes that belonged to Corrado Poccudu and remembered the irrational manner in which he'd played poker during that Monday evening.

"Have you close contacts with anyone inside the Florence branch of Nucleo Investigativo?" I enquired suddenly.

Morbelli pointed to the wall behind my right shoulder. Turning round I saw a photograph of him receiving an award from another officer dressed in a dark uniform. "The other person is Giovanni Regalia, now a Colonel of the Carabiniere in the Borgo Ognisanti down in Florence." He raised his eyebrows. "Why do you ask?"

"It's just a hunch I'm having but it could be well worth your time acquiring information about one Corrado Poccudu."

"Poccudu? An unusual name."

"He's a Sardinian."

"Ah."

I explained the manner in which Poccudu had been the last stranger to be given information as to the precise location of the apartment.

"But what reason might he have for taking the woman?" Morbelli was staring at the ceiling and appeared to be talking to himself.

"It might also be worth your while to run the name of

Domenico Mozzolino through your computer and see the information it provides," I suggested. "He was killed in a traffic accident several years before you moved across to this department. It must be a fair time ago but I've always had a hunch that the starting-point for this tragedy might come from an event in the past."

I waited for Morbelli to concur before continuing. "Poccudu's mood altered strangely after Byron mentioned Domenico Mozzolino as the name on his aunt's apartment.

"Then there was the way in which Byron gave Richard Strickland the address of his aunt, writing the same down on a slip of paper and passing it to him across the table so that Poccudu would have seen it." I paused. "To be fair to him, Byron could never have dreamt that such information might be used to someone else's advantage." I felt myself acting the role of counsel for the defence.

"Let's hope this kidnap leads to negotiation," Morbelli remarked darkly.

"And not to murder?"

Morbelli nodded. "But if money's demanded, who should we contact?"

"Her husband, Richard Wright. A successful barrister in the north-east of England."

"You know him?"

I shook my head. "Not yet. But I know about him. And Sian works from home as a translator. They've no children."

"A barrister?" He gave one of his cynical snorts. "Show me a poor barrister and I'll show you a fool. And there'll be money from the insurance companies, won't there?"

Morbelli lent back in his swivel chair and gave a smile of satisfaction. "But I feel," he touched his chest, "that this guess of yours might be correct.

"It's all fascinating, most fascinating." He glanced at his watch and an expression of surprise came over his features. "That late. You and the boy must return to your apartment and have the good long sleep you deserve. While you two are taking your rest I'll get ahead with replaying the recording, scanning through the documents from previous times and in a few hours' time I'll contact Giovanni Regalia in Florence." He strode to the other room to fetch Byron.

It might have been triggered off by that remark made by Morbelli but all of a sudden I felt exhausted. When Byron appeared, rubbing sleep out of his eyes, he seemed to be in a trance.

Before shepherding us down to the garage, Morbelli turned towards me briskly. "Signor Armstrong, I doubt whether you will have use for your handgun during the next few hours." He indicated the top of his desk. "Please leave it in my care. Thank you."

Without waiting for a reply he led the way along to the lift-shaft.

22

Wednesday, 28th February

Two men accompanied us back to Via Carlo Crivelli, a driver dressed in the midnight uniform of the carabiniere together with a sandy-haired officer in his forties.

"My men will take you to the apartment and wait in Via Carlo Crivelli until they receive further orders," Morbelli had said. "These might take several hours to arrive. Nevertheless," his voice became more excited, "you'll be pleased to learn that Sasso returned three hours ago and is busy stepping his way through various scientific procedures."

It was a difficult job waking Byron when we reached the apartment, and the driver helped to walk him up the steps and put him to bed in his own room.

I fell into a deep state of unconsciousness the moment after I'd taken off my shoes and lain down on the bed and only awoke at midday.

After I'd fully come to terms with the present I looked in on Byron, who was sleeping quietly, before I stepped into the bathroom to take a shower and rinse away the griminess of the previous thirty hours. I was impatient to telephone through to the *Questura* despite Morbelli's promise that he would make the initial contact when he'd received the relevant information from Florence. There seemed little that I could do but wait.

I therefore spent the succeeding period of time glancing through the books on the shelves. Although a few of them were in English the majority were in Italian, and many of them to do with the law. Several of the larger books were tomes concerned with the cult of witchcraft which had crept throughout Lombardy during the sixteenth and seventeenth centuries – and merely brought back memories of Gary's anxieties when living at Silkstone. One bore a letter written in a firm hand by one Sylvester Mozzolino, an ancestor of Sian's first husband.

The following moment I received a shock. Almost hidden behind the edge of the curtain was a sable-framed photograph of a man whose features were very like my own. Thinking back, I saw that this similarity might explain Sian's expression of wide-eyed surprise when she had first seen me at her home in Silkstone a week earlier. The man in the photograph was a few years my junior and had sleeked-down black hair, darker eyes and a nose that was more aquiline than mine, but I wondered whether this similarity lay behind Sian's attempt to seduce me, and recreate an episode from her past.

On looking more closely I noticed a thin scar that ran diagonally across his left cheek. The portrait was undoubtedly that of Domenico Mozzolino who had placed on the print a message to "*Carissima la mia Sian*" and had signed it with his name in glossy black ink. The scar interested me. It had the appearance of having been the legacy of a passionate exchange rather than a knife or blade. Are fingernails ever that strong? Or had the mark, instead, been caused by a swift slicing of a ring in a moment of passion?

What had Morbelli remarked? "The truth is closer than we probably realise." Coincidence can introduce unexpected drama to our lives. The most unexpected event yet in mine occurred over two years ago on a visit to New York. I'd attended a dinner at the apartment of some friends who lived in East 33rd Street, and much enjoyed an evening which didn't finish until after one o'clock in the morning. I found a cab soon after striding into Lexington Avenue and asked to be taken to the junction of East 56th and Madison, where my hotel stood. We could only have travelled three blocks when a voice from the front of the cab said in a very English voice. "Excuse me. Aren't you Ross Armstrong?"

All sorts of possibilities flashed through my mind about the identity of the owner, but it turned out to be Roy Elgood, two years my junior at school, who married a girl from Michigan and was helping to pay her way through art school. After having reached my hotel we spent a nostalgic couple of hours charting the whereabouts of certain common acquaintances before he went his way and I mine.

The discovery I was to make two hours after I began my search for clues in the Mozzolino apartment couldn't equal the ironic quality of that particular encounter (few things could) but it turned out to be exceedingly more significant. Following Morbelli's advice that the critical piece in the jigsaw might be close at hand I flicked carefully through all the books on the shelves before leaning down and sorting through the two lengthy lockers underneath.

One turned out to contain mainly materials for the mixing of cocktails while the other housed a collection of large china plates. On low shelving which ran along the opposite wall sat a voluminous library of records in addition to several dozen tapes. Peeking at the sleeves of some of them I noticed that most had belonged to Domenico Mozzolino and presumed that the same note of ownership must apply to the collection of cassettes. A Sony turntable was on the shelf above, the speakers being at the two corners of the wall where they adjoined the ceiling.

Byron awoke after I'd been up for roughly ninety minutes, entered the living-room dressed only in his shorts and gave me a fleeting smile. "I want to take a look around Sian's room," I said, "to try and find some clues as to where we should look next."

I indicated where we were at the present. "I've seen nothing here except books, records and valuable pieces of cut glass." These had been displayed along the shelving above the hi-fi equipment.

"Go ahead." Byron appeared to be an entirely rejuvenated person, plainly fortified by that lengthy sleep. "While you're doing that I'll make you a cup of coffee."

"Black, no sugar," I replied and entered Sian's room. It can often be embarrassing searching through other people's clothes, but the job had to be done, and I'd provided Byron with the opportunity of accompanying me, if he had chosen to.

The room gave off its bizarre character the moment I entered it. Although manifestly being used by a female, as shown by the assortment of perfumes and skin creams which sat close to the rear of the mirror attached to an ornate dressing-table in an alcove, the farther side of the room had a feeling of iciness and appeared to be entirely lacking in life. Peeking inside the teak wardrobe, alongside various dresses I noticed several men's suits, a label in one of which confirmed my surmise that it had belonged to Domenico Mozzolino.

Closing the cupboard I next looked inside a chest of drawers. Nothing unexpected in the first three – blouses, cardigans, sweaters as well as some underwear – but on opening the fourth and last drawer I sifted through clothes that were decidedly not feminine: shirts in pastel shades, ties, vests, underpants, socks and several pairs of glossy shoes. Sian's obsession with the memory of her first husband made more substantial the theory which I had presented to Morbelli at the questura.

I moved back into the living-room just as Byron was finishing his coffee. "You should have joined me," I said.

"I wouldn't have been much help. I've never been in that room until last night and so I would have been as lost as you."

"Never?" I found that astonishing.

"Never." He shook his head hastily. "Never. The only times I've seen this apartment were when I drove up to Milan to see Sian. The sight of cold gloating in her eyes when I passed over the money was terrible. I couldn't get away fast enough." His brow furrowed suddenly as he remembered what had happened the previous evening. "Where is she at the present? Do they yet have any idea?"

I brought him up to date with the events which had occurred since we'd left Via Carlo Crivelli 20 the previous evening. He himself, it transpired, possessed little recollection of these and I was often requested to repeat certain details for his benefit. The further into the narrative I went, however, the more agitated did he become and by the time I came to the very recent past his eyes had become as cold as ice.

"You've searched around this room?" His voice sounded brisk.

"Yes."

"It never hurts to take another look." Like me Byron had no clue as to whereabouts to start his search, and no clue either for what exactly it was he was seeking, but after a few moments looking around the living-room while whistling through his teeth, he started to read meticulously through the books on view.

"You've taken a good look through her personal effects and found nothing so why not sift through that drawer over there where she used to keep her correspondence." Byron indicated a point on the bookcase close to the window.

From four metres away it was almost impossible to detect. Just a razor-thin line across the teak told me the location of the drawer, and if I'd not been informed of its whereabouts I should have certainly missed it. The next problem lay in my inability to open it.

"See that black catch level with your eyes?" Byron asked without turning round.

It was above my left shoulder. "Yes."

"Press that and the drawer will be released." His voice had become less brusque, almost as though he was delighting in guiding me through this particular game.

When I'd done as he'd asked a deep drawer slid forward by a fraction, providing enough room for me to slip my fingers inside and open it completely.

"I discovered that when I came up in the autumn," Byron answered the question I'd been too slow to ask. "The evening I arrived I asked Sian a question, and before I knew it, there she was playing in the corner with that contraption." He gave a winning smile. "Ever since I was a child I've had a mind for tricks like that and committed that one to memory."

The drawer turned out to be packed almost to the top with bundles of letters and cards, handouts from restaurants and hotels, brochures about seaside resorts throughout Europe, and a few guide-books in both English and Italian. Those contents promised to keep me busy for several hours. Many of the letters were written by Domenico to Sian or vice versa before their marriage.

Most of the significant information they contained I'd already been told, but it might be vital to discover how much Sian had lied to me when we'd met a week earlier. I examined a curriculum vitae which she'd intended to send to a college intent on recruiting the most gifted teachers of English in Milan – but at that particular moment she had met and fallen in love with Domenico Mozzolino, a handsome young *avvocato*. Marriage had followed soon after. Corroboration of that particular story.

The correspondence was arranged in chronological order, and I soon found an account of Sian's first miscarriage. She had received some of the most privileged treatment that money could buy when she had been pregnant and found herself being cared for at the prestigious San Martino Clinic in the Galleria Buenos Aires. Only those who have suffered the tragedy of miscarriage could have any concept of how bleak life can become, but the letters from Domenico before, during and after the tragedy read like masterpieces of wisdom.

Although this was interesting confirmation of the story I'd been told a week earlier, it provided scant new evidence which might prove useful in the future. We'd been involved in our joint investigation for no longer than twenty minutes, however, when the telephone sounded. Out of instinct, I glanced at my watch. 4.22 p.m.

It was Morbelli, and a very delighted Morbelli at that. "Sasso has had an opportunity to run his tests," he exclaimed and then paused as if waiting for me to enthuse.

"And?" I said.

"There's no doubt that one of the people we would like to question about the abduction is Corrado Poccudu. It turned out to be blood like his that marked the settee. In addition Sasso found some human hairs. Presumably there was some kind of fight before the woman was bundled into the car." He paused, but I could tell that he was feverishly excited.

"Someone involved in seizing another person against their wishes surely wouldn't have attempted the feat without some help?"

"Indeed, there was a companion," Morbelli went on, answering my question, "but Sasso is not sure whether there was more than one. A driver might have been waiting in the car for them to appear." There was a long pause. "And *he* might have had a companion. We are continuing with our investigation."

"You're positive it was Poccudu?"

"One hundred per cent certain." Morbelli's voice became cold. "During the past few years Poccudu has been an inmate of the prison in Via Ghibellina on several occasions. Every detail concerning him is on the files."

"Giovanni Regalia must be an important colleague."

"Important, of course, but also influential. Already he's provided me with critical information concerning Poccudu, and has given me the make and number of his car – "

"Which are?" I interrupted. I'd caught a flash of the car driven by the Sardinian two nights previously.

There was a fleeting period while Morbelli checked his notes. "Lancia Fulvia, number FI 73286. Colour – metallic silver." His voice became more confident. "We've issued a bulletin giving that description to our cars in the area close to Milan."

"You've no clue about the identity of his collaborator?" I had a sneaking suspicion of the answer before I finished asking the question.

"We think the partner was one Antonio Nucera who, when last heard of, was employed as a chauffeur by a Florentine

236

businessman called Marcello Stirata." The voice of Morbelli had resumed its authoritative tone.

"You're certain of that?" I asked. There was a heavy feeling in the pit of my stomach and the temperature seemed to have become much colder.

"Certain, no," Morbelli replied. "Confident, yes. Sasso has yet to analyse several objects he has taken away but we feel that we're investigating on the right lines."

"When you yourself telephoned the apartment yesterday evening to discover whether or not the lady had yet arrived from Turin our friends must have been on the point of making their exit. Your call, I fear, can only have acted as an alarm. I presume that she broke free and managed to reach the telephone before she was overcome." He took a deep breath. "There must have been a strenuous fight until she was beaten into silence – "

"Mostly by Poccudu, I suspect." When I'd met Antonio Nucera on Sunday afternoon he hadn't struck me as being the type of man who would resort to brawling.

"By whoever." Morbelli's retort was sharp. "By whoever. You may be surprised to learn that Nucera has also been an inmate of that prison in Via Ghibellina."

I couldn't believe that.

"It's true. Six and a half years ago he was committed for being involved in the theft of some goods from a house in Fiesole." Morbelli's tone was emphatic.

Hadn't I heard details which were unnervingly similar only the previous day from Stirata? The principal difference lay in the number of years which had elapsed since the incident, and I felt more than a little annoyed with myself for having become far too obsessed with Poccudu and not been concerned with the previous escapades of Antonio Nucera.

"Did your friend Regalia provide you with the dates on which Poccudu and Nucera were sent down?" I asked at length, backing a hunch.

There was another rustle of papers before Morbelli answered. "Your suspicion is confirmed. Corrado Poccudu, three years for committing a serious assault, from August '77;" a brief pause, "Antonio Nucera two years for theft, from September '77. So these two spent twenty-odd months together in prison."

Knowing how prisons can be breeding-grounds for tyranny,

places in which might can so speedily equal right, I imagined Nucera was far too mild-mannered to stand up to an aggressive person such as Poccudu. Several years, however, had elapsed since the time of their first meeting, and presumably each had gone his separate route.

"That's it, Signor Armstrong. Thanks in the main to the help you provided we've been able to pursue every worthwhile lead. We are doing all we can." The more excited Morbelli was, the more pompous he became.

There came a brief silence before Morbelli's voice continued. "You'll have to stay in the apartment until after Sasso has completed his investigation. Is there anything that you require?"

There was nothing I could think of so we exchanged farewells politely.

The moment after I had replaced the receiver, however, I heard Byron say in hollow tones, "Do you think this is what we've been looking for?"

He was looking inside a slim edition of *Iphigénie en Aulide*.

However he wasn't concerned with studying the text of the tragedy, but instead passed over a map the size of a postcard which charted the route to be taken between Pavia and Castana, a hamlet just to the south-east of Broni on the southern side of the river Po. It had obviously been drawn in an haphazard fashion, was not to any particular scale and had presumably been used as a bookmark.

The copy of *Iphigénie* was inscribed with the name of a Donatella Spezia, and the initials "D.S." at the foot of the map suggested that she had been the cartographer.

"Where did you discover this?" I asked excitedly. I'd missed seeing it during my survey of the books on the shelves.

"Up there." He showed me a narrow chink between some folders that contained numbers of *Il Sole Ventiquattro*, law reports which appeared daily in certain newspapers. "I prised out one of the volumes and this fell out at the same time." He indicated the edition of *Iphigénie*.

"You've no idea as to the identity of this Donatella Spezia?" I asked after a moment. Her name was familiar, but only in the vaguest sense. "Sian never mentioned her?"

Byron shook his head.

I looked down at the sketch and presumed the map had been drawn to help Domenico find his way somewhere. On glancing at it closer, however, I saw that the final destination was a property in Casa Cristina, just beyond Castana, named Villacidro – which name had been printed in bold red capital letters.

"We must contact Morbelli again," I suggested. "This looks a most tempting avenue of interrogation." I glanced down at the map. "I assume that this word Villacidro means nothing special to you."

Byron gave a quick shake of his head. "Afraid not."

When I eventually got hold of Morbelli to pass on the details which could be learnt from scrutinising the map inside *Iphigénie*, he became as ebullient as I imagined he allowed himself to be in public. "Give me a few minutes while I feed these details through our computer. I like the feel very much." He paused briefly.

"Sasso, by the way, has provided me with further details concerning the apartment. We have confirmation as to Signora Mozzolino's identity because the blood-stains which were streaked down a cushion matched her very rare blood group. AB Negative." He then answered my silent question. "This we knew from the San Martino Clinic where Signora Mozzolino was a patient. Sadly the visit followed a miscarriage." Nothing, it seemed, was private.

"Her husband used to be a very celebrated lawyer," he explained. "When he married, naturally we took the precaution of opening a file on his wife. It always pays to be prudent. I'll be in touch again very soon." The line went dead.

I suggested that Byron listen in the next time on the extension in the bedroom. As good as his word, Morbelli rang back less than half an hour later, manifestly in a state of high excitement.

"The house Villacidro in Casa Cristina was purchased by Signorina Donatella Spezia in August 1975. Over one hundred years old, it is a farmstead which possesses two storeys and seven rooms. It seems that the Mozzolinos visited the place on several occasions during the succeeding year." He paused. "This we can deduce from the fact whenever he was down there Domenico Mozzolino was in the habit of leaving the telephone number of the property with his office.

"The decisive date was 29th September, 1977. Accompanied by an agent called Salvatore Brini, the three of them travelled that evening just to the south-west of Milan, probably for a

239

meal, and were on their return journey when the car belonging to Domenico Mozzolino careered into some roadworks, crushing him against the steering-column. His wife suffered only minor injuries but Brini was also killed while Donatella Spezia was discovered to be severely injured and her career on the stage was cruelly finished."

That was it. I remembered her from television. A striking beauty, she had high cheekbones, very light natural hair and moved with the most electrifying grace.

Another dramatic pause, and I suspected that Morbelli had further information to divulge. "And here's the part that should interest you." He gave a low chuckle. "Three months or so before the fatality Donatella Spezia broke off her engagement with the childhood sweetheart she'd known ever since her days in the village of Villacidro in Sardinia when she was called by her given name of Manuela Decchuras. Moreover, she started moves to purchase his half of the property which they'd bought together in Casa Cristina." He finished on a note of triumph. "Go on – ask me who it is?"

"Who is it?" I asked obediently, although I knew the answer.

"Corrado Poccudu." His voice sounded uncharacteristically fierce. "Corrado Poccudu. We'll collect you in twenty minutes' time."

"If not sooner," I replied. "And don't forget to bring my Beretta." But I was talking into a dead phone.

23

Wednesday, 28th February

They didn't arrive at Via Carlo Crivelli 20 until after thirty-five minutes had passed. But when they did, it was with all sirens sounding and alarm lights flashing as three Alfettas pulled up in the street.

Morbelli took my Beretta from the pocket of his coat and laid it carefully on the table, before pointing his right forefinger at me. "If any shooting is called for, leave it to us. All right? However I felt that you would like to have that back. I've taken out the shells."

When I'd reloaded the pistol he indicated the way out of the living-room. "You two can accompany us," he said.

The fog that had blanketed the city during the previous evening had given way to a clear night. Above the rooftops we could see the stars twinkling, their light made more sparkling by the coldness of the night air.

I pointed at the Alfa 90 and raised my eyebrows but Morbelli brusquely shook his head. "We'll travel in our own cars. Furthermore," his voice became steely, "on no account are you permitted to interfere when we reach Castana." He gave us both icy stares. "*Capito?*"

I murmured my assent but Byron stated in dispirited fashion. "Everything's understood, Captain, everything's completely understood. However, all of this is not at all important. At this moment what's far more urgent is the condition of my aunt." His voice suddenly rose. "Can we please hurry?"

"I've brought five men with me. Each has recently been on weapons training courses. They are all young, all very agile, all well versed in dealing with the sort of circumstances we might encounter." Morbelli shepherded Byron into the first car while I was directed to the second and placed in the custody of Luigi and Ernesto, two flint-eyed and unsmiling young men who were dressed in dark pullovers, black leather jackets and ebony trainers. The third car had another pair dressed in identical fashion but who were given no supernumerary to supervise.

We were the first to reach the city of Pavia, where we paused for the other cars at the Ponte Libertà, the bridge which crossed the Ticino, a tributary of the river Po. We weren't kept waiting for more than five minutes before both the other cars joined us, at which Morbelli's voice came over the car radio and ordered us to proceed straight away to Broni.

The countryside started to become more hilly as we wound our way between vineyards which dipped in towards the road. The third of the cars disappeared from sight at this stage, but when I enquired as to the reason I was abruptly told to mind my own business.

I assumed that we must be coming close to the property; a suspicion I attributed to the fact that whenever he could the driver put the car into neutral so as to cause as little sound as possible. Eventually we came to stop three hundred metres distant from the car that had brought Byron and Morbelli, who waited for approximately five minutes before deciding to issue orders on his car radio.

We were parked on the border of the farmstead, in the centre of which squatted what I assumed to be the relevant house. Despite boasting two storeys it failed to give the impression of height thanks to there being several trees grouped around it. Hundreds of vines stood in its hinterland and formed a screen around the lower part of the building, but from the window of a room on the first floor streamed out a yellowish light.

The radio crackled to life again. "Pietro and Beppe are in position on the opposite side of the house. Ernesto, you have a scout around the place. Luigi, you remain here." The whispering ceased.

We watched as Ernesto slid out of the car, raced silently across the road and disappeared temporarily from sight as he crept around a building. Ten minutes later he appeared again, and we could see him stealing fleet-footedly through the vines and the trees which skirted the house. He disappeared from sight for lengthy minutes while he reconnoitred the northern side of the farmstead but eventually he returned to the car, his survey having taken the best part of half an hour.

Ernesto couldn't be sure how many figures he'd seen: one for definite but he only had a suspicion of having seen a second. There'd been no sign of a woman, however – news which I could imagine going through Byron like an electric shock, reminding me of his concern as we had set off.

So far, of course, everything was mere supposition. As yet we had no definite evidence that Poccudu and Nucera had been involved in any crime.

We were informed that on the rear wall of the house was a steep stone staircase with no handrail. Morbelli ordered two of his men to attempt to secure a position mid-way up the staircase that would give a full view of the bedroom. "Beppe, you meet up with Ernesto," Morbelli ordered over the radio-phone. "Take those night-sights we brought. They could be useful when you are still some distance away from the house. Approach from contrary directions." He was evidently becoming edgy. "Off with you now, Beppe. Ernesto will follow in sixty seconds' time."

The next occasion I looked at my watch it was six minutes after four o'clock. We hadn't received any signal from members of the scouting-party that they had succeeded in discovering signs of Sian's presence in the farmstead or any information concerning her whereabouts. The orders which Morbelli had given his subordinates kept running through my head: that the prime objective of the mission was to save Sian from receiving further punishment.

One could imagine that, for her, the drive from Milan must have been a terrifying experience. She could have had no concept of her eventual destination and must have become increasingly distraught as the journey became longer.

"Remember," Morbelli had commanded. "We are almost certain that two of those who seized her are Corrado Poccudu and Antonio Nucera. You must take into account the fact that these men will probably kill her if they suspect that we are following their tracks. Let's determine first whether or not she is actually inside the house before we attempt to arrest the men. If we've no luck tonight then we can make another attempt in the morning reconnoitring the area disguised as road sweepers or officials of the Broni-Stradella regional *comune*. But it's the safety of the lady which is most pressing."

Looking up at the house I saw that a light had been switched on in an adjacent room and a figure appeared, drawing down the blinds at the window. I couldn't make out who it belonged to.

Two minutes later, however, my thoughts were dramatically

altered when two shots were heard, very close together. They sounded as if they had come from within, rather than outside the house.

I straight away controlled the urge to interfere, but the following moment a figure leapt out of the saloon three hundred metres in front of us, sprinted across the road and started to race up the slight incline towards the entrance of the house. Moments afterwards Luigi left our own car, chasing up in a similar direction, and seconds later two other figures moved out of the car in front – all giving me the perfect excuse to follow suit.

The front door was open but when I attempted to switch on the light in the hallway I realised that there was no bulb in the socket. As I scrambled upstairs I noticed about the house a dankness that suggested it hadn't been lived in for months, perhaps years.

A stunning scene greeted me when I entered the bedroom on the first floor. A dozen paper cups stood on various parts of the stone floor, all surrounding a radio which played popular music, while in a corner were some tins of food and bottles of cheap wine. Two books were lying face down and in the other corner stood a sizeable steel bucket.

Close to the centre of the room, and lying curled up on his right side, was Corrado Poccudu. Part of his skull was missing and he'd received a bullet in his heart. His left hand was pincered as though he had been trying to wrench out his innards. Morbelli was standing close to him as though he half-expected him to spring to life, while in one corner Antonio Nucera slumped on a chair, his left arm dangling by his side, his shoulder bloodied where he had been shot. He was being tended to by Luigi and Angelo, the driver of the vehicle that had ferried Byron and Morbelli.

Close to the window stood Sian, alongside Byron, who had thrown an arm around her shoulders to give her support. In a clear state of shock, Sian was resting her head against his chest and whimpering like a child. The jacket of her elegantly-cut maroon suit was soiled with marks and blood-stains, as was her cream blouse. She wore no jewellery, her make-up had been smudged and a vicious-looking welt ran across her right cheek. She was naked below the waist.

What Byron had told me on our journey up from Florence to Milan leapt into my mind, and I was astonished to find him so in control of himself, since memories of the previous occasion when he'd seen Sian naked must have been burnt into his memory.

I side-stepped my way past Beppe towards Byron and seized his other arm. "You all right?"

He nodded and gave a sad smile.

"Where's her skirt?"

Byron shook his head. "I've no idea."

I found it on the stone floor on the further side of the bed and brought it over.

Although still displaying signs of the trauma to which she'd been subjected, Sian eventually stopped making those uncontrolled noises deep down in her throat and opened her eyes when she heard me greeting her nephew. Tears of deliverance were streaming down her cheeks as though she had never wept before.

"Sian has not been harmed," Byron said to me before planting a lingering kiss on her crown. In reply she pressed closer to him and gave a shudder that kindled not tears but a smile.

After I'd helped Sian into her clothes I took a look around the room. Its décor was clearly based on a fixation. The entire area had been decorated with memorabilia of Donatella Spezia in roles which had been a triumph, from her childhood onwards. Portraits of her in various plays were punctuated with facsimiles, outlines, statues and prints. Those unframed were yellowing with age. She had dancing light brown eyes, skin the colour of almond and shoulder-length fair hair.

Byron indicated Morbelli by raising his left hand from Sian's back. "He can explain what took place."

The Captain drew me away into the musty stairwell. He was holding a Mauser P38 with the forefinger and thumb of his right hand. "Ernesto and Beppe were on the point of securing an entry through the rear of the building when they heard shots coming from inside the room. When they broke their way in they found Poccudu lying dead on the floor, while the other man was crouching on one knee, holding his left shoulder." He gestured with his right thumb. "Ernesto and Angelo are out scouting the locality to see if anyone else was involved – but we don't think so. Just those two." He indicated the room.

"Can you guess what happened?" I asked.

Morbelli shook his head. "Beppo has radioed for further

assistance. I think it best to wait until after that has arrived."
He tapped his temple. "I am 99.9 per cent certain what
occurred but it is always imperative to be sure as you can be."
He paused.

"There'll be a fair wait until I can have you escorted back to
Milan. We will want to question the woman, although it's such
a relief that we discovered her alive and comparatively
unharmed. In my career I've seen far, far too many victims
who've been killed for no reason whatever. You are very
fortunate." He paused, gave a half-smile and pointed to his
chest. "Forgive me – it is *we* who are very fortunate."

As we walked down to the car I couldn't help but reflect on
the unintended irony of his remark.

24

Saturday, 3rd March

When I was last in Florence many people I met enquired with a smile if I'd heard the scandal connected with the opening of a high-security prison at Solliciano, near Scandicci, in the western part of the city. It had just been discovered that the construction company had failed to use all the steel for which it had charged. As a penance for having cheated the authorities its president volunteered to serve a two-week sentence as an inmate of the prison which housed no female inmates and had been constructed primarily to look after terrorists.

Poccudu and Nucera had served their terms several years earlier, however, in a much older prison in the centre of the city, Via Ghibellina. Poccudu had been the earlier of the pair to take up residence by merely a few days but he had no need of this seniority to make the pacific Nucera dislike him intensely. Someone who'd grown up having to look after himself, and considerably more bulky than his cell-mate, Poccudu started to exercise his physical superiority from the moment they first met.

All the pleas that Nucera made to the prison authorities about being moved to a different cell went unanswered. Like water dripping on to a stone each of the insults, each of the torments and each of the beatings handed to the smaller man buried their way deeper into his psyche so that the day on which he was released became the most auspicious of his whole life.

Nucera was freed from the oppression for just under a year. He should have left Florence entirely, made a new life for himself in another part of the country or, better, moved abroad. But no. When Poccudu learned that his erstwhile slave had secured a good job driving a saloon for a wealthy businessman every aspect of the former tyranny was speedily reborn and Poccudu came to dominate Nucera even more cruelly.

As soon as he discovered the location of the apartment of "La

Strega Gallese", and the fact that she was expected to arrive in Milan the following evening, Poccudu determined to exact some form of revenge for the injury done to his fiancée. He'd no notion of exactly what had occurred in that fatal accident that had taken place twelve and a half years earlier. No one had, no one could have apart from the woman who'd helped to cause it. All that concerned him now was the opportunity to exact retribution on the sole unharmed survivor of the accident: Sian Mozzolino, known also as "La Strega Gallese".

I'd been despatched to Pisa on a fruitless mission so that Poccudu – together with Antonio Nucera whom the Sardinian had commandeered to be his driver – might be assured of arriving in the vicinity of Via Carlo Crivelli before me. The plane had been delayed, but this piece of ill-fortune for him had been balanced by our having chosen to dine out that evening. It had been a simple task to enter the apartment (expecting us to return from our meal Sian would have been caught unawares), to overpower "La Strega Gallese" and steal her away before we were able to answer her cry for help. The fog had been an added boon.

After being knocked unconscious by a blow from Poccudu's Walther P38, Sian had been bundled into the rear seat of his car. When she eventually came round she found her wrists had been tied together with a belt and that a stretch of masking-tape had been placed across her mouth.

Although she attempted to ascertain their eventual destination by taking covert glances out of the window, the density of the fog made signposts virtually impossible to read. She'd given up the attempt to memorise each twist and turn in the road and it hadn't been until they had come to the insignia for the small town of Broni that she had any firm idea as to where precisely they might be going.

She'd visited the farmstead named Villacidro on three or four occasions, but that had been more than a decade earlier. It felt so utterly squalid to revisit the place in this way – led from the car by two men she'd not seen before and forced to stumble up the path before being prodded into the large room on the first floor whose walls were covered with memorabilia of her former friend Donatella Spezia. She was then pushed on to the damp mattress on the iron-framed bed, but her wrists remained bound and her mouth was still sealed with tape.

The chill of the night helped to keep Sian awake, and as the long hours succeeded each other she tried to introduce a note of logic into this ocean of chaos. At the back of her mind was a sliver of memory which reminded her that Donatella Spezia had purchased the property in partnership with her fiancé. She'd never been shown any photographs of the man. Might not he be one of her captors? Soon after dawn the following day those suspicions were given form when the larger of the two quickly ventured outside to buy some groceries, leaving her to be guarded by the smaller man whose gentle brown eyes never dared to look into hers.

They continued to be evasive even when he was summoned to feed her. Although he tore away the stretch of tape from her mouth, Poccudu ordered to be left untouched the belt which bound together her wrists, and Sian found herself being fed with the contents of a can of beans which had been heated. Still the smaller man wouldn't look directly into her eyes, but preferred to stare at her mouth from an angle. She remembered that it had been he who'd displayed concern for her welfare when the two of them had burst into the apartment in Via Carlo Crivelli.

Unfortunately it was his boorish partner who was on guard duty when she needed to go to the toilet. He'd fetched a bucket from the kitchen which he arrogantly placed in the corner of the room and gestured at it.

Despite pleas that her wrists be freed Sian's hands had remained bound together. It took so long that she could only presume he gained some pleasure from seeing her being so humiliated. After she'd finished, she was ordered to resume her position on the bed.

In the long and lonely hours Sian tried to find some method in all this craziness. This was no ordinary kidnapping. That much was certain, and the way she had been left alone and allowed to answer the phone at the apartment suggested that her captors were amateurs. They had made no particular attempt to confuse her about where they were, and had not been in touch with the outside world, apart from that swift purchase of groceries. No. It was something else. Throughout she'd been very conscious that her every action, her every denigration was being watched and devoured. Devoured and relished. It was as though at least one of her guards was taking a special pleasure in delighting in her humiliation.

Although she'd been determined to stay watchful at all

times, Sian had eventually drifted off to sleep, exhausted by the happenings of the last twenty-four hours. Before she'd fallen fully into her repose, she thought she had overheard the two men whispering to one another. She could have sworn that one of them had uttered the word "Firenze". She thought next of her nephew and finally dozed off convinced that Byron might have set up this kidnapping as a form of vengeance for what she had done to him. When she was woken up two hours later all thoughts concerning who exactly was responsible were blasted from her mind, since at the foot of her bed stood the larger of her captors, his right hand still holding his pistol, his left hand releasing his belt.

The following second resembled a nightmare, and her eyes were still bulging with terror when Byron burst into the room. Antonio Nucera was standing motionless by the doorway that led to the other bedroom, the gun drooping from his right hand, blood still oozing from a wound in his left shoulder, his eyes registering his shock. At last he had carried out the deed to which he had often been tempted in the previous six years.

While the carabinieri were busy searching round the room, Byron scooped his delirious aunt from the bed, took her to stand by the window and released the strap across her mouth. Which was when I entered.

Thursday, 1st March
We didn't get back to Milan until the morning of the following day when we were taken to the *Questura*. Sian gradually recovered her poise but frequently rushed towards Byron whenever she felt alone, and I often saw him comforting her like a younger brother. In the car on the route northwards she'd insisted that they sat together, and it was only after she began to trust in Morbelli that she agreed to be alone when she made her statement.

I realised that the monthly payments of the "blood money" that Gary paid over must have been a constant reminder of the power she had over him. But in those years when he lived with her she had faithfully kept him in touch with his mother, and he gave her immense gratitude for helping to steer him away from a possible life of crime. I wasn't at all surprised when Gary later revealed that his companion as a "lookout" when the old lady had been mugged eight years previously was now serving a sentence in Wormwood Scrubs for having committed a murder.

A charming lawyer called Gino Desiena, whose English was perfect, was called in to help us in our dealings with the carabinieri. Not surprisingly, it was Sian who was in the most traumatised state, and after she had told everything to Morbelli, she always demanded to be close to Byron.

Also in a state of shock was Antonio Nucera. When Byron had initially burst into the room at Villacidro, Nucera had already started to enter his private world of fantasy. Having killed the man who'd made his life insupportable for the previous six and a half years Nucera had nothing more to live for. Or so it seemed. His attempt at creating a life of his own, acting as chauffeur to Marcello Stirata, had been eventually foiled. He'd tried to persuade Poccudu to leave him alone three years earlier – and had nearly been killed for his pains. This time he'd eventually been forced to take the most desperate measures.

Nothing we experienced could have prepared us fully for the coverage by the media. When we'd been inside the *Questura* for barely half an hour a uniformed member of the carabinieri was permitted to enter Morbelli's room and informed his commanding officer that the first reporters had presented themselves in the interview room, desperate to build a story around the heroism of Byron. In the end, Byron and I went to discuss what had occurred – but we were strictly chaperoned by three senior members of the carabinieri and informed which questions we might answer. Sian was allowed to be absent.

As a result radio and television programmes during that evening were entirely concerned with coverage of the story and the more energetic of the reporters sped down to Casa Cristina to capture either film or photographs of the farmstead. We were accompanied back to Via Carlo Crivelli by a positive snake of vehicles – most of which remained in the street on guard duty while we snatched a few hours' rest. Most fulsome of all, however, was Marcello Stirata who, on being fully apprised of the facts surrounding the events, flew up to Milan and instantly gave a press conference at which he stated that he would be prepared to offer Byron a three-year contract. Terms to be agreed.

Indeed when Byron came to speak to his chairman on the phone I was given a glimpse of the shrewdness of Stirata's character when he announced that he would be very honoured if the three of us would be his guests at the international match due to be held on the Saturday evening.

Talking to Morbelli later in the day I gathered that if he had a good lawyer Antonio Nucera might be given only a light sentence, if any at all. It could perfectly well be claimed by his defence counsel that he had shot Poccudu dead primarily to prevent the Sardinian committing a murder – but that explanation ignored the second shot into Poccudu's skull, the bullet that repaid those six years of tyranny.

I telephoned Tom Kennart in the evening to explain the reason for my not having been in contact as I had promised. Astonished to hear the story, he straight away passed on his good wishes to Byron.

"I'm not sure what effect these recent occurrences will have on his footballing talent," I said. "Or when he'll actually feel able to play again. He's not kicked a ball in the last fifty-odd hours and must be delighted that Fiorentina have no match on Sunday. That performance of his against Napoli will be a very difficult act to follow." I paused. "I'm sorry to be the bearer of bad news but I think that Gary Byrne may have changed his mind about wanting to return to England."

"You're probably right, but the most important thing is that Gary is safe." Typical of Kennart, I thought. "You're on the spot and you know what I want. Do what you can."

The three of us were requested to remain in Milan for three days afterwards to help the carabinieri prepare their documents completely. And we would all be expected at the inquest in addition to the trial that was due to follow.

Extensive coverage of the story continued to appear in all the daily papers with numerous photographs of the farmstead, the room in which Sian had been held together with those of the three major protagonists. There was an artist's impression of the final shootings which left little to the imagination, and done by someone who'd clearly not visited the scene of the crime. It came as small surprise that Byron found his nickname being used in forty-eight point headlines that praised his courage and audacity.

I waited until Sian and I were alone together in her flat later that night before I spoke my mind. "The two of us are going to be together for some time." I walked across the room and stood over her.

Although she'd physically recovered from her ordeal she looked emotionally rinsed-out and pale. "What do you mean?" she asked in a querulous tone as she looked up at me.

I wondered if she'd ever been able to understand. I was still astonished that Gary was so rational after what Sian had done to him. God only knows how she'd behaved before, but her behaviour must have led to the death of her first husband and her unborn child. As a result of that accident she'd been exacting vengeance on all she had been in contact with.

Gary had been placed in her custody, but she almost destroyed him. She crushed his belief in religion – a religion which was becoming a vital pillar in his life – and she almost succeeded in damaging his career as a footballer. She couldn't hear talk of Andrea Cornelius without becoming hysterical, though it had been Andrea who helped Gary find his way through bitter times. She couldn't hear talk of Giuliana without becoming insanely jealous though it had been thanks to Giuliana that Gary had settled down so well in Italy and had finally come to terms with all his tragedies.

"If you could have seen how he has behaved in these last few days, you would have been astonished. You owe him almost everything." I pointed at her. "I plan to stay in Milan for as long as I'm needed. Then I'll accompany you back to England. I'm not going to let you be alone. You're going to have a permanent security guard until you've handed over that diary."

A very solemn nod.

Saturday, 3rd March
As he'd promised, Richard Strickland showed up and we both accompanied Sian to watch Italy play Switzerland at San Siro Stadium, where we met Gary who'd had barely a moment's peace in these last three days. Imagine his delight that also in the box was Giuliana Stirata. Gary sat between the two women, who seldom addressed each other despite his attempts to act as a conciliator.

Eugenio Dal Bosco was able to fly over to talk to him, as well as to watch the match, and Marcello Stirata was also present. Apparently Sergio Taccone decidedly felt that by the start of the following season Roberto Cianfanelli would be one of the most-feared attackers in the championship and hinted that if

Byron was to perform every week with the flair he displayed at Napoli, he could become the undisputed play-maker of the team.

So Fiorentina might well renew his contract, and write off its interest in Pablo Cortes as a very expensive loss! In the circumstances all I was able to do for Tom Kennart was to extract from Byron a promise that his club would have an option on the services of the player when he chose to return to England. Of course if he wants to know fully what went on during my time in Italy he'll have to buy a copy of this book.

The match finished as a mistake-ridden 1–1 draw. The home team gave away an early goal, and appeared jaded and desperately in need of fresh sparkle. As expected, Dino Lanati played with great authority in its defence but it was only after the appearance as substitute of Roberto Cianfanelli during the second half that Italy looked like being able to save the game. He it was who scored the Italian goal and seems destined for a bright future representing his country.

Each World Cup final throws up an unknown name. Who knows but come June the media may be celebrating the exploits of Cianfanelli? It made me really wonder about the influence Byron could have played in the 1990 World Cup if he'd also been selected as a surprise player – the footballing equivalent of A Wild Card.

Epilogue

As he was driven northward, the passenger in the Lancia Fulvia cast his mind back over a story that had haunted him ever since he'd received news of the accident, a story that had its roots on a day in May 1970. Salvatore Brini was not the only person captivated by the girl at the festa that particular afternoon – but the other had been the faster to move.

Orange had been the background colour chosen for the festival to commemorate the recent winning of the championship by Cagliari. While in larger footballing centres victory of a scudetto *is always celebrated by communal rejoicing, in a much less prosperous island like Sardinia the feat bore added importance and festivities took place in villages and towns the length and breadth of the island. The village-folk of Villacidro made a singular effort to look especially dazzling, and the girls had been enchanting in their costumes with a motif based on dancing orchids.*

Although Angelo Decchuras rarely went out, despite becoming increasingly blind, he was determined to attend the celebrations. Why, hadn't he supported Cagliari since the team had been in the Serie C? Hadn't he journeyed frequently to the capital of Sardinia and back on a rickety old brown bus? The fact that his beloved only daughter would be taking part in the entertainment was an added reason to enjoy the festivities, and although he wouldn't be able to see her, his wife, Marita, had described her costume in minute detail.

Another to revel on that same day had been the taciturn Corrado Poccudv. He'd been employed in Villacidro as apprentice to the village cobbler for just over two years, and had been very slow to make friends. An orphan who'd been abandoned in Guspini, he'd been raised in an orphanage in Oristano forty kilometres to the north-west before being sent out into the world to make his living.

That day he had followed fixedly each and every movement made by the girl, whether she had been dancing or acting, and became entirely captivated by her. For the first time in his life he'd fallen hopelessly in love.

Although seven years her elder, he came to spend a vast amount of time in her house, and had grown to become treated almost like a son. In his spare time he would act as a guide-cum-chaperone whenever any member of the Decchuras family had ventured outside. He saved enough money to follow the girl to the mainland when she'd moved two years later, and had found work in the leather industry in Florence. Although they weren't lovers, he and the girl became engaged and together had purchased a house in the country.

Now she was as good as dead, and Corrado Poccudu was feverishly anticipating the chance of exacting revenge on the person he'd come to think of as being responsible for her death. As her former fiancé, and thus the closest male, hadn't he made a promise to the girl's parents that he would exact vengeance — the vengeance that had been demanded by her blind father?

While in prison he learned that the woman known as "La Strega Gallese" had had a miscarriage — and the fact that the foetus was that of a male had satisfied his dull peasant brain.

But there still remained the woman herself — first to be humiliated, and then to be killed. As he looked forward to the golden opportunity that was about to present itself, a smile of dark malice cut across Poccudu's mouth.